SHADOW OF DOUBT

HAILEY EDWARDS

Edited by Sasha Knight
Proofread by Lillie's Literary Services
Cover by Gene Mollica
Illustration by Leah Farrow

A special thank you to Branda Ericksen, who won the contest to name the rideshare app used in this series!

And big hugs to the ladies (and gents) in my reader group. You guys boost me on the low days, and your meme game is always on point.

Thank you for your support.

You make all this possible.

SHADOW OF DOUBT

The Potentate of Atlanta, Book 1

Hadley Whitaker is a liar, a killer, and a chocoholic, but she's getting better about the first two. Or maybe she's just getting better *at* them.

Some days it's hard for her to tell fact from fiction, but only one truth matters. Goddess willing, she's going to be the next Potentate of Atlanta. Even if it means playing nice with Midas Kinase, a shifter whose mysterious past might just be grimmer than her own.

When a bloodthirsty rogue begins hunting the city's paranormals, Hadley ropes Midas into letting her work the case. But that rope starts to feel more like a noose as they come closer to discovering not only the rogue's identity, but each other's darkest secrets.

I am enough

ONE

Regret tasted like a discount food truck taco. *Frak.* Sal swore on his mother's grave he had used real chicken this time, and I bought it. Literally. Goddess only knows what he had fed his regular customers until the health department caught up with him. Hence tonight's discount. He was trying to lure in a new crop of suckers, and my forehead must have looked freshly stamped.

Rinsing my mouth out with a gulp of flat soda of undetermined flavor, I was tempted to chase this bad idea with another one. The Italian ice stand the next block down made for a good palate cleanser, but they served at a glacial pace worthy of their product, and I wanted to finish watching *Robot Space Tentacles Attack Earth* before I called it a day.

The shadow pretending to be mine unspooled its grasping fingers across the sidewalk in front of me and made a *gimme* motion.

"Fine." I tossed my half-eaten meal, wrapper and all, into the darkness. "Don't come whining to me if it makes you sick."

The fingers shifted into a hand and formed the letter C. No. Wait. They mimed holding a drink.

"Are you serious?" I lifted my cup and got a thumbs-up in response. "Hope you like backwash."

The void swallowed my offering and snapped back into shape, mimicking me once again.

I never should have fed it one of the single origin chocolate ganache squares my boss gave me on my birthday. Flavored with champagne and dusted in pure cacao, they were heaven in the mouth and hell on the wallet. Now they were the only currency the shadow accepted as a reward for good behavior. Thankfully, indulgences at that price tier came magically treated against melting in my pocket. Benefits of living in the Deep South.

Halfway down Peachtree Street Northwest, I got a text from Bishop, who might as well have been my parole officer given how often he required check-ins when the boss was out of town. Rumor had it he had been a desk jockey prior to my arrival. Lucky me, he had decided—or the potentate had decided for him—to hit the streets to keep a particular eye on the newest member of Team Atlanta.

>>*We got trouble.*

Nice and vague, just the way I like it.

>>*Details to follow.*

An address popped on-screen that forced me to pull up the GPS app.

I had been a resident of Atlanta for a year and two days, but Peachtrees still looked the same to me.

On my way.

Using a rideshare app exclusive to the city's paranormal popula-tion, Swyft, I arranged for transportation. I didn't have to wait long for a sporty two-seater painted lime green with black racing stripes to squeal up to the curb. The driver honked twice, and when I didn't break an ankle sprinting around the car, she lowered her window.

Skin so pale it was translucent, I figured her for a vampire, but she hadn't sent a warning tingle up my spine. Her wide blue eyes, the color of her pronounced veins, locked on me like a tractor beam, as if her will alone could haul me into the passenger seat. Her spiked pixie cut highlighted the roundness in her cheeks, and the elastics on her braces matched her hair and her wheels.

Open palm smacking her outer door, she called, "Are you coming or what?"

Sizing her up, I felt my eyebrows climb. "Are you old enough to drive?"

Returning the favor, she leaned out farther. "Do you see a student driver sticker, lady?"

Another texted nudge from Bishop forced me to take my chances. "Let's go."

I climbed in beside her, noted the aftermarket stereo system that belonged on a spaceship, and exhaled through my teeth.

"I'm an ace driver," the girl snarled. "Stop huffing and puffing over there."

"Does your attitude get you many tips?" I strapped in. "How about positive reviews?"

Once upon a time, I had taken pride in the number of glowing reviews I collected on the job. Those were the days. I didn't get thanked for the work I did now, and I sure didn't earn any tips. Heck, I considered it a good night if I made it home without blood on my clothes or spit in my hair, and those were the more sanitary bodily fluids that got splashed on me. Maybe things would have turned out differently had I not embraced the role of villain, rather than heroine, in the fairy tale that used to be my life.

Used to be was key. I wasn't that person anymore. I had shed her and grown into a new skin.

I had buried the old me where no one would find her and risen with a new identity, a new purpose, and with hope that new and improved me would cancel out all the karmic debt past me had incurred. I was fully embracing the role of phoenix, which was only fitting since one graced the city seal.

Though I had to admit, as a necromancer living in a city teeming with paranormals, my old story hadn't ended so much as I had flipped to the start of the next chapter.

"I have to make rent." She stomped on the accelerator but mercifully left the radio off. "To do that, I zip as many slowpokes across town as I can in a night. Gas don't pay for itself. Neither do groceries. Keep that in mind when you're typing up the review I can hear you mentally composing over there."

That stupid taco came back to haunt me as she cut lanes, slashed through an exit, then slammed on her brakes.

I swallowed it back down, hit release on my seat belt, then reached for the handle. "Thanks for the lift."

"What's he doing here?" the girl mumbled. "Hey." She locked the doors, ensuring a captive audience. "What's he doing here?"

"You've got to be more specific." A manned barricade blocked the sidewalk. "Who?"

"Midas Kinase."

The sound of his name sent a shiver whispering down my spine. "I don't know."

But I could guess, and I only needed one.

The Atlanta gwyllgi pack wouldn't trot out its heir and chief enforcer for anything less than a capital crime involving a pack member. Crossing paths with him—or his keen nose—was the absolute last thing I needed tonight or any other night.

Gwyllgi scent memories filed away all sorts of information, meaning my true identity was only a sniff away. I had taken precautions, magical ones, to flesh out my new persona, but this wasn't how I wanted to learn if the witch had sold me the promised charm or just an old silver band that sometimes turned my middle finger green.

"You're Hadley Whitaker." Her eyes rounded until they swallowed her face. "*The* Hadley Whitaker. I saw your name pop up on the app, but...geez. You're really her?"

"Yep." I tapped on the window so she would take the hint. "I'm really me."

"No shit?" She all but bounced in her seat. "You know the Potentate of Atlanta?"

Linus Andreas Lawson III.

Appointed by the Society for Post-Life Management, the ruling body for necromancers, over which his mother presided, to protect and serve this city. He was Society royalty. Rich. Powerful. Influential. And engaged to my former best friend.

Yeah.

Our relationship was...complicated, even before I took a walk on the dark side.

Chills coasted down my arms, and my heart kicked hard once. "He's my boss."

"You're like his heir, right? Scion? I forget what you corpse-raisers call it."

Corpse-raiser.

This kid could teach a master class on how not to get repeat business.

"Right now, I'm a lowly employee of the Office of the Potentate. One day, if I play my cards right, I might get promoted to upper management."

"Wow." She sank back against her seat. "He's pretty hot if you're into the grim reaper type."

Once upon a time, I might have agreed with her, but on bad nights, I still dreamed of him.

The moth-eaten black cloak that hung from his shoulders, the threadbare cowl that hid his pale face. All that, I could stomach, but his scythe...the way moonlight glinted off its blade when he raised it to strike a killing blow...

I stood on the right side of the law these days, but one look at him had me feeling cold steel parting the warm flesh at my throat.

"Is this like official business?" She scanned the scene. "Did someone bite it?"

While she gawked, I manually unlocked my door. "That's classified."

"That's a yes." She grinned at me, metal glinting over needle-sharp teeth that made me wonder if she wasn't as pixie as her hair-style. "I'll be in the area if you want to call me up special." She passed me a crumpled piece of paper trimmed into a lopsided rectangle. On the front, she had painstakingly drawn a business card with colorful markers. On the back, she had crossed out the last four digits of her debit card number on a receipt for takeout. "The app won't let you pick who you get, but I'll charge their rates for a private ride."

"I appreciate it." I tucked the slip into my wallet so as not to ding her pride. "See you around."

As I stepped onto the curb, she peeled out, blasting rap music that rattled my bones from three feet away. She hadn't given me a chance to shut the door, so she yanked the wheel hard to one side and let momentum slam it for her.

"Goddess," I muttered, grateful to have survived the experience.

"Buy a car," Bishop advised on his way to greet me. "You won't suffer so many near-death experiences."

Adrenaline still pumping, I glanced behind me. "Do you have one?"

"Hell no." A shudder rippled through his broad shoulders. "People drive like maniacs here."

The snow-white hair he kept trimmed short and styled neat was streaked with russet brown. Not much. Just enough to tell me he had fallen off the wagon. His eyes, usually a brilliant titanium, were tinted the milky green of the corpse he had no doubt left in his wake. But he and I had an unspoken agreement. I didn't ask how he fed, and he returned the favor.

"I heard Midas Kinase is here."

"Yeah. The victim is gwyllgi." Bishop studied me. "That a problem?"

"No," I lied, and he pretended to believe me.

"Come on." He led me to where sentinels, necromancers working undercover with the Atlanta Police Department, held the line. "The pack reps are waiting for you."

"Goody." I had successfully avoided all remnants of my past life since arriving in Atlanta, but it looked like my number was finally up. "It just had to be a gwyllgi."

"You got this," Bishop murmured, misreading my hesitation.

Ahead, two men cut from the same cloth stood watch over their dead. Gwyllgi varied in height, but they ran toward beefy—in a sink-your-teeth-in kind of way—and these two made a girl think about taking a bite. They lifted their heads in tandem upon scenting us and joined us at the barricade.

"Hadley," Ford said, his voice warm. "This your scene, darlin'?"

Ford Bentley, who had cracked a joke about his name the first time we met, wasn't laughing now. As the pack liaison with our office, he and I were on friendly enough terms that I recognized the endearment wasn't a come-on or condescension but simply habit.

Sorrow had turned his lively blue eyes dull, and his wild black hair showed tracks from where his fingers kept tunneling through its jagged length.

"Yeah." I locked my gaze on him to keep it from sliding to his left. "The POA is in Savannah."

That meant this was my case to solve, the first one I would tackle as lead.

Just my luck, Midas was here to bear witness. A ghost from my past, come to haunt me.

Perfect.

"Have you met Midas?" Ford twitched his head toward the slightly taller man. "He's our beta."

"We haven't been introduced." I dropped my gaze to the victim, using the gruesome tableau to help regulate my pulse. "I'm Hadley Whitaker."

"Midas Kinase," he said, his voice sandpaper rough, not with emotion, though I heard that too, but from an old injury no one so much as whispered about behind his muscular back. "Are you sure we haven't met?"

Predator that he was, he scented my nerves and eased in front of me for a better look.

In response, the predator in me unfurled, creeping across the asphalt, stretching shadowy fingers under his boots, tapping on individual treads, as if counting all the ways it could kill him.

"We both live in the city." I kept my voice bland, eyes focused on the stag logo branding his tee. Fine. I was ogling the way his pecs stretched the thin fabric to its limits. He had packed on serious muscle since the last time I saw him, but he hadn't been the heir then. His sister, Lethe, had held that title until deciding to break ties with Atlanta and start her own pack in Savannah. Guess her defection had landed him a promotion. "You must have seen me around."

The new cut and style reinvigorated my blonde hair with short layers and plenty of curls, and the hazel contacts, heavy on the green, plus a few magical augmentations, meant Midas would see only Hadley. Just the law-abiding citizen and enforcer of justice. Not the homicidal maniac our mutual friends would have warned him about.

"Your scent..." Flaring his nostrils, he parted his lips. "It's familiar."

"I work a kiosk in the mall, and I run the Active Oval in Piedmont Park five days a week." I held my ground. "You could have picked up my scent anywhere."

Crowding me, he ducked his head, attempting to force eye contact, a dominance tactic that didn't work half as well on necromancers as it did on gwyllgi and did nothing for me. "What was your name again?"

"Hadley." I caved to the challenge and my annoyance, which never failed to land me in hot water, and met his gaze. "Hadley Whitaker."

The full force of his shifter magic pooled in his eyes, turning the tranquil aquamarine to vibrant crimson. I should have been terrified. I *was* terrified. Goddess, I couldn't glance away after verifying he was every bit as gorgeous up close as I remembered from all the glimpses I had stolen of him through a curtained window in that other life.

Sun-streaked blond hair fell in waves to his broad shoulders and framed a face so beautiful in its austerity that I wanted to reach out and touch it, see if he was real. His jaw was hard, and muscle twitched in his cheek. His mouth was full, perfect. Soft, I bet. But his eyes. That's what captured and held my attention. The sorrow in them tugged on my heartstrings, and I understood in that soul-bearing moment when our gazes clashed that he was dangerous to me on levels I hadn't conceived of before meeting him in the flesh.

The one thing I had been warned against doing—instigating a staring match—was exactly what I did while Bishop and Ford looked on in horror.

Clearly, they expected Midas to strike me down for the offense. I did too. And yet, I kept breathing.

"I have exceptional control," he rumbled, "but you're testing it."

Bishop stomped on my instep, and the jolt of pain yanked my attention to him and away from Midas.

"Fire ant." Bishop made a production of searching for more on the sidewalk. "Little bastards."

"Bastard is right," I groused at him before redirecting my focus to Midas's chest to avoid another standoff. "Mr. Kinase, I'm sorry for your loss. I respect your right to be present, but I have a job to do. I would appreciate it if you stepped aside and let me do it."

Midas yielded no ground but let me ease around him. If he figured my willingness to do so proved his dominance, well, bless his heart.

Ditching him and Ford at the barricade, I continued on with Bishop. "That went well."

"Yeah," he said, ignoring my sarcasm. "It did." He crouched over the body, what remained of it. "The pack isn't required to cooperate with us. Not when the victim is one of theirs. They could throw their weight around and block us from investigating. Their alpha prefers to handle these matters internally."

"There's no guarantee the person who did this is gwyllgi. That puts the ball back in our court."

Though I couldn't afford to let assumptions cloud my judgment this early in the investigation. I had to get this right, or I lost points with the POA, who would not want to cut his trip short to play pack politics.

"That's why I like you." Bishop chuckled under his breath. "You're so gosh darn optimistic."

"Har har." I flicked my fingers at the shadow nosing the corpse. "Make yourself useful."

The vague outline of me snapped out a salute then made a production of diving in headfirst.

"Showoff," I grumbled then caught Bishop staring. "What?"

"I'm never going to get used to that."

"All potentates have wraiths."

"That is *not* a wraith." His gimlet eyes dared me to lie to him. "It's so...*Peter Pan*. Do you remember the part in the cartoon where Wendy captures his shadow one night then sews it back on him the next?"

"No?"

"You never watched *Peter Pan*?" He clucked his tongue. "What kind of childhood did you have?"

A dull throb spread beneath my left eye, a distant memory of pain, and when I ran my tongue along my teeth, I almost tasted blood in my cheek. I would have spit to clear my mouth if it wouldn't have contaminated the scene.

Some girls learned makeup to entice, some learned it to claim their spot in the girl hierarchy, but others learned it for more practical purposes. Makeup had never been armor for me, it had been camouflage. I learned how to apply concealer, how to set a proper foundation, so no one, not even my siblings, saw what happened to the family's spare when the heir misbehaved.

Goddess forbid we got a speck of dirt on the precious family name.

Thinking about how thoroughly I raked that name through the mud before discarding it once and for all, I almost laughed, but freedom from that life had cost me everything.

Every-frakking-thing.

Most of them, I didn't miss. Some things, two in particular, I missed a whole heck of a lot.

"A long one," I rasped, drawing on the good times to erase the bad.

Motion caught my eye as darkness seeped from the body, giving no warning before it leapt into mine.

Cold plunged into my chest, wrapping my heart in an icy fist, squeezing a gasp out of me.

"Play nice, Ambrose," I snarled under my breath. "Or I'll put you in time-out."

Warmth returned to my torso in a petulant creep, but the biting chill speared my skull in the next second, giving me an epic brain freeze.

At least, once I thawed out, I had the information I requested. Since he had more or less behaved, I tossed a piece of expensive chocolate into the darkness spilling from my soles across the concrete.

"You're training your shadow to do tricks." Bishop watched the confection vanish. "That can't be healthy."

"Nice streaks," I said sourly. "Who does your hair?"

"Point taken," he grumbled then gestured toward the body. "Walk me through it."

"The victim is a black female, early twenties." Squatting for a closer look, I started off easy, with the stats. "Five-nine or five-ten. Maybe one-sixty. Brown hair. Eye color is also brown." Next came the hard part. "The cause of death is..." I searched my memory for the technical jargon the POA would have used but came up empty. A gaping hole started below the victim's throat and ended at her hips. The soft parts had been devoured, the hard ones gnawed on. "She was eaten."

Bishop didn't dock me, just listened while I tried to keep the fumbling to a minimum.

"There are claw marks on the body as well as teeth marks." Bruising where the creature pinned down the victim while it ate made clear which was which. "There are defensive wounds on the forearms and hands." That stupid taco made its thoughts on the carnage evident, but I wasn't going to hurl in front of an audience. "She was alive when the creature started feasting."

The shadow I cast across her thighs turned its head, interested in something behind me.

"You keep saying *the creature*," Midas rumbled, a dangerous edge to his voice. "Are you implying the killer was one of us?"

"I'm not implying anything." I kept my back to him. "No gwyllgi did this."

Ambrose, being a parasitic entity that consumed paranormal energies, had what you might call a refined palate. The flavor, according to him, wasn't gwyllgi, wasn't anything he could pinpoint, and I bowed to his superior taste buds.

Midas squatted next to me, our elbows almost brushing, close enough I smelled the cedar and amber soap he must use. "How can you tell?"

"It's my job," I said flatly, but Ambrose shook a warning finger, chastising me for taking all the credit. "What I can't determine—yet—is the killer's species." There was no delicate way to ask, but I figured I might as well put him to work if he was going to hover. "Can you identify its scent?"

"No," Midas said after a pause that made it plain he was deciding if the question insulted him.

I conducted the rest of my examination in silence, as much to keep my thoughts contained as to give the illusion I knew what the heck I was doing without the POA there to dictate my every move.

"I'm done here." I stood, ready to bluff my way through the pack reps, when Midas rose beside me. "Mr. Kinase, I will keep you and your alpha apprised of any further developments."

"No need."

"Are you...?" I squared my shoulders, cleared my throat. "Are you taking the case from me?"

"I thought about it," he admitted, and I had to swallow a plea to let me have this one chance. "I have a lot of respect for Linus, and he chose you as his potential successor. That means, if you ace your apprenticeship and trials, you and I will be crossing paths for the foreseeable future."

Relief fluttered through me on butterfly wings. "Thank—"

"I can't allow this investigation to continue without pack oversight."

"—you," I finished dumbly.

"Ford." He gestured for him to join us. "You're with Ms. Whitaker."

Surprise flickered in Ford's eyes, but he smothered it quickly. "Happy to oblige."

Bishop, who filled the roll of aide to me when I wasn't doing the same for Linus, goggled.

"Looks like it's you and me against the world, darlin'." Ford grinned at me. "Let's give it a swift kick in its axis."

A soft laugh escaped me, totally inappropriate given the location, and I caught Midas staring at me, watching my mouth like he expected me to crack up again. Blanking my expression, I angled my chin higher. "Anything else?"

"Give me your number."

The moisture evaporated from my mouth when he captured me in his gaze, but I found enough spit to lubricate my tongue. "Ask me nicely, and I might."

"Please," he said flatly. "Give me your number."

Figuring that was as good as I was going to get, I rattled off my digits and waited, but Midas didn't offer his in return.

He didn't say goodbye, either. Just turned on his heel and left me questioning who had won our rematch. Bishop trotted after him, likely hoping to clarify our arrangements, but I was done here.

"Women." Ford blasted out a sigh as I watched Midas go. "Y'all always want what you can't have."

"True." I reeled my attention back to him. "I want to be home watching TV with a bowl of extra buttery, extra salty popcorn on my lap while I marathon the *Robot Space Tentacles* trilogy, but it doesn't look like that's happening."

"You're a geek."

I swung my head toward him. "So?"

"A huge geek." He flared his nostrils. "That's probably what Midas smelled earlier."

"And?" Used to being picked on, I reined in my temper. "There's no law against being a geek."

As a matter of fact, Atlanta hosted one of the largest science fiction and fantasy conventions in the world.

"You, being a geek, would know."

A flicker of shadow coiled near Ford's boots, but I stomped on it and sent it skittering.

"Fire ant," I mumbled when his brows winged higher. "Little bastards."

The rest of the on-site work fell to the cleaners. A neutral entity comprised of all supernatural factions in any given area, they documented each paranormal crime scene in photos and video, collected blood and tissue samples, then made it all disappear before humans caught wind of a disturbance. There wasn't much I could do until they finished and uploaded their findings into their database, so I was done here.

"Come on, Lee." He reached in his pocket. "Can I call you Lee?"

"Sure." The almost familiar ring of the nickname shot a pang through me. "Where are we going?"

"Dawn will be here soon." He squinted at the sky. "I'm driving you home."

"Necromancers don't have sun allergies like vampires do."

"I know." He jingled his keys. "Hurry and you can still catch *Robot Space Tentacles Encircle the Earth.*"

"Ah." I nodded sagely. "I thought I caught a whiff, but I wasn't sure."

"This isn't the start of a wet-dog joke, is it?" He pointed out a jacked-up white pickup truck, a gleaming off-roader without a speck of dirt marring its glossy wheels, one I would need a boost or a ladder to climb in. "I'll warn you now, I've heard 'em all, and not a single one made me laugh."

"No." I made a show of sniffing him. "Geek." I wiggled my nose. "You reek of it."

Grinning when he hooted with laughter, I headed for his truck, shadow obediently in tow. For now.

TWO

Ford drove the posted speed limit, always used his turn signals, and kept to the slow lane, proving he was every bit the gentleman behind the wheel as he was on the street. Even the classic R&B station he hummed along with registered as an indistinct murmur to my less sensitive ears.

Without prompting, he took me straight to the Faraday, and I wasn't sure how that made me feel.

The Faraday was all glass, gloss, and glitter. It was also a human-free zone where paranormals in the city could relax, unwind, and be themselves without censure or fear of inciting a panic. Its trendy address was so exclusive, I half expected the doormen to charge admission on the rare occasions when I had no choice but to enter through the lobby.

The security staff was also one hundred percent gwyllgi, explaining how he knew my address.

"You look right put out with me, darlin'." The smile on his lips crept into his eyes. "You'll have to forgive me, but I asked around about you."

Pins and needles swept through my arms, a primal warning a predator had me in its sights. "Why?"

Intrigued by my panic, a curl of darkness slithered across the seat, its jack-o'-lantern grin sinister.

"You're easy on the eyes," he flattered as he idled at the curb in front of my building.

Flattening my palm on top of the creeping stain, I dug in my nails until it quit spreading. "Try again."

"And...you're attached to the Office of the Potentate."

Professional curiosity I could handle, as long as it didn't go any deeper. "What did you find out?"

"That you're Adelaide Whitaker's little sister. That you suffered from fibromyalgia and chronic fatigue syndrome all your life and became a shut-in to the point most folks thought you had died. Until Adelaide got herself engaged to Boaz Pritchard, who is family friends with Grier Woolworth, who happens to be engaged to your boss." He slid his gaze toward me. "Most folks now believe Linus cured you using one of his experimental sigils as a favor to his fiancée. He brought you to Atlanta with him, and he's training you in his place supports the conjecture. Some of the less charitable speculate it was a trade—your life in exchange for his." At my startled look, he clarified, "His fiancée went and named herself the new Potentate of Savannah. He won't want to stay here while she's there. He might have given you a second chance at life, but he's getting one out of the bargain too."

The facts were close enough to the truth to make me sweat, but they fit my cover story like the lid on a pressure cooker.

All warm drawl and kind eyes, he asked, "Any reason why digging into your past would bother you?"

"It's hard for me to talk about that period of my life with new people," I said, and I wasn't lying. I just wasn't telling the truth.

"I get that." He let himself relax. "You spent so many years isolated, it's got to be strange moving to a big city, being all on your own. You must miss your family."

Family was a sore topic with me, one I didn't want anyone else poking, so I let it pass.

"Yeah." I hit the release on my seat belt and told him another truth. "I'm a new person here, with a whole new life."

"How are things in the friendship department? It's gotta be hard making connections when you've had so little experience socializing with strangers."

I had no friends. Not a one. Not anymore. I would much rather blame my self-imposed solitude on social ineptitude than face the real reason why I had no one to hang with after work. "I've been focused on learning the job."

"You gotta have balance, Lee." He twisted in his seat. "How about I hook you up with some training wheels until you get the hang of it?"

"Um..."

Toying with the piping on the seat, he shrugged. "How about I be your friend?"

"Does this have anything to do with you keeping a closer eye on me?"

Midas had paired us up for a reason, and I had no doubt his justifications went deeper than this case.

"You're hurting my feelings." He clucked his tongue. "Friends don't hurt each other's feelings."

I had done more than hurt feelings. I had ruined lives, ended them. That was then, and this was now. I had to stop letting the past overlap the present. Otherwise, what was the point of a second chance? "I'm sorry I hurt your feelings."

"Hey, you're getting the hang of it." He clapped for me. "Friends always say they're sorry when they're wrong."

"I didn't say I was wrong." I smiled at him, all sugar and spice. "Only that I was sorry I hurt your feelings."

"Okay." He gripped the wheel. "Back to remedial you go."

"Are you sure friendship isn't a conflict of interest when it comes to our partnership?"

"Nah." He waved off the notion. "Now if we were dating..."

The slight rise in his tone on the last word made it sound like a question I didn't know how to answer. "We're not."

"No," he agreed, his mouth pinching. "We're not."

"I can't tell if you're being nice because Midas told us to work together, or if you're hitting on me."

"Am I that rusty?" He scratched his cheek, glanced out the windshield. "I haven't dated in...a while."

"That makes two of us." I was creeping up on a twenty-month dry spell with no end in sight, even if Ford was a tall drink of water.

"Do you remember the night we met?"

Try as I might, I couldn't pin it down to one defining moment. "No?"

"The first time I saw you, you were standing over a decapitated chupacabra, a short sword in each hand, and its head at your feet." Nostalgia tinged his voice. "Not gonna lie, darlin'. I got heart palpitations."

I remembered the kill, one of my first, but I didn't remember him bearing witness.

"Only when you're hunting big game, huh?"

"You might have noticed the POA is a fan of decapitation."

I, his faithful apprentice, was one year into lessons with twin kopis blades already stained with more blood than a lifetime of scrubbing would cleanse.

"Does it bother you?" He put a pin in his amusement. "The killing?"

"No." The shadow reveled in it, took sustenance from it, and I... had made my bed. There was nothing to do but lie in it. "It's part of the job."

"You've seen gwyllgi?"

"Shifted?" I locked down the shiver that wanted to roll through my shoulders. "A few times."

Gwyllgi, this pack at least, had descended from the matings of gwyllgi born in Faerie to wargs born here.

In their natural form, gwyllgi reminded me of that flipbook where you mixed and matched heads, torsos, and legs from other animals to create a new one. They weren't mishmashes, but a seamless blend of a large dog and a monitor lizard. A bullmastiff and Komodo dragon maybe. Their pelts, as far as I could tell, ran toward earthy colors. Tawny or rust or black or some combination.

"You don't sound scarred for life," he noted. "Does that mean you can deal with that aspect of my nature?"

"You can't be worse than Midas."

A prickling curiosity honed his voice. "When did you see Midas shifted?"

Frak.

I hadn't meant to let that slip.

Memories from my old life were crowding my new one, and I was at risk of getting trampled.

"The POA is big into assigning homework. I watched footage from the Siege of Savannah."

Fifteen months ago, vampires had seized the city and held it for the better part of a week. Gwyllgi had fought alongside necromancers to regain control and stomp out the vampire uprising. Midas had missed the action, but he had been present during the initial stages of the rebuilding process, lending a hand to his sister and her newly established pack.

I really had watched the video as part of an assignment on how to secure Atlanta against a similar attack, so it wasn't a total lie. Even if I had seen Midas shift in person, on more than one occasion.

Nodding, he seemed to accept that. "What did you think?"

He meant what did I think of Midas, of gwyllgi in their natural form, but I faked misunderstanding. "The siege was long and bloody but not half as bad as it could have been."

Ford narrowed his eyes on me, clearly not fooled, but he didn't push me for a real answer.

"I should go." I pointed out the sign near his bumper. "No parking zone, remember?"

"I'll give you a holler tomorrow."

"Works for me."

I slid out of the cab and waited on the sidewalk until he drove off before skirting the front entrance, and the regular nighttime gwyllgi doorman who always eyed me with distrust, to slip down the alley between buildings. I wasn't kidding about not tempting fate. I kept to myself as much as possible to avoid giving myself away.

That meant avoiding the doormen, the lobby, the elevators, and common areas where I would establish a scent trail over time that anyone could follow straight to me. Using the fire escape to reach my apartment was safer with warm summer rains and hot breezes erasing the buildup before it seeped into the cracks and stuck.

"What are you doing back here?"

Midas.

Instincts honed over a lifetime warned me to hunch away from the snap of his anger, from the certainty pain would follow, but I didn't take hits anymore, not from anyone, and so I straightened my shoulders. "Going home."

"Hadley," he said, the rasp in his voice going soft. "I don't hurt women."

Fists balling at my sides, I hated how easily he read weakness in me. "I never said you did."

"No, you just recoiled like you were waiting for a slap to land." He considered me. "Or a fist."

Playing it off as a misunderstanding, I shrugged. "Hazards of the job."

"That's not what I—" He shut his eyes, but his lips kept moving as he counted to ten under his breath. Who routinely annoyed him enough that he had adopted such a coping mechanism? "Please use the front door from now on. The fire escape is for emergencies, not for cardio."

"I've been taking the stairs for the past year, and the supports have yet to pry free of the building, crash to the asphalt, and put me in an early grave. I don't see the problem." I spun the interrogation around on him. "What are you doing here?"

"Notifying next of kin."

A grimace twisted my lips before I could smooth them, but he only watched my mouth.

Maybe I had a sour cream mustache from that travesty of a taco?

"You didn't mention you knew the victim," I said casually. "That might have been helpful."

"She's pack," he replied simply.

Meaning Ford had known her too, and he had kept just as silent while I stupidly followed procedure and waited to see if the cleaners identified her based on her fingerprints. He had handled me like a pro, and I had bought into his *aww shucks* routine without blinking because he was so darn likeable.

Credit where credit was due. Or, in this case, blame. I was the one who made the verbal report to Bishop as fast as I could rattle off the pertinent details, and I did it without input from the pack reps. All in order to avoid Midas's notice, which I had attracted anyway.

The shadow I cast across the wall slow clapped for me until I wanted to punch the bricks where his face ought to be. "Do you want me to go with you?"

"Nothing will make this easier for her mother, but it will help if I'm the one who delivers the news." He might have tried to hide his short, quick breaths, but the flare of his nostrils drew my eye. "Wounded predators don't respond well to other predators in their dens."

"I understand."

Surprise flitted through his impossibly blue eyes, which I wouldn't have noticed if I hadn't been gazing into them again. Likely that's why he let it show. Most folks had more sense than to make eye contact with him.

"No false modesty?" He canted his head, looked his fill. "No argument against your predatory nature?"

"This job requires a predatory nature."

"True."

Heels clicked on pavement, and a woman's tremulous voice called down the alley, "Midas?"

"On my way, Bonnie." He lingered with me a moment longer. "If any staff member has threatened you, propositioned you, or otherwise made you feel uncomfortable in your own home, you can tell me."

As tempting as it was to throw him off my scent by blaming my anxiety around him on another gwyllgi, I couldn't toss someone else under the bus. "It's not like that."

"Midas?" the woman tried again, her voice going impossibly softer. "The Randalls are waiting."

"I have to go." He blasted out a sigh. "The victim was Shonda Randall, by the way."

"Thanks for that." I could tell this was costing him, so I paid a little back. "For giving me a chance."

"You're welcome." He glanced over his shoulder. "The offer stands."

"Which offer is that?"

"You can come to me if you have any problems at the Faraday."

"I can manage."

A slight dent appeared in his right cheek a more charitable woman might call a dimple. "I'm sure you can."

He turned and started toward the slip of a woman doing her best not to cower when he got close.

"Come on, Bon." He didn't reach out, didn't touch her, and they both seemed relieved to avoid the contact.

Maybe I was misremembering the chapters I read on gwyllgi as part of my training, but I could have sworn this pack, thanks to their distant warg ancestry, were big on touch as a means of reaffirming pack bonds.

Since it was none of my business who rated skin privileges and who didn't, I tabled my curiosity and hit the stairs.

I lived two stories up, which suited me fine. High enough to easily defend but low enough to jump if I had no other choice. Why yes, those were the selling points the potentate mentioned before showing me to my shoebox—I mean, apartment.

The intricate exterior lock on the window was my doing. Since I only used the front door when accepting deliveries, I considered this my primary entrance and locked it behind me every time I left. There was no point, really, considering how tight security was at the Faraday. Yet another reason for its sky-high rent and exclusivity. I never could have afforded this address without the potentate, who lived several floors above me, footing the bill as a thinly veiled attempt at keeping tabs on me via job perk. Not that I was complaining. Free is free.

Sadly, the POA's generosity hadn't extended to a decorating budget, so I managed to furnish it for pennies since that's all I had to rub together these days.

The layout was a perfect cube. As with most efficiency apartments, it came without interior walls. The front door, which opened onto the hall, stood opposite the single window I used to come and go. The other door, on my left, led to the extravagant, if compact, bathroom. The microkitchen managed to fit everything a girl needed to survive and sat on my right, and the dining table where I sometimes ate but mostly sewed was on my left. The living room/bedroom occupied the corner right of the front door.

The futon where I spent my days was a Vampslist find and cost me fifty bucks after delivery. I could have traded for it in blood, but that was too risky. The mattress, such as it was, had been wrapped in cotton batting until it was cloudlike, and slipcovered in lavender fabric. Pillows in every pastel color imaginable covered it from head to toe, and most nights I collapsed face-first into them without bothering with underwear, let alone pajamas.

With a little help from a staple gun, a dollar hula-hoop, and Velcro hanging strips, I had created a wall-mounted canopy in complementary shades whose draping lengths could be tied back when I was watching TV or pulled closed against the sun when I was ready for bed.

With yards of fabric left, I'd made another one using the light fixture in the center of the room as my starting point. From there, the material fanned out to cover the entire ceiling, spilled down the otherwise white walls, and left behind a splash of color and texture before pooling on the polished concrete floor.

All in all, it was very *Arabian Nights*, if I do say so myself, though most of that was to blame on my day job rather than personal taste.

Four days after moving to Atlanta, in order to establish my new identity, who was sorely lacking in credit scores among other things the average person cultivated over a lifetime, I invested a whopping two-thirds of my life savings in a Peachy Keen Sheets franchise I ran out of a kiosk at Haywood Square, a Society-owned mall, funding my new life with my old one. As my apartment attested to, the freebies had to go somewhere.

Plus, it was a great excuse to put the MBA I had worked my butt off earning in my past life to good use.

Most importantly, being my own boss gave me the flexibility to close shop when my real job required me to put in extra hours. That was probably the reason I didn't make as much selling sheets as I had hoped, but what can you do? The stipend I was paid as the POA's apprentice was enough to keep me solvent. I could make it another year on the cheap. Then it was make-it-or-break-it time with this gig. Either I would be elected as Potentate of Atlanta or—

No.

There was no *or*.

I had no backup plan.

I *would* be the next Potentate of Atlanta.

Full stop.

Since Ford had been nice enough to give me a lift, I had time to watch the last movie in the *Robot Space Tentacles* trilogy, but working my first solo crime scene had wiped me out, and dealing with Midas—twice in one night—had left me drained and a little spooked.

After a shower scalded off the night's miseries, I skipped the pajamas and flopped naked on the futon without bothering to lower it. Honestly, I reserved the bed setting for off days and other special occasions. Otherwise, I was usually too tired to make all the heave-hoing worthwhile.

The massive screen extending from the wall across from me on its full-tilt mount was my one splurge, a fifty-inch UHDTV with sound-bar. I might not have the gumption to sit through the whole feature, but I could let it lull me to sleep. And I did. Like the dead.

Right up until a brisk knock sent me rolling out of bed with a muttered curse, ready to gouge out the eyeballs of whoever expected me to put on pants at this hour. *Surprise!* I was tired, and I wasn't putting in the effort. After wrapping a sheet around my torso, I opened the door with a squint for the bright hall lights.

Midas, whose eyes bore fresh shadows, said, "You need to get to Perkerson Park."

Dread squeezed my heart in a merciless fist. I was in over my head and sinking fast. "Let me get dressed."

Midas dipped his gaze to where my fist clutched the sheet then glanced away just as fast. "I'll call Ford."

"It won't take but a minute," I protested, shocked to find I had followed him out into the hall when he fled my seminudity. "Just wait."

Without a backward glance, Midas left me standing with a fistful of sheet and hit the elevator.

"This is the job," I reminded myself. "Sleep is never guaranteed."

Urgent texts from Bishop yanked me out of bed a few days a week, and I hadn't been half as grumpy about those times.

Ending the free show, I returned to my apartment to scrounge up jeans and a tee from the armoire I kept hidden behind the fabric draping the walls. About to pull on underwear, I wobbled off-balance when a second knock on the door startled me. Clutching my sheet, I rushed to answer it. "I thought you...left."

Ford stood there, his eyes wearier than they had been, his clothes more rumpled, but he still found a smile for me after he noticed what I was wearing. He glanced away, but slower than Midas.

"Nah." He jangled his keys. "I had to see Mrs. Randall. Shonda's mom. She babysat two of my brothers."

"I didn't realize you knew the victim." I bit my tongue to keep from reaming him out for not mentioning that, or the victim's name, during our cozy ride. "Personally, I mean."

"I didn't really." He bowed his head. "There was more of a chasm than gap in our ages."

Having fae roots meant gwyllgi lived a long time. Necromancers averaged five hundred years or so, but it was believed that gwyllgi could clock two or three times that if dominance fights didn't kill them first. The gap between Ford and his siblings could span decades or more.

"I'm sorry in any case." I hitched my sheet up higher. "I'll get dressed, and then we can go."

"How did you...?" He flared his nostrils, and then his eyes held comprehension. "Midas told you."

"Midas told me to go to Perkerson Park, not what was waiting there."

"Take your time getting ready," Ford said, eyeing the hallway with mild interest. "There's no rush."

No rush was code for no survivors. "I would invite you in but..."

"I've been in plenty of these units. Hard to keep modest without walls."

At the rate I was flashing skin, I wouldn't label modesty as one of my virtues. "I'll be right back."

After I shut the door, I dropped the sheet and pulled on fresh clothes. Since popcorn hadn't happened, and the taco was best forgotten, I pocketed two individual baggies of the trail mix I whipped up once a week before joining Ford in the hall.

"Here you go." I tossed him one then opened the second for myself. "It'll put hair on your chest."

Ford nodded his thanks then dug in. "What's in this?"

"Pecans, almonds, cranberries, buttercrunch toffee covered in dark chocolate, and a pinch of sea salt."

A slow whistle parted his lips. "Are you sure you should be eating beforehand?"

I cradled my bag to keep it out of his hands. "I notice it's not slowing you down any."

"I'm a hunter. I've seen my share of dead bodies, caused my fair share too."

I had too, but I wasn't in any hurry to admit my sins. Or share my chocolate. "I'll manage."

"All right." He crunched his way through his entire stash before we hit the elevator, which I took as a compliment, then stuffed the trash in his pocket. "You ever been to Perkerson Park?"

"I stick to Piedmont." I let him push the buttons, otherwise it would have been obvious I had to search for them. He didn't need to know I could count my total number of elevator trips on one hand. "Perkerson's near Capitol View, right?"

"Yeah, south of the BeltLine."

"I didn't realize how many parks Atlanta had until I moved here."

"That's why they call it a city in a forest."

"That's why the gwyllgi are so at home."

"Who do you think fought to keep every inch of green space we have?" He snorted. "Humans?"

"Got beef with humans, huh?"

"Every ecologically minded species does, or they should." He eyed me. "You're descended from them?"

"Yep." I hadn't studied the Whitaker family tree enough to get specific, but there were human ancestors in their branches. "I'm Low Society."

He pondered what that meant before it clicked for him. "Linus is High Society?"

"Yep again. His bloodline is one hundred percent dyed-in-the-wool necromancer."

"Your line is half and half?"

"Originally, yes. Now? I can't do that math without a genealogy chart and a calculator in front of me."

"It's the same for us. Our original line stems from a pack of gwyllgi who left Faerie to roam Earth. They interbred with wargs, and that's where we came from, what gave us our toehold as a species, and the ability to argue with the powers that be we belonged here and not there." We hit the lobby, and he led the way to the exit. "For a while, we kept that mix, but these days we're true mutts. Gwyllgi, warg, human, and who knows what else."

"That doesn't divide your society?"

"Why should it?" He laughed. "Your Society are the separatists, not ours."

He wasn't wrong. The Society frowned on its necromancers mingling with other species. Vampires were the sole exception. They were our creations, and therefore immune to the unspoken rule.

Less *our* than *their*.

Only the High Society had enough magic to turn willing humans into vampires. Low Society practitioners didn't have the juice to perform resuscitations.

All the magic in me I owed to Ambrose. Every last ounce. I had been born without a single drop.

And I had proven I was willing to go to any lengths to rectify that.

Careful what you wish for, you just might get it...and spend the rest of your long life regretting it.

"I didn't mean to step on your toes," Ford ventured when I didn't offer a comeback.

"You didn't." I trailed him past the nightshift doorman, working yet another double. Just my luck. He narrowed his eyes on me, more suspicious than ever. Until Ford firmed his mouth. That was all it took for the doorman's expression to relax several degrees. "I was thinking that must be nice. Not to have your worth decided by your blood."

"I wouldn't go that far." He opened the passenger-side door on his truck, cupped my hips, and lifted me. "Gwyllgi decide everything by blood. Usually by how much they're willing to spill to prove a point."

Ford's boost left me bouncing on the seat when he let go and made me curious how often he interacted with other species for him not to know his own strength. The pack's heir might not be the only one who'd benefited from a recent promotion.

Then again, it might be a reminder of what he, and his kind, were capable of should I fail to get justice for Shonda.

Paranoid? Nah. Not me.

Once I settled in, Ford shut the door and jogged around the truck to join me in the cab.

"You're the best driver I've had since I got here," I confessed as he merged into traffic.

"Momma always says it's one thing to drive a monster of a truck and another to drive like a monster in a truck."

"Your mom is wise."

"Yeah, she had to be to survive raising four boys on her own."

"There are three more of you? Two brothers were bad enough, but *three*?"

The slip caused my breath to catch, my heart to thud louder in my ears, and my palms to go damp.

Hadley didn't have brothers. She only had a sister. I had to keep it straight. I had to sell him on me.

Luckily, he seemed to think I was referencing his earlier mention of his brothers and not my personal experience with having them.

"All older." He was grinning now. "I'm the baby."

"So, you're spoiled."

"Harsh." He cut his eyes toward me. "I wouldn't use that word exactly."

"What would you call it?"

"Lucky? Besides, you've got no room to talk. You're the baby too."

"No, I'm—" *The middlest.* I bit my tongue so hard it bled. *Frak.* This was why making friends was dangerous. Too much potential for blowing my cover, especially with Ford. He was slick as spit. "Sick kid trumps birth order."

"Yeah," he said after a minute. "I could see that."

With that brilliant zinger, I single-handedly managed to kill the vibe, and we settled in to listen to the radio for the rest of the trip.

THREE

Fresh from visiting the Randalls, Midas sat with his back against a ratty pine gnarled from abuse and rotting from the inside out. The sun was rising, the air warming, but the earth remained cool beneath his palms, and a faint breeze nudged the warped plank he and his sister had fashioned into the seat for a rope swing what felt like a million years ago.

This was his thinking place. He came here to escape when life closed around his throat like a fist. The only corner of the city left where he could breathe without choking on duty, on expectations.

Here he vented all the things he would never breathe to another person, even Lethe, though he still directed his gripes to her out of habit.

"You screwed me over, sis." He tipped his head back against the trunk. "I don't want this. I never did. I'm not like you." He grimaced when the coarse bark tugged on the long hair he ought to trim soon. "Shonda is dead, the Randalls are demanding justice, and Mom is sitting back to see what I'll do to get it for them."

Nine out of ten gwyllgi deaths were what Hadley would call open-and-shut cases. Dominance fights kept the highest-ranking pack members from enjoying their full lifespans, and an accidental sneeze on the wrong person could spark a throwdown that spun into an all-out brawl.

Hadley.

A frown carved his mouth when he realized her name—and not Linus's—had popped into his head first.

"I met Linus's apprentice. There's something about her." A growl entered his voice. "I know her from somewhere, but I can't place her. Yet." He rubbed his face. "It'll come to me."

Overhead, the frayed rope creaked in the only agreement he was likely to get.

"I paired her up with Ford, but it ought to be me. I'm the beta. It's my duty to protect the pack, not his. I did what Mom would have done. I passed the buck." He gritted his teeth, grinding down on the insubordination in his tone. "She does things a certain way, and it works for her, but it's not working for me. I was trained to be a soldier, not a prince. You were supposed to take the mantle, not me."

That was all water under the bridge now that Lethe had her own pack, her own home, her own city.

She was an alpha, and one day he would be too, whether he wanted to be or not.

"Mom has booked my Friday and Saturday nights with her hand-picked potential daughters-in-law since I got sworn in. I haven't gone on any second dates, and she'll run out of candidates before I agree to one." His sigh left him sagging on weary bones. "You'd think she would understand why I..." He snapped his jaw shut, unwilling to speak of it, even to the empty air. "Some days I'm tempted to let Mom arrange a match. Just mate someone and get it over with."

Then she would expect grandkids, and procreation required a level of physical intimacy that broke him out in cold sweats, even after all these years. Whatever unlucky female he chose might expect love when all he had to offer any woman was elevated rank. For some, it would be enough. More than enough. Those were the ones he ought to focus on.

Fingers bumping over the crosshatch scars raised down his forearms, he conceded it was no less than he deserved. To be used. Though he had trouble breathing when he pictured sharing a life, a purpose, a *bed*, with another person.

"You should have left me there," he said, not for the first time, but added the words he would never utter to his sister, who had tried so hard for so long to fix him. "You didn't save me." He let his eyes close. "No one can."

FOUR

erkerson Park was a fifty-acre oasis for the city dweller in southwest Atlanta. Beyond the tennis courts, basketball courts, disc golf course—whatever that was—ball fields, rec center, and pavilion, I saw what must appeal most to the gwyllgi. Shady woods crisscrossed with walking paths, open fields prime for frolicking—though they would never call it that—even a stream for a quick dip in the summer heat.

Parks like these were a veritable paradise for the urban predator.

Hmm.

Can I get away with asking Ford if he can doggy paddle?

Probably not. Unless I was willing to find out how it felt to get bitten by a gwyllgi.

Ford parked without skimming signs the way I had been, so I assumed he was familiar with the area.

Unsnapping my seat belt, I scanned the otherwise vacant lot. "Anyone meeting us?"

"Midas returned to the den."

The den made it sound primitive when the truth was the seat of the pack was a sprawling estate with an elegantly modern home flanked by miles of forestland. The alpha lived there, most of the pack did too, but I had never been invited for a tour. All I knew about it I'd heard in secondhand accounts from the POA.

"I was thinking more along the lines of the cleaners or the witness who discovered whatever it is we're about to see, but good to know."

A grimace twisted his features. "Beg pardon."

He got out, and I sighed into the empty cab. "Men."

"I heard that," he said through the window.

Contrition was difficult to fake, but I like to think I managed as he opened the door for me.

"Gwyllgi tend to get protective fast, both the male and the female of the species," he explained. "Midas paired us up, and that's that as far as my inner wild man is concerned. I don't mean to snap and snarl, but those same instincts make it hard when another male is encroaching on my territory, so to speak."

"You haven't snapped or snarled." I gave credit where it was due. "You've been downright kind to me, but you will have to work on your Midas fixation. I'm starting to think you've got a crush on him."

"All that golden hair, those flowing locks..." Ford batted his eyelashes. "He's so dreamy."

Despite the reason for our early-morning trip, I burst out laughing. "You're horrible."

"Yeah, well. Every pretty girl wants an equally pretty boy, and he's as pretty as they come. I don't have to want to date him to be honest with myself. Doesn't hurt I've heard dozens of lovelorn women ticking off his attributes over the years. I could recite them for you, and you could write them down. Just think of all the time you'd save not making your own list."

"Jealousy is poison." I gentled my tone to avoid coming off as reprimanding. "It warps your outlook on life *and* the object of your envy."

"Voice of experience?"

"Oh, yeah. I had a friend like yours. The best, the brightest. I wanted everything she had. Her magic, her status, her family, her whole life. I made a bad bargain to get a poor imitation."

Tension shot through his shoulders. "Not with Linus?"

"No, not with Linus." Ford must have superpowers that caused you to blab your darkest secrets. That, or I had starved myself for companionship until I was ravenous enough to vent a year's worth—a lifetime's worth—in one go. "He saved me, in more ways than you can imagine."

As his posture relaxed, he pointed toward the creek. "That's our destination."

A petite woman stood where he indicated, arms crossed over her frail chest, delicate hands cupping her opposite elbows, bony finger-tips digging into delicate skin.

"That's Bonnie Diaz."

I jerked my head toward him. "The same Bonnie from the Faraday?"

"Yeah. She's Midas's new PA. He's not thrilled about it, but she has office experience. She suggested it, and he didn't have the heart to turn down the offer."

Mud had soaked through the hem of the ankle-length dress she wore, cream with tiny pink flowers, and her shoes were ruined. Her cardigan was a complementary petal-pink shade, and her hair was bunned up so tight it gave me a headache looking at her. Her face was scarred, a cruel swipe of claws across one cheek, but she was lovely, and she trembled when she spotted Ford.

"I got a t-t-tip." Head down, she kept her eyes averted. "I followed up before bothering anyone."

Ford gawked at her. "Alone?"

Bonnie curved her shoulders inward, making herself even smaller, and whispered, "Yes."

I couldn't say why I did it, except I had often wished for help that never came, that I never dared ask for, but I stepped between them and wrapped a supportive arm around her narrow shoulders.

"Ford isn't mad at you," I soothed in tones that would have

calmed me back then. "He's just worried. No one wants to see you get hurt."

Happy to plaster herself against my side, she turned her face into my shirt.

"I didn't want to lose my job," she mumbled against me. "I just got hired, and I need it to stay in the pack. Everyone has to contribute. *Everyone.* Alpha Tisdale told me so. If it had been a crank call and Midas came out for nothing, he might..."

The sentence hung there unfinished, and I hoped I read her implication wrong.

"Midas doesn't hurt women." I repeated what he'd said to me because I believed it. I wasn't sure how she could doubt him after spending any amount of time with him, but past trauma had a way of coloring the present in shades of the familiar. "You come tell me if that ever changes."

"I c-c-can't do that." She shivered at the sound of his name, or maybe at the thought of standing up for herself, and she burrowed close enough it felt like I gained a second heartbeat. "You're not p-p-pack."

"You're right. I'm not. I'm the POA's apprentice. I operate outside pack law. That means if the pack ever gives you trouble, right on up to the alpha, you come to me, and I'll keep you safe. I will set you up with a new job and arrange a place for you to live."

The Office of the Potentate did more than enforce Society law. We protected all those who were subject to them, regardless of species, when those same laws failed them.

"Okay," she breathed, barely a whisper.

Remembering the empty lot, I asked, "Did you take a Swyft?"

"I shifted and ran." She plucked at her ruined dress. "I'm stronger that way."

She was braver than she knew, reckless too, but I wasn't about to kick her for it when it was obvious life had knocked her around enough.

"There's a bench over there." I pointed down the path winding back toward the parking lot. "How about you wait for us, and when we finish up, we'll give you a lift wherever you need to go?"

Peeking up at me, she wet her lips. "You're sure you don't m-m-mind?"

"Not at all." I winked at her. "It's not my truck. It's his." I laughed at Ford's pinched expression. "What's a little mud between friends?"

"Friends?" she repeated with so much hope I didn't have the heart to tell her she had misunderstood.

"Yeah. Friends." I patted her bony shoulder awkwardly. "Sure. Why not?"

Bonnie was strong, *ridiculously* strong, as I learned when she hugged me until my head threatened to pop off like a cork stopping a bottle of shaken champagne. "Thank you."

"Go on." I pried her off me and shooed her in the right direction. "We won't be long."

With a quiver in her limbs, she padded to the bench where she sat facing us. The bright intensity of her stare made my spine prickle when I turned, giving the absurd impression she was watching my back when a strong breeze would knock her off her feet.

"You handled that well." Ford toed off his boots, rolled his jeans up over his ankles, then stepped down into the shallows. I took the high road, keeping to the edge of the shore, and left him the wet one. "Her fear makes it tough to spend much time with her. Her timidity makes our submissives withdrawn, which draws out the protective streaks in our dominants, and you wouldn't believe how fast those brawls turn ugly."

Given her reaction to males of the species, I could imagine. "Who hurt her?"

"She won't tell." A low growl entered his voice. "Midas found her in one of the women's shelters where he volunteers, recognized her as gwyllgi, and brought her home with him. It's been a week, give or take, and you're the first person she's allowed to touch her."

Abuse recognizes abuse was what I thought, but what I said was, "Let me know if I can help, in any way."

"I'll do that." He slowed a dozen or so feet upstream from where Bonnie had been standing when we first arrived, and grimaced. "There."

Kicking off my sneakers, I hiked the hem of my jeans up to my calves. About to wade in, I startled when Ford scooped me up in his arms with a wide grin that told me he thought he was quite gallant.

Though he might very well be, I was on the job, and I wasn't about to explain to my boss how I solved a crime without my feet ever touching the ground. The Prince Charming routine only worked on girls with stars in their eyes, but all of mine had long since fallen, and no amount of twinkle from him would put them back.

Bracing a palm on his broad shoulders, I used him as leverage when I snapped my hips to execute a twist that flipped me out of his grip. I hit the water in a crouch, soggier than I would have been had he left well enough alone, but admiration sparked in his eyes that made the damp worthwhile.

I wasn't interested in a boyfriend or a booty call. I had to focus on me, on proving myself a worthy successor, but that didn't mean I couldn't appreciate a handsome man sizing me up like he might consider both, or either.

"You're quick," he said, and it came out as a growl. "And flexible."

"I run, and I do yoga." I stood and splashed out to meet him in the ankle-high water. "Gotta have an edge."

"I would pat you on the back for landing that move, but your edge is so sharp it might cut me."

Rolling my eyes, I sloshed past him to what had drawn his interest before my moves distracted him.

Tangled in a tree limb was an arm chewed off at the shoulder, making it look as though the grasping hand had tried holding on until help came. We were here now, but we were too late.

"Scout the area," I told my all-too-invested shadow quietly. "Tell me if we're expecting company."

Ford made his way to me. "Want me to call this in?"

"Not yet." I took out my phone and snapped pictures from every angle before wading on. "I want to see what we can find before more evidence gets washed away."

I had no beef with the cleaners, but I wasn't taking any chances. I had to get this right.

Tipping the brim of an imaginary hat, he nodded. "You're the boss."

Not yet I wasn't, but it still had a nice ring.

"The water is usually deeper than this by a few inches," he murmured. "There must be a blockage."

For our sake, I hoped the creek was a victim of our recent dry spell and not something worse.

"There's another one." I picked my way across the slippery rocks and found a foot, its heel wedged between two rocks. "Two separate victims."

Thanks a lot, hope. You continue to fail at your one job.

"First was Caucasian," he agreed. "This one looks Hispanic, maybe Indian. Hard to tell in this condition."

Crouching for a better angle to snap a photo, I pointed. "See the design across the top of the foot?"

"Henna, right?" He scratched his jaw. "Atlanta has a large Indian population."

"Henna tattoos are popular with non-Indian women too." I thought of a kiosk on the opposite end of the mall that offered henna, as well as other temporary tattoos, to anyone with an hour and twenty bucks. "We need to nail down any meaning associated with the design. It might give us a lead on how or where the victims were selected by the killer."

Please don't let them all be gwyllgi.

Not that I wished this epic heartache on anyone or any faction, but three deaths? Even in a pack the size of the one in Atlanta, it would equal a catastrophic loss.

We found more victims as we traveled upstream, pieces of them anyway, and the freshness degraded with every yard. I had a bad feeling about what we would find at the apex, but I got no sense from

Ambrose that the person or creature responsible was still in the area. That was something.

As I catalogued each hand, toe, finger, and foot with my phone, I kept wracking my brain for a species that might fit the profile I was building, but I didn't have enough information. I was getting ahead of myself. Again. There was no time to slow down, not with a killer—or killers—on the loose.

Argh.

Ford made a choking noise behind me, and I turned to find him covering his nose with the neck of his tee.

Thankfully, my senses weren't as keen. "I don't smell it yet."

"You will."

We kept documenting as we went, as much to keep track of our macabre findings as to pinpoint their locations, and then I spotted the reason for the low water. A dam made of torsos in various stages of decay stretched across the modest creek, causing the water to over-flow its banks on the far side while it trickled on ours.

Shock numbed me even as I said, "I count seven."

"Eight," he rasped, his flirty coping mechanism as broken as his voice. "Look there."

A girl, maybe seven or eight, lay tucked between two women's bodies, as though they had tried to protect her, even in death.

"The victims are all women." Wishing I had enjoyed the clean air more while I had it, I had no choice but to breathe in the stench of decomposition. "You can put in that call now. We can't touch this without cleaner oversight."

Calling it an obstruction felt wrong. Paranormal or normal, they had been living, breathing, laughing, crying people until whatever did this hunted them down and killed them.

Throat tight, I followed procedure and shot Linus an update. I could have called, maybe should have for the sake of expediency, but I was too raw. I worried a tremble in my voice or catch in my breath would betray the doubt threatening to rise up and swallow me whole.

I'm not enough. I'm not enough. I'm not enough.

I never had been. Not even for my own family. These poor souls were mine now. I was all they had left, and I would stand for them.

For the past year, as I scurried in the wake of the POA's tattered cloak, I had champed at the bit for this: a shot at proving myself, a case of my very own, an opportunity to shine. Now that eagerness tasted as sour as the air in my lungs.

The POA was *not* the coddling type, but I would dump this case in his lap in a heartbeat if he were here, and he would let me. Justice before pride, always. If I let myself start to doubt, there would never be an end, and that alone got my fingers moving over the screen.

We have more victims.

The pause between me hitting send and him replying never ceased to amaze. He rarely slept for reasons above my paygrade, and so he replied within seconds.

>>*How many?*

The number has yet to be determined.

Until all the pieces fit together again, we could only guess, but eight was a start.

>>*Can you handle it?*

A tremor shook the phone in my hand. *Yes.*

>>*Are you certain?*

Nerves jittering, I forced myself to seal my fate. *Yes.*

>>*All right.*

The first victim was gwyllgi. For that reason, Midas Kinase assigned Ford Bentley to act as my temporary aide and represent the pack's best interests. The other victims have yet to be identified. Until such time it is determined the first victim is their only casualty, I felt accepting Midas's offer was prudent.

>>*You mean he left you no choice but to accept oversight or surrender the case.*

Pride stung, I deflated on the spot. *I like how I said it better.*

>>*Our alliance with the pack is critical to maintaining the balance of power in the city. Accepting Midas's offer tells them that you're willing to cooperate in the gray areas where our laws overlaps*

theirs. You made a judgment call, one I happen to agree with under the circumstances.

Relief sang through me upon reading his validation. *I'll keep you updated.*

>>*Please do.*

"Checking in with Linus?"

I sent Bishop the same update then pocketed the device. "Is it that obvious?"

"You scrunch up your face when you text him. If you were one of us, I'd say you were baring your teeth." He shrugged. "Makes sense, really. He's your superior, and you're looking to move up. If you were gwyllgi, you'd probably be at his throat."

"If I were gwyllgi," I said, willing to be distracted. "Who do you think would win?"

He didn't hesitate. "You."

"You would bet on me against the POA?" I barked out a laugh. "You are insane."

"Linus has a home, a family, a fiancée, a whole other life south of here. For all that he does his job and he does it well, his heart hasn't been in Atlanta since Grier Woolworth put that ring on his finger."

"Award me a sympathy win, why don't you?"

"Let me finish." He shushed me with a raised hand. "You're hungry, and you'd have to be blind not to see the chip on your shoulder. You walk lopsided because of it. You've got something to prove, and you believe this is the place to do it."

"I don't have anything to prove to anyone."

"Not even to yourself?"

A pang resonated through me when his jab landed too close for comfort, but I ignored the hurt. I was an old pro at that. "Can you pick up the scent of whoever—or whatever—did this?"

"I'm not a bloodhound." He pushed out a long sigh. "But yes, I smell it. That is to say I smell something. I'm not sure what. The rot and the water make it hard to parse the individual strands."

"So," I nudged, "you can't tell if it's the same as what you scented on Shonda's remains."

"No," he said patiently. "I don't have the best nose, and I can only do so much with it in this form."

Before I goaded him into shifting forms, which may or may not do us any good since he had been on two legs then as well, I flexed my toes on the slick rocks and considered other options.

"The predator scent is hours old." He filled his lungs, humoring me. "The killer isn't here."

A shadow on the water confirmed his assessment with a wavering nod, but Ambrose had already told me as much. I just had no way to convey that information to Ford without telling on myself.

Potentates were expected to bond with a wraith or even multiple wraiths, if they had the power to leash more. They used them as backup on the streets, but—as Bishop had pointed out—Ambrose was no wraith. Until I earned the title, I couldn't afford to take any chances.

"I'm getting pruney." I started back. "I'll go sit with Bonnie until the cleaners arrive."

There was nothing more for me to do here, and I bet questioning her woman to woman would go over better.

"I'll wait here."

I could have told him the dead didn't need him to stand watch, but gwyllgi protective instincts demanded he stay put, and I wasn't going to convince him otherwise.

After I stepped out of the water, I yanked on my socks and shoes then joined Bonnie.

The smaller woman trembled despite the heat. "Did I do the right thing?"

Unsure if she meant her ill-advised solo recon, which we had already addressed, or calling Midas instead of me or the cleaners, which might land her in hot water if these victims were anything but gwyllgi, I kept my answer as vague as I felt.

"It's good we got a look at this scene before it was disturbed." I dragged a damp hand down my face before remembering where it had been. "Ford got a hit on the scent before we had to deal with cross-contamination, and that might make all the difference."

Tension shot through her spine. "He can track the person who did this?"

"We can hope."

"Oh." A frown gathered across her brow. "Can he tell if it's a warg or another gwyllgi?"

"No," I admitted. "We're stumped on that front, but we'll figure it out."

Hopefully before another innocent paid the price.

"The cleaners should be here in a minute. I hear vehicles approaching." She relaxed her rigid posture and inched closer until our hips brushed. "I don't like them. They smell like death and chemicals."

Given their line of work, I wasn't surprised they carried their profession in their scent. "If I can keep you out of it, I will. If I can't, then I'll stay while they question you."

"Okay."

Once even my weak hearing picked up the sound of approaching footsteps, I rose and went to greet the four men dressed in waders and carrying crime scene kits. They each nodded on their way past, about as much of a *hello* as you could expect from cleaners, who did their best to avoid on-scene interaction to keep their impartial reputation intact, but the red-faced man who arrived next made a beeline for me.

"You should have followed standard operating procedure. You should have called us immediately, not waited until it was convenient for you." He stabbed a finger in the direction of his team. "You contaminated the scene, you compromised this investigation, and your superior *will* hear about this."

"Don't raise your voice," Bonnie whispered. "Please."

"I don't take orders from you," he spat then turned back to me. "Or you." His cheeks puffed with outrage. "Not yet." His face kept mottling. "Not ever if I have anything to say about it."

"Please," Bonnie said again, barely an exhale.

The man slanted her an annoyed glare that slid toward panic in the next instant. "What is wrong with—?"

Crimson magic splashed up Bonnie's slight frame, washing away her human form as it crested over her head in a tidal wave of power. As it drained, I got my first look at her other self, and I almost wet my pants.

Bonnie might be submissive, but she was a giant submissive. Frakking gargantuan.

She was also snow white from tip to tail minus her button nose. It, and her eyes, were as pink as the tiny flowers on her dress had been. Her scales were translucent and shimmery like they had been sprayed with glitter, and even her claws were clear to the quick.

All that might have been fine if she hadn't been the size of a robust pony, easily twice the height of any gwyllgi I had ever seen. In this form, she came off as a lot less timid and a lot more willing to eat people who frightened her.

Bonnie growled at the cleaner until he backed down, then she came to lean against my side, almost knocking me down with her heft.

"I would go if I were you," I told the man, and I wasn't being snide about it. "Maybe tell Ford to come? Quickly? Not run, you understand, but to walk swiftly and with purpose?"

After smoothing a hand over his balding pate, the man sauntered off with as much dignity as he could muster. Until Bonnie huffed in his direction. Then he squeaked like a mouse before skittering away to safety.

"You can change back now," I told her, and I hoped she didn't notice the faint tremor in my voice.

Don't get me wrong, I had seen gwyllgi shift, but usually there was a pane of glass between them and me. Never had I stood this close to one on all fours, where all those details I had missed—the sharpness of her teeth, the pinkness of her gums, the brightness of her eyes—were crystal clear.

A soft whine escaped her, and she rested more of her weight against me, reminding me of a Great Dane who thought it would fit in its owner's lap as an adult the same as it had as a puppy.

There was no delicate way to ask, but never let it be said that stopped me. "Are you...stuck?"

Another pitiful, whistling exhale more or less confirmed it.

"Do you want me to call Midas?" A shake of her head nixed that idea. "Okay then. We'll wait on Ford."

The man in question arrived five impossibly long minutes later, torn between awe and horror when he spotted Bonnie. I didn't understand the combination, but his gawking caused her fur to stand on end.

"She's stuck," I said when he didn't make a peep. "Can you help her?"

"Stuck?" He wiped the back of his hand over his mouth. "Well, damn."

"She's an albino," I prompted when he continued to stare. "Does that have any special significance?"

"Yeah." He blinked a few times. "It sure as hell does." He leaned forward to get a better look, but even that intrusion into her personal space made her snarl. "This explains why Midas took responsibility for her."

"How would he know the color of her fur based on a sniff test?"

"Not her color, her species," he explained. "She's gwyllgi."

"I got that part." I gestured toward the hulking beast. "Are all albinos this huge?"

"No." He checked to make sure we were alone. "I mean, she's gwyllgi."

"Oh."

Fae.

That's what he meant. She was fae. As in a pureblooded fae. As in born-in-Faerie fae. A fae-fae.

The exact thing all good necromancers are forbidden to approach, speak to, interact with, etc.

As if I needed a reminder I wasn't good by anyone's standards, my shadow perked with sudden interest.

Fae didn't just have magic, they *were* magic, and Ambrose strained against his leash for a taste. He was eyeing her like a starving man handed a plate at a buffet, but I smashed his dreams with a tug on the bond that connected us, reminding him who was in charge, however thin the margin.

Bonnie nudged me, a soft cry in her throat, like she was pleading with me for understanding.

The fact the Atlanta pack harbored an undisclosed number of their Faerie relatives was a secret very few knew, and it was information they would kill to protect. Bonnie's identity was a burden, a huge one, and I wished I could shrug it off, but now Ford knew I knew she was the real deal.

"She must have been using a charm to mask her scent," he decided. "Only on her human self, since I can smell her loud and clear now that she's shifted."

The subject of magical augmentation hit too close to home, so I redirected him. "Okay, so what about white is special?"

"Gwyllgi born with albinism are always, without exception, powerful healers. They're kept under lock and key. No pack who has one will let them go without a fight, whether the gwyllgi is on board or not."

That might explain why she fled her old pack, but it's not like we could ask with her currently embracing life on four legs. "Can you communicate with her?"

"She can understand us," he told me, "but I would have to shift to converse with her, and I can tell you right now that's a terrible idea. She would view me as a threat, and she would attack. She can barely control her instincts with me on two legs."

"What are we going to do with her?" I tipped back my head, annoyed at the rising sun and how its bright glare made my head ache. "I can't bring her home with me."

I almost mentioned I hadn't paid a pet deposit, but that was the exhaustion talking.

"She lives at the Faraday," he confessed. "She was uncomfortable at the den."

That explained how she joined Midas within minutes. She definitely hadn't been on-scene with us.

"How are we going to get her inside without anyone seeing her?"

"Will you consent to being taken to the den?" he asked her. "Just until you can shift back?"

Bonnie flattened her ears against her head and bared her teeth.

Panic must have been fueling her reaction. More like *over*reaction. There was no reason for her sudden aggression at the mention of the den. The alpha was there, and if anyone could unstick Bonnie, it was Tisdale.

"I'm guessing that's a *no*." I joined him in a sigh. "Let's get her loaded into the bed of your truck."

"Okay, but how is that going to get her inside the Faraday without exposing her to rubberneckers? It's almost lunchtime, darlin'. The streets will be packed downtown."

"Leave it to me." I started walking and trusted Bonnie to follow. "I know a guy."

The guy was Bishop, and boy was he in for a surprise.

BISHOP MET us at the Faraday with an industrial laundry cart on fat wheels, stuffed with heaps of pastel fabric that resembled the contents of my scrap heap. He tossed a few sheets in the bed of the truck where Bonnie lay flattened on her side, then parked the cart beneath the tailgate, which he lowered after she chuffed her readiness.

I palmed my forehead when the lump no one would believe for a hot minute was a pile of laundry started wagging its tail.

"Help me hold this up," Bishop said, passing me the corner of a sheet. "This will give her some cover to hop down."

Doing as he asked, even though it put me close enough to the zoom of ravenous motorists that I felt a breeze from each passing vehicle, I pretended this was a totally normal activity fit for human consumption while silently thanking my lucky stars this was a pack problem and not one I had created.

Except Bonnie obviously hadn't shifted since the pack took her in until now, since no one except Midas had a clue what she was, and she hadn't felt the need until she met...me.

Well, frak.

"Ready?" Bishop rippled the sheet. "Olé!"

Bonnie leapt into the cart, which made a popping/grinding/screeching noise that couldn't be good.

After closing the tailgate, Bishop, Ford, and I lifted the cart out of the road and back onto the sidewalk.

"Where did you even find this?" I panted at Bishop. "The Faraday doesn't have a laundry service."

"You would be amazed at the props I keep on hand for just such occasions."

"You stole it, didn't you?"

"I'm an attaché to the Office of the Potentate of Atlanta. I don't steal. I acquire."

I throttled a laugh as we pushed Bonnie to the entrance in time for the doorman to step in our path.

"What the hell is in that?"

Clearly, he had been watching the show, and we had to give the man an answer. "Bonnie Diaz."

His eyebrows shot so high, he almost struck a low-flying aircraft, and he cranked his head toward Ford. "Is she serious?"

"Oh, yeah." He nudged the cart forward. "Now, get out of our way."

The doorman did as he was told, and we squeaked past him into the safety of the lobby, but Ford didn't follow. He lingered outside, and I might have felt the sudden need to bend down and retie my shoe.

"Midas has a special interest in Hadley," Ford said. "So do I. Unless you want to get busted down to janitorial work, I would do my damnedest to hide whatever problem you've got with her—or any other resident—before our beta makes an example out of you."

"Ford—"

"She's a predator. It gets your back up. I feel it too, so I understand, but there are bigger and worse here."

"I'm not sure about that," the doorman murmured after noticing I hadn't kept going.

"I am." Ford clapped the man on the back. "Suck it up or get demoted while you work on your poker face. Your call." He entered the lobby and squatted in front of me. "Here, let me help you with that. The bunny goes over the—"

I batted his hands away. "I can tie my own shoe."

"I can't tell. You've been kneeling here long enough to rethread your laces."

Annoyed, I jerked a knot in my bow, which made him chuckle under his breath, but I played it off like I had meant to do it.

"I'm going to bed." I waved to the laundry cart. "Night, Bonnie." I singled out Bishop next. "Thanks for the assist. Call a full meeting at dusk. We need to put our heads together on this."

The elevator doors had closed behind me before I heard the first shout. I smacked my palm against the emergency stop button, but it ignored me. Probably because the glide from the lobby to my floor was so short, I was practically there by the time the red light flashed.

Not trusting it a second time, I shoved open the emergency exit door and crashed into a wall of pale fur. "What in the—?"

"Bonnie," Ford yelled. *"Bonnie."*

"Bonnie?" I caught the breath she had knocked out of me. "Explain."

The last bit had been directed at Ford, since Bonnie had yet to shift back.

"She saw you get in the elevator and lost her ever-lovin' mind." He wasn't winded from the run up two flights of stairs, but he was flustered enough his cheeks had reddened. "She tried to pry you out of the booth. The doors are shredded from her teeth. God, her teeth. She bit through that metal like butter." He tried, but he couldn't hide his admiration. "Once she saw the shaft was empty, she used her nose to depress the access bar for the stairs and started climbing."

Tail between her legs, Bonnie whined pitifully, all but calling Ford a big meanie for chasing her down.

"What floor is her apartment on?" I exhaled. "Tell me it's above mine."

"First floor," he admitted. "She's got a thing about heights."

From what little time I had spent with Bonnie, she seemed to have a thing about a lot of things.

"Can she read English in this form? Did she maybe miss her turn?"

Pity twisted his features into what wanted to be a smile. "Afraid not."

Though she was half the size of my apartment, I still asked, "Do you want to sleep over?"

Her ears perked, she yipped once, and then she spun around on the stairs.

"That's not the potty dance, is it?" I asked Ford. "I don't have enough paper towels for this."

"I'm sure it will be fine." He backed down a step, then another. "I'll just leave you ladies to it."

"Chicken," I growled, which earned him a dirty look from Bonnie.

"Bawk, bawk." He winked at me. "Night, darlin'."

"Come on." I pivoted on the stairs and started climbing. "I'm beat."

On the landing, I held the door for Bonnie and showed her into my apartment. I worried I might have to fight her for my futon, but she curled up on the mountain of scraps and half-sewn projects

Bishop had dumped out of my supply bin during his hunt for sheets. Would it have killed him to steal dirty sheets *and* a laundry cart? I seriously doubted Bonnie cared if her escape route was springtime fresh.

Sometimes the fact my boss, and therefore Bishop, had access to my place really tweaked my nose, but I had agreed to the terms. I understood why the POA felt I warranted unrestricted access. And, now that I thought about it, maybe that utter lack of privacy was another factor in the absence of any personal life.

Sharing myself with another person was hard enough without turning it into a spectator sport.

"Bathroom's through that door," I told Bonnie. "Everything else is in plain sight."

Her contented huff rustled the cloth beneath her enormous muzzle.

"I have a meeting to attend at dusk, so we'll have to make arrangements for you then."

A faint whine whistled through her nose.

"Don't pout. You'd be bored out of your mind."

All that was left to do was turn out the light, change into pajamas since I had company, and hope she didn't snore.

FIVE

A troupe of chainsaw-juggling lumberjacks woke me ten minutes before my alarm got the chance. Cracking open my eyes, I caught sight of Bonnie, still on four legs, all of which were currently sticking up in the air as she snored louder than some woodchippers.

A firm knock jolted me upright, making me rethink where to cast my blame, but my sleepover buddy kept right on sawing logs. Probably sequoias. A whole forest of them. Into toothpicks.

When I opened the door, I wasn't all that surprised to find Midas standing in the hall, but I was glad I was decent. The red *Star Trek* pajama set I got on sale at the mall might not give off a professional vibe, but I was home and off the clock, so he could deal.

"I heard you made a friend." His gaze slid past my shoulder. "I came to see if you needed anything."

"Do you mean a harness and a leash?" I covered a yawn with my palm. "Or a crate and newspaper?"

The fine hairs rose down the back of my neck when crimson bled into Midas's eyes as my joke fell flat.

"Look, I just woke up. As a matter of fact, I'm pretty sure you woke me up." I gave him the stink-eye for that. "I didn't mean I would cage Bonnie or that she was my pet. I was thinking out loud how to disguise her as a dog, which I can tell by the glowing thing your eyes are doing isn't working for you."

A steady rumble filled the space between us, and a wet nose bumped the back of my hand in solidarity as Bonnie sidled up to me, but I shushed her before things got worse.

"I had a long, miserable morning. I didn't get much sleep today." I risked scratching Bonnie behind her ear when I spotted her lip still quivering in silent warning at Midas. "I'm sorry if me trying to be funny before I've had my morning café mocha came off as offensive. I didn't mean anything by it. I know Bonnie is a person, even if she's a four-legged person at the moment."

Goddess, someone needed to shove something in my mouth to shut me up. Preferably some form of chocolate.

"Bonnie is special," Midas said gruffly, reining in the temper I excelled at provoking in him. "It's my understanding you're aware how special, so you'll grasp that allowances must be made."

"While it's light-years beyond cool I have an actual fae in my apartment, it's also illegal for necromancers, such as myself, to fraternize with them. Ignoring that, I can't afford to sit on my hands until she irons out her kinks." I checked my phone and grimaced. "I have a meeting with Bishop in an hour. Can you resolve this by then?"

"Are you a cat person or a dog person?"

"I don't know." Most Low Society necromancers performed no magic, so we required no familiars. "I've never had a pet." I lifted a finger. "Or a sentient not-pet-friend-woman-person." I pointed at him. "Don't give me that squinty-eyed look, mister. I'm trying here. This is as good as it gets without caffeine."

A twitch in his cheek below his right eye left me unsure if he was smothering a laugh or seconds away from a stroke.

"Bonnie." He kept his voice firm but polite. "You have two choices. You can shift and come to work with me, or you can glamour yourself and go to work with Hadley."

She whined at me, soft, pathetic noises, and her eyes glimmered, huge and impossibly liquid.

Basically, she dialed her pouting before bed up ten degrees. She might not be an actual dog, but she knew how to make the schtick work with a sucker like me.

"Fine." I exhaled through my teeth. "How does glamour work?"

"Magic," he said, and this time I *knew* he was laughing at me.

"Can we get this pony-sized dog show on the road?" I started tapping my foot. "Bishop is waiting."

"Pick a form that won't be out of place in a city," he told her. "A dog is more practical if you're dead set on patrolling with Hadley."

Bonnie plunked on her butt, the claws on her front paws flexing like fingernails drumming, and then her outline shimmered and shrank.

"What is that?" The snow-white breadbox on knobby knees barked at me, a surprisingly big sound out of such a small body. "Wait. It's that meme dog. Not Doge, that Shiba something. Shiba Inu? That's a breed, right? This is..." I snapped my fingers. "A corgi. Yeah. That's it."

"A Pembroke Welsh Corgi." He examined her with interest. "Look at her tail."

"She doesn't have one."

"Exactly."

"Why didn't she do this last night?" I turned the question on her. "Why didn't you do this last night?"

The much smaller dog, about twenty-five pounds' worth, lolled her pink tongue at me.

"Bonnie hasn't shifted since she joined the pack," he answered for her, confirming my earlier assumption. "Ford told me she shifted to protect you. When she got stuck, it must have panicked her. She wouldn't have risked compounding the problem by casting magic she might have trouble controlling."

"The city has leash laws," I reminded him. "She'll have to wear a collar or harness and a leash."

With a twitch of her huge ears, she manifested both and wagged her nub, mostly her butt, with pride.

Since I wasn't getting out of this, I accepted my fate. "What do I feed her?"

"Human food is fine." He dragged a hand over his mouth. "Hopefully she won't stay like this for long."

"Are you laughing?" I planted my feet and crossed my arms over my chest. "This is funny to you?"

The tempting curve of his lips thinned, but a gleam sparked in his eyes, which I shouldn't have noticed but did. Clearly I hadn't learned my lesson from our earlier clash of wills.

"No," he said with false solemnity that hinted at a wicked sense of humor.

Bonnie woofed at Midas, proving neither of us believed him.

"Ford's in the lobby." He braced his hand on the doorframe, rubbed a scuff with his thumb. "He brought a casserole from his mom for the Randalls." He gouged the wood with his fingernail. "He's waiting on you."

"He told me Mrs. Randall babysat two of his older brothers."

"She has many children in the pack, but Shonda was the only one she birthed."

They say it takes a village—or a pack—to raise a child. "He okay to work this case?"

"His brothers need the closure."

That explained why Midas volunteered him. The buffer of years between Ford, his siblings, and Mrs. Randall also clued me in on how he could cut up with me without breaking down over her daughter's death.

Curious despite myself, I found myself asking, "Does Ford usually cope through humor and flirtation?"

"For as long as I've known him." Midas rolled his shoulders. "We all grieve in our own ways."

During the past year I had spent enough time around sentinels, most employed with the Atlanta Police Department as a cover, to know he was right. Laughter and jokes were popular coping mechanisms. Alcohol was too. Drugs. Sex. Other vices. Humor was the least harmful, in my opinion, even if the release valve of laughter often got tutted as being in poor taste.

Stretching until my shoulders popped, I yawned hugely. "Tell Ford I'll meet him downstairs?"

Midas noticed the bare strip of skin exposed between my pajama top and shorts, shut his eyes on an exhale, then turned his head. "What happened to using the fire escape?"

"First Snowball couldn't fit through the window, and now she can't manage the stairs. Look at those stumpy legs. Cute? Yes. Practical? No."

"Snowball?" he echoed. "Her fae name can't be pronounced by human—or necromantic—tongues, but you're going to call her Snowball?"

"Between us," I mock whispered behind my hand, "I hope the nickname shames her back onto two legs."

Snowball flattened her ears against her skull, but it was no use. The fluffy butt ruined the stone-cold-killer vibe.

"I could call her Bonnie," I told him, "which I assume is the name she chose for herself, not one you gave her, but it's safer if people think I adopted a dog. Snowball will draw less attention, especially from the pack, who might notice me naming a dog after a woman I met just yesterday—today?—who has coincidentally vanished." I gave her a reassuring pat. "The fewer people who know what she is, what she can do, the better."

"I'm starting to see why Bonnie opened up to you."

"Thanks to you, Ford has adopted me, and now I've adopted her. Maybe it's contagious. Don't come any closer, or you might get adopted too."

"I'm current on all my shots."

This time he didn't hide his smile, and it was every bit as devastating as I imagined it would be.

"You have a nice smile. You should use it more often."

"If I told a woman that, she would kick my family jewels so hard a crown would pop out on top of my head."

The resulting spurt of laughter would have sprayed him had he been six inches nearer.

"I have to go." I wiped my mouth. "I've embarrassed myself enough for one night."

Before I made an even bigger fool of myself, I shut the door and contemplated a shower. I was going to be late to the meeting. There was no getting around that. I might as well be late *and* clean, right?

Bonnie padded after me while I gathered clothes, and I would have felt her judgment from a mile away, let alone from across six hundred square feet.

"What?"

She barked while she tossed her head toward the door.

"Don't sass me." I grabbed a towel. "It's called interdepartmental cooperation."

Her angular head reminded me of a fox, especially when she pivoted her oversized ears forward.

"Wipe that look off your face." I scowled at her snort. "I wasn't flirting with him."

Clearly the girl rule of *new haircut, new woman* applied here. Or maybe *new fur, new woman*.

Bonnie the gwyllgi and Bonnie the corgi were both far more assertive than Bonnie the woman, and none of them knew what they were talking about when it came to me and a certain blond beta.

Midas couldn't have *hands off* written more clearly across his face than if he tattooed it on his forehead.

I shut Snowball out of the bathroom while I indulged in a shower that tested my water heater's stamina, then dressed for patrol in jeans gone splotchy from previous bleachings, a tee with a dancing chocolate bar on the front that said *Bite Me*, and sneakers.

Presentation was everything in my past life. Not so much anymore. I got to schlub it, and I liked it. There was no point in wearing trousers or blouses or cute boots when goddess only knows what you would step in before the night was through. Jeans, tees, and sneakers? Those could get tossed in the washer along with a capful of bleach, and they would be ready to go again.

The only time I made a slight effort with my appearance was when I manned my kiosk, which wouldn't happen tonight.

"I need to hire an assistant." I eyed Bonnie thoughtfully. "Do you think Midas would loan you out?"

An employee who could run the business when a tough case required all of my focus would be *amazing*. Dare I dream, I might even start turning a decent profit that way too. Anyone I hired had to be trustworthy, trustworthy, and trustworthy. They also had to have big ears to catch all the latest supernatural gossip and have no qualms about passing it on.

Hmm.

Bonnie mentioned the alpha expecting her to pull her own weight, so maybe not. Still, it was an idea.

I would ask her about it tomorrow night, assuming she got herself unstuck by then. Otherwise, I would have to ask her to glamour up a service dog vest.

Shoving all the *maybes*, and *it might be nices* out of my head, I checked my foggy reflection.

The big reason I cut my hair to jaw length was so I could shower and go without the hassle of drying my thick hair. All I had to do was dump goop on my hands, rake my fingers through it, and I was styled and ready to hit the streets.

When I exited the bathroom, Bonnie was waiting on me with the handle of her leash in her mouth.

"Are you sure you wouldn't rather shift?" I looped it over my wrist. "This doesn't embarrass you?"

Tugging on my arm, she led me to the door and scratched at the bottom corner. Since she hadn't, to my knowledge, gone to the bathroom since we got home this morning, I didn't hesitate to let her out into the hall, where any puddles would be a pack problem, if you asked me.

We hit the elevator, and I saw myself scowling in the silver panels at the scent trail I was establishing throughout the building.

Down in the lobby, Ford was chatting up two women who resembled one another enough to pass for sisters. One noted my arrival and wrote on a business card she pulled from her purse, then handed it to him while maintaining eye contact with me. The other scowled at her sister, who must have called dibs on him.

The pair walked off before I reached him, who looked at the card, then at me, and tore it to pieces.

"Don't snub her on my account," I teased. "We both know you'll end up taping the jigsaw puzzle back together when you get desperate enough."

"Nah." He dusted the bits into the nearest trash can. "I would have done the same with or without you."

"Off the market?"

The question came out too interested, and I immediately regretted how easy it was to talk to him. I was starting to worry he wasn't handling me, that he was genuinely a nice guy and it was my expectation everyone had their own agenda that jaded me into seeing what I expected and not what was there.

The problem with lying about who and what you are is you expect others to do the same.

Sadly, most people don't disappoint. Vanity, ego, insecurity all drive lies out of mouths. I might be hiding for nobler reasons, but I was still a liar. Hard to feel entitled to expect truth from someone when you can't offer it in return.

"Not exactly." He stuffed his hands into the pockets of his jeans. "I am waiting for the right kind of woman to come along."

Flirting.

He was flirting with me.

Again.

There must be something seriously wrong with him if he thought this hot mess was just plain hot.

"Good luck with that." I did what I did best and blew him off before the spark fanned into a flame that burned my new identity to the ground. "The right person always seems to come along at the wrong time. Or maybe I got that backwards, and it's the wrong person who always seems to come along at the right time."

"Either works, as near as I can tell." A beat later, he addressed the dog at my feet. "Corgi?"

"Midas says she's a Pembroke? Pemberley? No, that's Jane Austen. Definitely Pembroke."

"Midas." He slid the leash between his fingers, his skin throwing off warmth but not touching mine, and rubbed the nylon between his fingers like he couldn't quite decide if it was real. The leash or his attraction, I wasn't sure which piqued his curiosity more. "That explains your new pet."

"This was our compromise. I have to work, and she has to blend."

"Have you checked DORA? The cleaners have uploaded their preliminary findings."

The best thing about the cleaners had to be their expansive database. Thanks to their in with all factions, they collated historical data on every crime involving supernaturals within city limits. Bishop nicknamed her DORA, and it caught on, but I had no idea what it meant, and no one would tell me.

A year later, I was still enduring my hazing with good humor. Mostly.

"Not yet." I slanted Bonnie a pointed glance. "I'm heading for a meeting now. Bishop will brief me then." Ford made no move to let me pass, so I tacked on, "I would invite you to tag along, but it's OPA only."

"OPA?"

"Office of the Potentate of Atlanta. Bishop likes OPA because he likes having an excuse to yell 'Opa!'"

"He's Greek?"

"No, he's annoying." Bonnie started tugging on her leash, and I took the hint. "Nature calls."

I almost said *duty*, but I didn't want to jinx myself since I didn't have any doggie poop bags.

"Lee," he implored, eyes downcast. "I don't want you to think I'm pressuring you to cooperate with the pack, with *me*, but I do need you to keep me in the loop—in your loop—until we resolve this." A grin hit his lips. "Think of me as your substitute Bishop."

"Bishop is part of the team. There are things I could tell him that I can't tell you."

"I get that." He shifted his weight, scuffed a heel. "I only want you to keep me in mind."

"I'll do that," I promised. "Just like you have hard lines, I do too. I won't cross them."

"I can't disobey my alpha," he confided in a tone that hinted at secrets, and I heard the warning even if I didn't understand it. "I always follow orders. It's not a matter of conscience, it's a physical compulsion for me."

"Midas isn't your alpha."

"Yet."

"He can exert that level of control over you?"

"The power makes him uncomfortable," he neither confirmed nor denied. "That's why he was happy playing second fiddle to his sister, but Lethe squirmed under her mother's thumb. None of us were much surprised when she started her own pack where she can run things her own way."

"He didn't seem all that uncomfortable when he was staring me down last night."

"Lee, darlin', had you pulled that stunt with his mother, Tisdale would still be picking you out of her teeth."

"Well, that's comforting." I ran a finger along the collar of my tee, but I had trouble swallowing. "He did say his control was excellent."

"His position comes with certain...benefits. Midas isn't fond of those either. He's used to making eye contact with whomever he likes, so he gets frustrated when folks won't look back. He snares them, like he did you. That's why he didn't punish you. It was his fault, and he knew it."

Curious about that very topic, I prodded him. "What's the deal with that anyway?"

"You can make brief eye contact with any pack member, with the exception of the alpha and the heir." A pause told me he was thinking how to frame the rest. "Friends and lovers earn certain exemptions to the rules over time, but only with the gwyllgi they're involved with, and only for as long as the relationship lasts."

"I look at you all the time," I pointed out. "I'm looking directly into your eyes now, as a matter of fact."

"We're friends, remember? I can look at you all day, and you can look right back, and it won't ruffle that side of me."

"I thought you said it happens over time? It's been like twenty-four hours."

"I've watched you for a lot longer." He tapped the end of my nose. "You just recently made the mistake of letting me wedge my foot in the door is all."

"Don't blur the line between friend and stalker, Ford."

"Gwyllgi don't stalk." Ford acted affronted as he escorted me out onto the sidewalk. "We're not cats."

Touchy, touchy.

With a promise to touch base soon, I set off under the pretense of walking my dog, which made her kind of handy as far as exit strategies go, then pulled out my cell to text Bishop.

HQ, which was less of a tongue twister than OPA, was fluid. Its location, I mean. Ask anyone on the POA's team, and they would tell you we have several bases numbered one through twelve scattered throughout the city. They would also admit they had never stepped inside one.

Members of the team, aside from the POA (See what I mean about it being a tongue twister? Or maybe a brain twister. I mean, really. *The POA is at the OPA.* What's with all the acronyms?), Bishop, and me, were kept anonymous.

Only Bishop knew their real identities, and he acted as a go-between. Yet another reason why he had been a desk jockey pre-Hadley. Maybe he was grateful I provided an excuse for him to venture out into the world, take a break from his computer screens. Or maybe he hoped I would fail in spectacular fashion, and the POA would remand him back to his techie temple to worship in peace.

I had a more pressing issue on my hands than whether Bishop liked or merely tolerated me. What to do with Bonnie. Only one person could grant her clearance to enter HQ with me, and I regretted there was no choice but to have the conversation in an unsecure location.

"Watch my back," I told the shadow sniffing around Bonnie, hoping for a contact high. "I need about ten minutes."

Slinking away, it began canvassing the area while I sucked in a fortifying breath and dialed the POA.

"Hadley."

Even the way he said my name gave me chills. "Linus."

Warmth tempered his voice, but it failed to thaw me. "To what do I owe the pleasure?"

"I have a pet. Temporarily. A dog."

"Congratulations."

"Um, the thing is, she's actually a friend's dog. You know who I mean? The friend with a whole pack of them? So I guess I'm dog-sitting. Kind of."

Even with Ambrose on the prowl, it was dangerous, so dangerous, to name any names.

"I see."

"She got stuck, and she's my responsibility until she gets unstuck."

"Let me see if I have this straight. A pureblooded gwyllgi under Tisdale's protection has glamoured itself to appear as a dog who is now in your custody. Did you perform a service for it? Or it for you to create this debt between you?"

Yet another reason why he was scary. He read between lines where air molecules wouldn't fit.

"A little of both," I supposed. "She doesn't like men, so I acted as a buffer. We bonded over it, I guess. She took it personally when one of the cleaners got in my face about procedure. That's when she...got stuck."

"She was a witness?"

"She received a tip sent to her boss and followed up personally. We met her on-scene to assess the situation, and...it escalated from there."

"Necromancers are forbidden to interact with fae."

Since fae were more or less immortal all on their own—the very nerve!—and therefore required nothing from the Society, the Society viewed them as lesser beings rather than peers or—goddess forbid —superiors.

Our factions indulged in commerce—no surprise considering the Society prized wealth over life, or undeath—but those transactions were handled through specially bonded solicitors who negotiated on behalf of their clients.

"I didn't knowingly interact with...her, but then it was too late. For what it's worth, no one outside the, uh, top dogs, are aware of her...condition?" I bit the side of my cheek. "This covert stuff is harder than I thought it would be."

All the awkward pauses made me sound like I was doing a Captain Kirk impression.

"You need clearance for your guest to accompany you to the meeting?"

"Yeah. That's why I called in the first place."

"Can you hold the phone to her ear?"

"Sure." I crouched on the sidewalk, certain I'd fit right in with crazy dog moms everywhere for letting my pooch burn a few of my unlimited minutes. "Here you go, Snowball."

Linus spoke to her for a minute or two, and Bonnie barked once at the end before nudging the phone away with her nose.

I held the receiver to my ear. "You speak dog?"

"Glamour doesn't impair her comprehension. Her mind is just as sharp, no matter what form she takes. You would be wise to remember that if you're going to work this closely with the pack."

"I'll do that." I reconsidered Bonnie. "What did you tell her?"

"I explained she is more than welcome to stay with you for as long as you'll have her, but if she expects to accompany you everywhere you go, and be privy to the details of your current investigation and beyond, she must swear an oath to our office."

The oath prevented her from divulging the location of any or all HQs she visited, from sharing any case-related information she overheard, or spreading identifying information on the team, etc.

"Will it supersede any contradictory oaths?" I searched the darkness, but my shadow blended too well. "Her...owner...can order her to spill her guts. So can her owner's son, apparently."

"That is true to a certain extent. She will do as she's commanded, a submissive seldom argues, but she's fae, and fae can't lie. She gave her word, and her vow is magically binding."

"A bark is binding?"

"Yes."

"Okay." I absorbed this information, filing it away. "You're the boss for a reason."

"Lethe has been attempting to educate us for our own safety now that a pack, and therefore its distant relations, will be living next door."

Lethe Kinase, Midas's sister, the former Atlanta heir and current Savannah alpha, had purchased the home next door to Woolworth House, where Linus would live after he married Grier.

No doubt those close ties were to thank for the prosperous relationship between HQ and Tisdale Kinase.

Yet another reason for me to keep my nose clean. The Savannah alpha knew my secret. The Atlanta one...did not.

Thinking of Ford, and Midas, I hazarded, "Maybe Lethe can send me some tips via email."

"I'll mention it at dinner."

That was a polite way of saying I was holding him up, so I mumbled thanks and ended the call.

Then I gave myself a few seconds to just breathe.

Linus trusted me.

He believed in me.

He wouldn't go off la-di-da to dinner if he felt Atlanta was burning in his absence.

I got this.

I can do this.

A sharp bark drew my attention to Bonnie, who had finally noticed Ambrose. Not everyone did. It required a smidgen of magic to see him, a dollop to track his movements, and a dash to comprehend his full range of motion. Most folks only saw a blur, if that, which made life easier for me.

"Ambrose, knock it off."

While Ambrose bristled at the command, Bonnie made her move. She snapped at him, but her teeth—

"Goddess," I hissed. "Bonnie, *no.*"

Jaw locked on a corner of shadow, she slung her head while snarling, and I hit my knees.

Stars sparkled on the edges of my vision, growing brighter, closer.

"Kill him," I panted, "and you kill me too."

Bonnie spat out the mouthful of darkness then reared up on me, licking my face while she whined softly.

"You didn't do anything wrong." I waited until I caught my breath. "This was my fault for not telling you. Most folks can't see him, let alone touch him. I should have given you a heads-up."

Only the POA had ever strong-armed Ambrose into submission, and that was before we fused into this...thing.

Learning gwyllgi, full-blooded ones anyway, could tear into Ambrose both comforted and terrified me.

I appreciated the need for fail-safes, but I didn't enjoy discovering new vulnerabilities the hard way.

"Come on." I checked for physical wounds, but there was only a sharp pang that radiated throughout my body. One thing was certain. Bonnie had just guaranteed I would have to feed Ambrose to heal him, and I didn't mean chocolate ganache squares. "Bishop will have a conniption if we don't hurry."

For the next half hour, I exchanged long strings of code with him that guided me through the city toward the base selected for tonight's meeting. About the time I started to worry I might have to carry Bonnie, her short legs flagging, a final text informed me Base Four was expecting me.

After tucking my phone away, I led Bonnie to the parking deck on the corner.

A swirl of shadows darker than the rest shot past me to race us to the stairwell.

Accepting the challenge from her new archnemesis, Bonnie barked at the top of her lungs and gave chase, straining against her leash. Until she remembered it was her own construct, anyway. Then it stretched like taffy between us as she ran flat out for Ambrose.

Frak.

Just my luck she would suffer delusions of grandeur while dressed in her fur suit.

"Snowball," I yelped, belatedly realizing she might be small, but she was mighty. "Slow down."

Ignoring me, the corgi dragged me clear across the bottom floor to the emergency exit doors. She cornered the shadow, who leaned down and patted her shadow's head, which incensed her to new volumes of pissedoffedness. She didn't bite him again. Thank the goddess.

"Ambrose," I sighed, scooping up Bonnie so she would hush. "Why are you like this?"

The shadow gave an exaggerated shrug, returned to its usual Hadley shape, and started climbing to the correct floor, not waiting on me to follow.

Out of breath by the time we arrived on an abbreviated landing tucked between floors, I set Bonnie down and braced my hands on my knees. "You weigh a lot more than twenty-five pounds. What are you, fifty?"

She spun a tight circle and gave me a face full of her fluffy butt.

"Yeah, yeah," I groused. "That was rude of me."

I punched in my code and entered HQ before the overwhelming urge to smile set a bad precedent. I already had a misbehaving shadow who expected artisanal chocolate in exchange for not indulging his murderous whims. I refused to stuff jerky in my pockets for dog training too.

A quick glance at Bishop's command center, which I preferred to call *the bridge*, as in his equipment was so advanced he could pilot a starship from here, told me I hadn't missed the meeting.

The wall in front of me was painted an unrelieved black, and the two rows of monitors anchored there blended in when not in use. The upper row held four monitors, each about thirty-four inches, and they were blank. The lower row mirrored the one above it, but those were always on and flashing surveillance mooched off city cameras as well as our own private mounts. That or cartoons. Depended on if business was slow.

Bishop strolled in from the kitchen cupping a steaming mug that perfumed the air with its bright copper fragrance.

Since I wasn't a practicing necromancer, I hadn't built up much of a tolerance for blood. The way it smelled, the way it looked, the way it felt running through my fingers. I gotta admit, I wasn't a big fan, but I was getting used to it. Mostly because Ambrose *was* a fan. That didn't mean it was any less weird to watch someone walk around sipping it like the café mocha I forgot to brew on my way out the door.

Ugh.

No wonder I was so crabby tonight.

"You're late." Bishop licked his lips with a smacking noise when he caught me staring at his blood mustache. "We've been waiting."

"An hour. Half that was spent talking to the POA. You saw me."

I gestured to the live feeds. "You have a billion cameras mounted across the city, and you watch my every move like I'm the star of your favorite television series." I indicated the blank monitors. "No one is waiting. They're probably running late, as usual, just like me."

As much as I would like to claim I set a sterling example for the team by showing up on time to every meeting, I would be lying through my teeth. Between the circuitous route I took to get here, and never knowing where *here* was, I ran late as often as everyone else.

Gathering this many people, with lives and jobs outside the OPA, and on short notice, was plain hard. We were lucky when two-thirds of us showed and blessed when we had a full house.

On his way past, he caught sight of Bonnie and almost dropped his mug. "That is *not* a corgi."

"No, it's an Andulian liver worm from the planet Balfonz that I stuffed into a fur suit I bought off eBay. Using its newfound powers of adorableness, it will infiltrate our society. Soon we will all call it master."

"Can you stop being a geek for five seconds and tell me what the actual hell you're doing with that gwyllgi on a leash? I hope you asked her permission first. Otherwise, it was nice knowing you. She'll kill you when she gets free." He swept his gaze over her again. "Unless... Is the leash spelled?"

"It's not spelled." I dropped it. "It's not even real."

To illustrate my point, Bonnie vanished the leash and the collar.

"Can I pet her?" He squatted in front of Bonnie, a smile on his face. "She's so much cuter pocket-sized. I just want to—"

Between one blink and the next, my corgi morphed, becoming a slavering beast ready to devour the arm he extended toward her.

Guess she didn't like guys getting handsy with her in any form.

"Fuck." He toppled back like a turtle stuck on its shell. "Damn it."

The POA trusted Bishop with no caveats, and that meant I did too, whether I wanted to or not.

"We're investigating the mutilation of nine people, and no one has considered this might have done it?"

A warning growl revved up Bonnie's throat, and she took a menacing step closer to Bishop.

"Remember what we talked about?" I tugged on a handful of her fur. "The whole wearing-glamour-in-public thing? You need to stay, dare I say it, in*corg*nito. You're also going to have to not eat people."

Grumbling under her breath, Bonnie reactivated loaf mode. Back in her cutesy form, she trotted over to Bishop and offered her head to him for a pat.

"I'm not going to fall for the act twice." He scrambled back. "Call off your dog, Hadley."

"Snowball, behave."

Now, I'm not saying normal dogs can do smug, I hadn't been around enough to know, but this one sure managed.

"You had no problem with her before," I pointed out.

"Then she was your problem." He flexed his hand. "I'm a programmer. I need all my fingers."

"Come on." I clasped palms with him and hauled him onto his feet. "Let's get this meeting started."

Keeping a wary eye on Bonnie, he returned to his desk. "Her name's not really Snowball, is it?"

"Only when she's on four legs." I shrugged. "And a corgi." I noticed her sniffing a pair of his boots left out to dry from the last time he'd worn them, and I was grateful she wasn't a boy who could hike her leg. "The rest of the time, she's Bonnie."

"Bonnie." He tapped a finger on his chin. "Bonnie." He cocked his head. "Bonnie Diaz? Joined the pack about eight or nine days ago?"

I wasn't surprised Bishop knew her name and situation, at least the official version. He was a shameless gossipmonger, both officially and unofficially. We couldn't afford to be caught unawares when we shared a city, what some might consider hunting grounds, with so many often opposing supernatural factions.

Even though I grew up a measly two hundred and fifty miles from here, Atlanta felt like a long way from home. There I mingled with necromancers, vampires, and humans, but that was as diverse as it got. Now I toed a dangerous line by willfully keeping company with a fae.

I wasn't a necromancer, not really, not anymore. Maybe the Society's rules no longer applied to me.

Ha.

As if I'd ever been that lucky a day in my life.

Bishop mashed a few buttons, and the shadowy outlines of two men and two women filled the topmost screens. Filters masked their features, and their voices to a lesser extent, but the POA insisted the team remain anonymous for their protection.

I knew the quartet as Lisbeth, Reece, Anca, and Milo, but I had no idea if they used their real names or pseudonyms.

Three of them weren't just techs but had been deputized to patrol the streets. They wore black garbs to mimic the POA when he was in what we jokingly (except not) called Grim Reaper mode. The overall effect was of him being omnipresent, that you couldn't walk a dark alley with bad intent without bumping into the guy.

As far as strategies go, it was ingenious. I had to give him that. It did make me consider if I would be expected to pick up the cloak and cowl if—no, *when*—I took on his role in order to maintain the image.

The apprentice gig meant I had to show my face, the same as the POA, so it's not like the city wouldn't know a new POA had been named. They were well aware I was in training, and I got no veil to hide under. I had to be transparent in all my dealings with the citizens of our fair city in order to build their trust in me. The public didn't get a vote about who became their next potentate, but their good opinion was still worth bonus points in my favor...or against it.

Bishop clearing his throat interrupted my navel-gazing, but the squeal of delight that came next left my ears ringing.

"I'm in love," Lisbeth announced. "That dog is the cutest thing I have ever seen in my whole entire life."

"Who's a little bread loaf?" Milo cooed. "You are, doggo. I bet you're the tastiest bread loaf."

Without knowing Milo's species, I couldn't decide if he was being funny, but that's how I chose to interpret his comment for his own safety. Though it might be entertaining to watch a warg or vamp attempt to make a snack out of Bonnie only to have her explode into full-on gwyllgi mode and devour him in a hilarious role-reversal.

Proving she didn't mind the opposite sex, as long as they stayed on their side of the monitor, Bonnie preened for Milo while he continued to call her various bread-based food items: bun, home slice, toasted ciabatta... As I was starting to reconsider, that he might be envisioning her as the meat in a corgi sandwich, Bishop muted his screen.

"What a lovely creature," Anca murmured. "Her color is quite extraordinary."

I noticed she didn't call Bonnie a dog, but I let it slide. "Who knew they came in white?"

Not me. Probably not Bonnie either. Albinism—or was that amelanism?—occurred in all species, right?

"The cleaners uploaded their preliminary report on Shonda Randall," Reece interrupted, unaffected by the cuteness. "You're not going to like this." He shared his screen with all of us. "Saliva and hairs found on the body indicates the killer is a warg."

"You're right," I agreed. "I don't like that."

The booming gwyllgi population had all but shoved the three warg packs who used to run the streets out of the city. One pack, the smallest of the three, hung on by keeping their membership exclusive. The two larger and more aggressive packs had been forced to the outskirts. They weren't happy about it, but they couldn't fight Tisdale for more territory and win.

The Atlanta gwyllgi pack held more land, boasted higher numbers, and had diversified into security among other specialty fields to financially support their current size and stockpile funds for future growth. They were more than a pack, they were a local institution.

"This could be retaliatory," Lisbeth mused. "Mendelsohn is the youngest and the hungriest."

"He's also the horniest," Milo chimed in, fresh from his unmuting. "Deric would have to stumble out of his harem and put on pants long enough to notice he'd been driven from his territory first, then he'd have to sober up before he could orchestrate this. Even then, he isn't known for his violence against women. Why kill this one?"

Deric Mendelsohn was a young alpha, just shy of thirty. Bloodthirsty? Yes. He ripped out his father's throat to claim the title not six months ago. According to gossip he was too busy knocking up every unmated female in his pack above the age of eighteen to care he had lost prime digs in the city.

That Deric. *Super* classy guy.

"The Clairmonts get my vote," Anca said. "Ayla is clever enough to see the power vacuum Tisdale's reign has left among wargs in Atlanta. However small the territory, she may hope to step in and claim it."

"They would never be able to defend it," Bishop argued. "They don't have the numbers, and they're afraid to get their manicured hands dirty. They establish dominance via savings balance, for pity's sake."

"I'm inclined to agree." I exhaled through my teeth. "That leaves the Loup."

Garou, a title, not a surname, was alpha of the Loup Garous. His great-great-great-whatever grandfather thought *loup garou* sounded edgier than *warg*. Guess when your hobbies include mugging, stealing cars, and running drugs, branding is important.

"They're thugs," Lisbeth said, "not homicidal maniacs."

"They're plenty homicidal." Anca snorted. "Their murder-for-hire numbers hit triple digits last year."

"We hit them back," I reminded her. "Hard."

Five of their members were rotting in jail. Two more had received death sentences.

"The Loups are all about the bottom line," Reece added. "Gender and age don't mean anything to them. They take special requests for cause of death, charge a nice fee to get specific too. Nine kills costs, big-time, so what's a few bucks more to make them memorable?"

"Where's the link?" Anca interjected. "What's the motive?"

"We haven't seen the cleaners' reports on the Perkerson Park bodies yet." I held up a hand when the protests started. "We can't afford to get ahead of ourselves."

Until I received confirmation in print, we had two murder scenes, not one serial killer.

Without IDs on all the victims, we couldn't run full backgrounds on them, and we had no way of knowing how, or if, their lives had intersected.

"For all we know," Milo added, "this was a Loup hit on a competitor."

"Until you've got evidence to support your theory, keep it within these four walls. We do not need to piss off the pack with unsubstantiated hypotheticals." An itch started on the back of my neck, but it was only Bonnie. Ears perking under my notice, she scooched closer to me. "Who wants to draw straws for the dubious honor of interrogating Garou?"

"You're the one who wants to be the next POA," Lisbeth singsonged. "How much do you regret your life choices right about now?"

A great many things I had done in my life were regrettable, but not this. "I need volunteers for patrol. I'm not going to make it out there tonight."

"I'm game," Lisbeth chimed in. "I need to get in my steps anyway. The EDJ kept me stuck in my cubicle."

"Count me in too." Milo yawned. "My evil day job isn't so much evil as it is mind-numbingly dull."

"I'll meet with Ford." Cooperation, here I come. "We'll start interviewing the alphas."

The henna lead would keep. It was present on one victim out of nine. This one burned hotter.

"I wouldn't mind putting in some OT with him," Lisbeth sighed dreamily. "Would dating him be a conflict of interest?"

"Yes," I told her without thinking. "He said so himself."

"You talked to him about dating?"

"Yes?"

"You, who haven't gone out once since you got here, talked to my secret crush about *dating*?"

"As your crush was a secret, I didn't realize you had a thing for him, and it was hypothetical."

"Hadley, Hadley, Hadley." Bishop patted my shoulder. "A man doesn't bring up dating unless he wants a woman to start getting ideas —about him."

"Too bad Lisbeth called dibs." I shrugged off his hand before he started giving me pointers. "Good thing I have a case to distract me from the heartbreak over what might have been."

"We've got an update." Reece pulled up his personal screen on a lower monitor then used his mouse to highlight a block of text for us all to see. "There's a slight—I'm talking blink-and-you'd-miss-it—hormonal difference between a warg's body fluids when it attains each form."

I got a bad feeling about where he was going with this. "Please tell me it didn't kill Shonda with its human teeth."

"I can't do that," he said in his scientist voice. "The evidence is inconclusive."

"A warg, on two *and* four legs, killed and ate her instead of shooting, stabbing, or any of the other things people enjoy doing to one another?"

"That's how it looks."

"How individual is the hormonal signature?" Anca asked.

"Enough that it would skew one way or the other, depending on the individual?"

"It's possible," he allowed, but he didn't sound happy about giving her theory legs.

"What about the bite imprint?" I massaged my forehead. "Do we have that yet?"

"It shows a mixture of human and canid teeth," Reece said, pointing it out on a second report.

"Are we talking one person?" Backing up, I clarified, "Pre and post shift, I mean?"

Killing on four legs, dining on two. Or, I suppose, the reverse might be equally true.

"Or do the hormones indicate two different individuals?" Bishop finished my thought. "One human and one shifted warg?"

"I would need a saliva sample to be certain." He hummed under his breath. "I'll see what I can do."

The cleaners did a damn fine job, and they saved us a hell of a lot of time, but they raced against the clock. Sometimes we had to pinch the minute hands and rewind them a bit to decode the exact chain of events.

"Skip Shonda. There are too many eyes on her. Get your sample from one of the Perkerson Park victims." I hated the political aspect of the job, but no office was ever held without playing the game. "We can always double back to Shonda if we need verification."

"All right." Reece made a thoughtful sound. "I should be able to crosscheck my findings in a noninvasive manner."

"Good deal." I scanned each screen. "Anything else?"

"No."

"Nope."

"Nah."

"No."

"In that case, meeting adjourned." I tried to resist, but in the end, I caved to the geek in me. "Tune in tomorrow—same Bat-time, same Bat-channel!"

A chorus of groans met with that gem of a catchphrase from the 1960's *Batman* TV show before their screens went dark.

When I dropped my gaze to Bishop, he was staring a hole through Snowball. "Not this again."

"What I said earlier might have been out of line, but that doesn't mean I'm not on the right track."

"We covered too much ground, and I haven't had any chocolate. You'll have to remind me."

"Bonnie showed up a week ago, give or take. What do you bet the oldest of the bodies from Perkerson date back to the same time frame?"

"Are you saying this because she tried to bite you or because you think she's involved?"

"You had Midas Freaking Kinase on-scene for Shonda Randall, and he couldn't place the killer's scent. Your buddy Ford couldn't positively link both scenes either. That's not normal. They're both familiar with wargs, the local packs in particular, so how do they not recognize a warg if that's what it is?"

"Bonnie," I addressed the corgi pretending to nap. "Care to defend yourself?"

A fake snore, albeit an adorable one, sealed the deal.

"She can understand us however she appears," I told Bishop, "but she can't talk without shifting back, and she's stuck."

"How sure are you she can't?" He eyed the dozing loaf. "How sure are you she won't?"

"I'll bring it up to Ford."

"Do you trust him?"

"I don't know him well, but I've always pegged him as a decent guy whenever our paths have crossed."

"Midas handpicked him to play liaison with OPA."

The fact he resisted the urge to yell *opa!* told me he was dead serious. "I figured."

"He got promoted days before you arrived in Atlanta. The shine wasn't off the apple when he introduced himself to you. He set himself in your path at the first opportunity." He kept going, hitting me over the head with facts, hammering nails in the coffin of any possible friendship with Ford. "Since then, he's overseen every gwyllgi-related crime in our jurisdiction."

"That's kind of his job, right?"

"Yeah, and his predecessor did what you'd expect. He prioritized. He only showed when it mattered."

"Maybe Ford enjoys being thorough."

"Or maybe he was planted in a position where the pack could keep an eye on you. The first opportunity Midas got, the very first, he paired you with Ford. I can tell you right now that has never happened in the history of this office. We've always been friendly with the other factions in the city, the gwyllgi in particular because of the POA's personal connections, but he's never worked a case with them. He's never partnered with them. They would rather snatch a case off his desk than look over his shoulder while he did his job."

"I get that but—"

"Now here you are, with a gwyllgi—a *fae*—in tow, in our HQ. What better spy than one who can change their face?" He wrapped his knuckles on his desk. "Watch your back, kid. That's all I'm saying."

The warning pinched my heart, not because I liked Ford, though he was likeable, but because it meant my first instincts had been correct. He was playing me. Tisdale, or her son, had set him on my trail. They wanted me vetted for the position to their satisfaction. For me to waffle, even for a second, proved he was good at it.

"I will." I bent down to collect the leash Bonnie had manifested after sensing an end to our visit then started for the door. "Thanks."

"You've got friends here," he called to my back. "I'm not as pretty as Ford, but I care."

I didn't slow to answer, because I wasn't sure about Bishop either. The POA had stuck us together, much the same as Midas had volunteered Ford. Neither of them had chosen to work with me. They were both doing a job, and I was a part of that.

On the landing, Bonnie pressed herself against my ankle, and her full weight almost tripped me.

I saw through what she was doing. The action warmed my heart, but I didn't let her make a dent in it.

"I get it." Loud and clear. I leaned down to scratch behind her ears. "You're a true friend."

Her bark was loud, sharp, and left no room for argument. I wished I could believe her.

"As much as I hate to agree with Bishop," I said, straightening, "he's right. The timing is too coincidental. You need to shift sooner rather than later so I can ask you some basic questions."

A pitiful whine made it clear talking was the last thing she wanted to do, and it lent weight to Bishop's concerns she was hiding behind me by choice. If that were true, she wasn't leaning on a friend, she was using me to avoid an interrogation that needed to happen.

Calling it a draw for now, I pulled out my phone and called Ford as Bonnie and I took the stairs.

"I'm hungry."

"Um." I held it away from my ear then checked to make sure I had dialed the right number. "Okay?"

"How about lunch?" His truck's engine was a steady hum in the background. "I know this great taco—"

"No."

"No to tacos, or no to lunch?"

The chat with Bishop had spoiled my appetite, but we had work to do, and I had questions for him. "Tacos."

"Tell me you didn't eat at Sal's."

I twisted the leash around my finger. "He promised."

"You can't go around believing everything that everyone tells you, darlin'."

"Say it ain't so." Bonnie and I hit the ground floor and took the sidewalk to put as much distance between us and Base Four as possible. "Here I took everyone at face value."

"I'm going to tell you a secret." His voice softened, saddened. "You can't trust anyone."

Bam. Bam. Bam.

More nails hammered in the coffin of our friendship left my ears ringing.

"I learned that early," I rasped, torn on how far to trust him, how far I could let him trust me.

"I hate to hear that."

"What sounds good that's not tacos and is on the way to Loup territory?"

"We'll talk about why we need to visit Garou, but first— How does pho sound?"

"Pho-nominal."

"You're a hoot." He chuckled like he meant it. "Where should I pick you up?"

"I'm at the Gas-N-Go on West Peachtree Street Northeast."

"Be there in ten."

The call ended, and Bonnie swiveled an inquisitive ear my way.

"Remember the rules." I held a finger to my lips. "We don't talk about HQ to outsiders."

Accepting that, despite her outsider status, she trotted off, butt wagging, for the gas station five blocks down.

We had enough time for me to purchase a bottle of water to split with Bonnie before Ford pulled in and lowered his window.

All smiles, he leaned across the seat. "Need a hand up?"

Remembering how he tossed me in the last time, I was quick to reassure him. "I got it."

After he popped the locks, I opened the door then scooped up Bonnie. I set her on the seat, intending for her to ride between us, but she had other ideas. She waited until I climbed in before claiming the window seat.

"I showered." Ford lifted his arm, sniffed. "I even applied fresh deodorant."

As much as I wanted to joke about it not being strong enough to cover his geek, I suspected his geekiness was an act for my benefit. If Bishop was right and Ford had been placed to monitor me, he would have learned my hobbies by now. Including my love for old sci-fi movies. What better way to bond than over a shared interest?

Blergh.

"I figured she would be more comfortable between us, but I wasn't thinking about the man-factor."

"Man-factor." He grinned wider. "I like that. It sounds…manly."

A snort escaped me. "You're ridiculous."

"With your taste in movies? You have no room to talk."

"I have excellent taste in movies."

"Prove it."

Stumped by the dare, I fumbled. "Do you want my top five?"

"Invite me over for a movie night. I'll watch your all-time favorite, and then I'll render judgment."

Ears still ringing, I didn't play as nice as I probably should have with him. "That sounds like you want an excuse to snoop around my apartment."

"If I do?"

"I would prefer you ask me outright rather than pretending to be something you're not—namely interested in me personally when this arrangement is professional."

"Life isn't black and white, Lee. There's a whole spectrum. You can't go through life colorblind."

"You sure have a lot of wisdom to dispense tonight." I cut him a look. "Are you sure you don't want to go for Chinese? You've already got a leg up on the fortune cookies."

"I like you." His eyes crinkled until they almost vanished. "I really do."

And damn if I didn't believe him.

WE ATE our pho on the shady patio of a hole-in-the-wall restaurant you had to know existed to find, and no one gave me a second glance when I ordered Bonnie her own portion of pho bo vien. I paid for the three of us, which scandalized Ford and his gentlemanly sensibilities, and made the food taste all the sweeter.

Bonnie slurped her compliments to the chef under the table while Ford and I hashed out strategy.

As much as I wanted to quiz him on Bonnie, which shelter Midas found her in and what they knew of her past, I also didn't want to offend someone who would be alone in my apartment with me while I was sleeping. I didn't think she was a slavering murderer, but that didn't mean she hadn't run away from one.

For now, my questions on that topic would have to wait. I could always text him later.

Ford must be a frequent customer. The proprietress herself, a delicate woman who moved with the casual grace of a predator, brought us a plate laden with bánh tằm khoai mì, which Ford explained was steamed cassava silkworm cake, on the house. She also kissed him on the mouth, which flustered him, but she didn't let his discomfort stop her from also testing his biceps with a squeeze before leaving us to our dessert.

Biting into his first piece, he growled, "Don't say a word."

"I'm sitting here, enjoying my freebie. Whatever do you mean?"

"She wants me to mate her granddaughter."

"Mmm-hmm." I nodded with proper solemnity. "That must be why she test-drove the merchandise."

Mouth stretched thin, he gave it one last try. "Would you believe me if I told you it was cultural?"

"Nope."

"I didn't think so."

We polished off the treat in amused silence. Oh wait. That was me. He gave off more of a horrified vibe.

He left the tip, which was fine by me, and we headed back to the truck.

"You've got to work on your endurance," Ford tsked as I struggled to lift Bonnie onto the seat without hurling. "What about second dessert?"

Gwyllgi are walking stomachs. Ford was sated, but he could go for another bowl of pho or another piece of silkworm cake without busting the zipper on his pants. I, on the other hand, wished I could pop my top button and make some breathing room.

"I'm not a hobbit, or a gwyllgi. I only have one stomach, and it's about to burst."

A pleased sound rumbled in his throat that raised Bonnie's hackles.

"Chill." I smoothed her fur with gentle strokes. "He's doing that guy thing where he feels good about having fed me until I can't move. It probably originated with men who couldn't woo the girl of their dreams with riches or wit and had to resort to stuffing them until they couldn't outrun them."

The corgi made a snickering noise then pressed her nose against the glass.

Ford blasted out a low whistle as he rolled up to the last-known address for Garou and his Loups.

"Looks like Momma was finally wrong about something." He peered through the windshield. "Crime does pay."

"No, the victims pay. None of this was earned. It was stolen." I pointed at Bonnie. "Stay."

The corgi bared more teeth than I felt a dog of her size could fit in its mouth, but I wasn't cowed. Much.

"Midas," I said patiently, "will swallow me in one gulp if you get hurt on my watch."

Ears pinned back, Bonnie snarled until foam dripped from her sharpening canines.

"Midas will not swallow you whole," Ford was quick to counter. "He might be put out, but he wouldn't harm a hair on your head."

Accepting him at his word, Bonnie wiped her mouth clean on his seat.

Next to me, Ford shut his eyes and tightened his hands on the wheel.

"I'm sure fae slobber won't stain." I patted his shoulder. "I bet it wipes right off leather."

A pained groan slipped past his lips, and I almost felt bad for teasing him.

"Scoot over." I nudged Bonnie aside as I opened the door. "I'll get down, and then I'll get you down."

Before the scream trapped in my throat escaped, she had leapt onto the driveway without stumbling.

"Are you kidding me?" Fingers glued to the door, I gawked down at her. "You could do that the whole time?"

She turned wide eyes on me, all innocence, and I wished for Bonnie the woman back. The four-legged version had my number and wasn't shy about calling it.

Ford beat me to her, and she spun a quick circle, urging me to get a move on.

I joined them in the driveway, and we didn't have to wait long for the Loups to roll out the welcome wagon.

Two men and one woman prowled down the marble steps leading up to a mansion tackier than a toddler's fingers after a lollipop. They wore black leather, head to foot, and one of them must be breaking in new pants. They creaked when they walked like an old door whose hinges needed oiling.

"Are you lost?" the woman called, swinging a scarred bat in one hand. "I'm real good with directions."

The shadow pretending to be mine curled its fingers with want and seeped toward her, a dark stain, and his hunger beat at me until my vision doubled with sympathetic pain.

"I'm Hadley Whitaker." Blinking my eyes clear, I stepped forward to intercept the trio and was relieved Ford didn't fling any misplaced chivalry at me while I was on the job. "I'm with the Office of the Potentate. This is my associate, Ford Bentley, and we're here to speak to Garou."

"You're that skank Grim is training?" the guy next to her asked. "Heard you like to cut people."

"I am that very skank," I agreed amiably. "As to the rest... The POA trained me. What do you think?"

The third man rubbed a hand across his throat, confirming the POA's reputation for decapitation via scythe was still holding strong on the street.

"Do you have an appointment?" The woman looked me up and down. "Garou is a busy man."

"I bet he is." I looked her up and down right back. "Criminal enterprises don't run themselves."

"Garou is a businessman," the second man informed me. "A businessman with a clean record."

"That's the funny thing about dirty money," I mused. "It's good for washing the hand holding it clean."

"I'm Lou," the third and most timid of them announced. "That's Lara, and he's Landry."

"Definitely sensing a theme here..." I whispered to Ford. "Nice to meet you. Where's Garou?"

"Thing is, I'm second in the pack." He puffed up at the title. "She's third. He's fourth. You don't get through us, no one does."

Lightning struck, and I grasped the reason for their unbalanced dynamic. "You're Garou's son.

Lou tipped his head down, like he had taken a hit on his chin. "So?"

"So, tell Garou I'm here. I won't take up much of his time."

"Forget it," he snarled, pissed at having the reason for his spot in the pack hierarchy exposed to outsiders. "Dad's in a meeting."

Dad.

Yup.

I was working on his temper, and it burned hot.

Nepotism had no place within a healthy pack. The Loups might tolerate Lou, but they would rip out his throat the second his old man kicked the bucket if he didn't show them he could bite back.

"You heard him." Lara smacked the bat across her palm. "Hop back in your redneck limousine and drive."

"Redneck limousine?" Ford clutched at his chest. "That's my baby."

"I have a show on in fifteen." Langley rolled his shoulders. "Season finale."

Change was slower for wargs than it was for gwyllgi, and it hurt. Worse, it left them contorted, exposed, and vulnerable. These goons weren't going to risk shifting. That didn't make them any less dangerous, but it evened the playing field.

"I'm a TV junkie myself." I reached for Ambrose, dipped a hand into his black mass, and ice-cold leather wrapped around a carved pommel filled my palm. "I can respect a guy who prefers to watch live rather than DVR."

"Lessens the experience," he agreed, lips curving.

For the past nine months, I had been training with twin kopis blades. Linus tended to dispatch his justice at the edge of his scythe, but I vomited up my toenails the first and only time he let me hold his, and we never spoke of it again.

Two months after that humiliating debacle, he showed up with my two new best friends. I'm not sure why he opted for two over one. I never asked him. I was too grateful he hadn't written me off as a loss. That was the thing about the POA. He enjoyed teaching—used to be a professor, actually—and was willing to invest in students he felt showed potential. Since he included me in that rarified few, I was determined to live up to whatever he saw in me.

"Oh, shut up," Lara huffed. "No one cares about your stupid show or your idiotic viewing preferences."

That was all the warning she gave before she cocked her bat and charged me.

The short swords sang as I retrieved them, one after the other, and she stumbled in shock at the trick. Or maybe at the fact I was now holding two swords like I knew how to use them. Possibly even at the snow-white ball of canine fury yapping at my feet. Definitely one of those things.

"Did you see that?" Lou's eyes widened. "I thought only he could do that."

The POA was a showman, and he had perfected the sleight of hand that made it appear his scythe manifested in his palm when it was held by one of his wraiths until he required it. It wasn't some mystical weapon with magical powers. It was a symbol. The Grim Reaper schtick was no accident if you asked me, and no one had, since no one was dumb enough to critique the boss.

I may not have the death-incarnate thing happening—I was too blonde and too short to pull it off, honestly—but he had taught me the one trick that made it clear I was his chosen successor. If knuckleheads like these thought that meant he had bestowed some mumbo-jumbo powers on me, well, that would only help me build my rep.

"Are we doing this or what?" I asked Lara. "You heard Langley. He's got a show coming on."

"I'll tell Dad you're here." Lou retreated up the stairs. "Just wait there."

Lara didn't back down, but she didn't advance again either.

"Damn," Ford whispered, his lips almost brushing my ear. "That's hot."

Bonnie turned her growl on him. He raised his hands and backed away.

About the time I was ready to stomp up the gaudy marble stairs to the gaudy marble foyer I could see through the gaudy gilded door Lou had left open, he reappeared with a man who resembled him down to the mole on his left eyebrow. Only the fan of wrinkles at his eyes and graying hair at his temples distinguished them physically, but Garou was an alpha to the bone while his son couldn't fake it skin-deep.

"Ms. Whitaker," Garou greeted me, all smiles. "What a pleasure to see you again."

"I wish I could say the same." I returned his fake bonhomie. "I need to ask you a few questions."

"Of course." Distaste pinched his features. "Might I ask you to put that away first?"

"Sure thing." I passed them back to Ambrose, but the trick appeared to reassure rather than alarm Garou.

"Come." He waved me over to the garden beside the house and held out a chair for me at a delicate bistro table painted metallic gold to complement the gilded veins in the marble monstrosity behind us. "Sit."

There was no point in being rude since he was cooperating, so I let him get his jollies playing host. Just like I let Ford get his playing muscle as he fell into parade rest behind me.

Leaning back, all ease and comfort, I crossed my legs. "Does the name Shonda Randall ring any bells for you?"

"No." He tapped scarred fingers against his chin. "Should it?"

"That's what I'm here to determine." I linked my fingers at my navel. "Shonda was a member in good standing of the Atlanta gwyllgi pack. She was murdered, brutally, two days ago."

"I have no beef, as the youngsters say, with Tisdale or her people."

"Mmm-hmm." I rubbed my thumbs against each other. "Unless you're paid to have one?"

"I thought you were asking a strictly personal question." A twinkle brightened his clever eyes. "Business is a different matter."

"Can you tell me if anyone put a hit out on Shonda?"

"Tsk, tsk, tsk. There's no cause for such language." He brought out his phone and hit a button. "Let me summon my aid. She will know if we had any dealings with this Randall woman."

A tall woman dressed in a flowy black silk gown exited a side door and padded over to join us.

"Leanna," he said cordially, "do you recall if we had any business with a Shonda Randall?"

"A Miles Randall in 1978, a George in 1999, and a Huron in

2000," she answered less than a minute later. "No Shonda. No Randalls at all since our business with Huron concluded on May 21, 2000 near the intersection of Oakview Road and Hosea L. Williams Drive."

Impressed despite myself, I wished I possessed half her recall. "Eidetic memory?"

"One of her many talents." He patted her on the butt. "Now, Ms. Whitaker, is there anything else I can do for you?"

"Not at this time." I stood to leave but hesitated. "I appreciate your cooperation in this matter."

"You are the future of Atlanta. Never let it be said I do not embrace the future."

Without another word, I left Garou to continue embracing other things, namely Leanna's backside.

While the alpha had been busy entertaining us, his pack had gathered, cutting us off from our ride.

So much for cooperation. Guess Garou wanted to make an example out of me after all.

"Skim them," I whispered to Ambrose. "Skim, not drain."

Ford, who must think I had a muttering problem, eyed the gauntlet. "How do you want to handle this?"

Given free rein, the shadow punched in and out of bodies with manic glee, sipping on their magic to replace what he had lost when Bonnie attacked him. "Give them a minute to reconsider their life choices."

Cocking his eyebrows at me, he made his doubt clear. "You really think that will work?"

"I really do."

Bonnie watched Ambrose, her interest keen on her cute doggy face, but it appeared Ford was blind to his shenanigans. Thank the goddess.

After about a minute, the dozen or so Loups gathered started swaying on their feet, groaning, clutching their stomachs, and otherwise glaring at me like I was a plague fairy come to dust them.

To be fair, I kind of was.

"I think they're repentant enough now." I led the way, Bonnie on my heels, and shoved over anyone who got in my path. Most curled in a ball on the ground, but a few crawled after me. "Ford, now would be a great time to unlock your truck if you haven't yet."

"Yes, ma'am." He mashed a button on the fob he took from his pocket, his myriad other keys jingling, but his eyes were locked on me. "Hop on in."

"I'd have to be half grasshopper to make that jump," I said, hoping to deflect his sudden interest.

At the truck, I opened the door and dared Snowball with a look to expect me to play elevator for her.

She stuck her nose in the air then leapt like a frakking gazelle onto the seat.

"Normal corgis can't do that," Ford remarked after we had resumed our usual seats.

Their short legs did make it seem unlikely. "Normal corgis also don't weigh fifty pounds."

Bonnie yelped with affront, which made Ford laugh and me grin.

"There's just more of you to love, Bon-Bon." I ruffled her fur. "You're a badass, and you know it."

Just slightly more *ass* than *bad* in this form. Corgis had serious swagger and the butts to go with it.

Mollified, she curled up on the seat and dozed. For real this time.

Eyes on the road, Ford still managed to award me his full attention. "What did you do back there?"

"I didn't do a thing." Ambrose did it for me. "Don't get too excited, though. It's a rare occurrence."

Letting Ambrose off his leash was only slightly less dangerous than handfeeding a starving lion a prime rib fresh off the hoof. Too little, and he was no use to me, and I became physically ill. Too much, and he regained his former power, and he could exert his will over me. A precarious line to walk if I wanted to keep the body count to a minimum, but I was getting better at balancing.

Shaking his head, he let it go. "Did you get what you came for?"

"I buy that Garou and the Loups didn't have an official stake in Shonda Randall. That doesn't mean an individual didn't harbor a grudge."

"You don't believe that."

"No." I only had a gut feeling to go on, but the evidence would come. "I don't."

"Nine bodies." He gritted his jaw. "That's a whole lot of grudge."

"The cleaners haven't conclusively linked the victims," I reminded him. "The Perkerson report will verify if we're looking for one killer or a pair."

"Why a pair?"

I debated how much to share with him, but he had a stake in the outcome where Shonda was concerned, so I came clean. I told him what Reece discovered, that a warg and/or human was involved, and that eased the frown lines that had bracketed his mouth since hearing I wanted to meet with Garou.

"That explains a few things." He flipped on his blinker. "I'm guessing you want to meet with Clairmont and Mendelsohn too?"

"That was my plan."

"Do me a favor and let me in on the plan next time?"

"Oh, I will." I got comfy. "I don't want to lose my chauffeur privileges."

He huffed out a laugh, and I did too, but I don't think he was laughing at the same thing as me, considering I was imagining a gwyllgi behind the wheel, wearing a little black cap, steering with his paws.

Yeah.

Best I keep that under my proverbial hat.

SIX

The Mendelsohn pack resided in tents pitched in the woods off the interstate, and that suited them just fine. I couldn't remember if this is how they had chosen to live within the city, congregating under overpasses, or if they were embracing nature in their new locale.

"I might need a shower after this." I rubbed my eyes, but my vision didn't clear. "Goddess."

The Mendelsohn pack had also, apparently, embraced nudism.

"I've never seen so much junk in my life." I wasn't talking about the piles of garbage left for the city to pick up when road crews worked the area either. "I'm not a prude, but come on."

When Ford didn't comment, I expected to catch him ogling the boob parade since the jiggling was kind of hypnotic, but he had tucked his chin to his chest and glued his eyes to the floorboard.

"I can handle this solo," I offered.

Unimpressed, Bonnie barked once, loud enough to make me wince.

Wiggling a finger in the ear nearest her, I worked out most of the pain. "Bonnie can watch my back."

"Bonnie can't drop her glamour to help you. Even if she could, we don't need to give the wrong impression." Heat blazed in his cheeks. "I'll go."

Ford made his point, and it was a good one. This was a delicate situation, and I didn't want her presence to cause friction between the packs when there would be strife enough to go around once the victims had all been identified. Corgis were much less intimidating than gwyllgi, so corgi she would stay.

"All right."

I didn't ask what made him uncomfortable. I didn't want him to be more likeable than he already was, and I didn't want to respect him either, but it was hard not to when he treated women like people and not sex objects created for his personal gratification.

Unlike our visit to Garou, no one spared us so much as a glance as we walked the main aisle. They were too busy getting high, rocking out, and having sex against trees, up trees, beneath trees, and anywhere else but on their cots in their tents. A moaning, writhing mass caught my attention in the center of the circle made by the tents.

The star of the show was a very buff, very handsome, very well-endowed young man busy plowing into a woman from behind while she mewled like a bagful of kittens. Other women surrounded him, offering him their breasts on their palms and other things to feast on until his spine snapped straight, and he roared.

I expected—no, I hoped—that would be the end of it, but he only motioned for that woman to roll aside to make room for the next.

Unwilling to stand too close, I called out, "Can I have a moment of your time?"

"It'll take me longer than a moment." He shoved the eager woman away and patted the flattened grass he'd cleared in an invitation for me to join him. "I'm willing to put in the effort, though, for as long as it takes."

"I'm Hadley Whitaker, with the Office of the Potentate." I let that sink in. "I need to ask you a few questions."

"Sure." He wet his lips as his gaze slid down my body. "We'll talk in my tent."

A dangerous rumble poured over my shoulder, but I couldn't blame Bonnie. This was all Ford.

I leveled a hard stare on him, and he quit, but he didn't look happy about it.

Territorial males. They're so cute. Except not.

"I appreciate the offer, but I forgot to pack Lysol."

Rising to his full height, Mendelsohn scratched his left butt cheek. "What does that have to do with anything?"

Nothing at all, stud.

Disinfectant spray probably wasn't strong enough. Bleach might work. A hazmat suit would be ideal before entering his lair. Even then, I bet everything crunched underfoot.

"It's a beautiful day." I indicated the nice paved road away from his tent. "Why don't we take a walk?"

"All right." He glanced back at the woman he'd slighted and winked. "Gotta hurry back, though."

"Yeah." I ignored the daggers she threw at me with her glare. "I can tell you're a busy man."

The next spokesman for Energizer, folks. He might not be a bunny, but he was breeding like one.

Once we hit the road, I got to the point. "Do you know a woman by the name of Shonda Randall?"

"She pack?"

"Not your pack, no."

Thinking, he started scratching other things. "Did I meet her at a party in the city?"

"I'm not your secretary. I don't know your social calendar."

"Do you know your hips are ripe for childbearing?"

"I'm not the maternal type," I said, barely suppressing a shudder at the thought of my own mother.

"God put you here to bear fruit," he said to me, but then he spoke to Ford. "Is she not fertile?"

Pretty sure Ford would have dug a hole and climbed in then raked the dirt over the top of him had a shovel been handy. He looked ready to shift and use his claws. He didn't know me all that well, but he had seen my handiwork, and he had to know I was itching to leave Mendelsohn with a sample.

Hot and tired, and way too close to an aroused nudist with no concept of personal hygiene, I stuck out a hand, and Ambrose obliged, allowing me to draw one of my kopis blades. I doubted I needed the other. I held the tip to Deric's throat, and he attempted to swat the sword aside then acted shocked when it cut him.

"What is your problem?" He cleaned his hand on his thigh because that was totally sanitary. "Your man needs to teach you some manners."

"I tried polite, and it didn't work." I held the weapon firm. "Do you know a woman by the name of Shonda Randall?"

"No? Maybe? Who can tell?" He flung out his arm, encompassing his harem. "A woman is a woman."

"From what I can tell, your little head got all the brains, so let me break this down for you. Shonda was a member of the Atlanta gwyllgi pack, and she was murdered. Right now, a warg is our prime suspect."

Eyes widening in comprehension, he examined the wound on his hand. "I'm a warg."

"I'm done here." I wrinkled my nose at Deric and sheathed my blade. "Happy humping."

Ford waited until we had put distance between us and the horndog in charge. "On behalf of my gender, I apologize."

"What a waste." All this emotional scarring for nothing. "His brain might be the size of a hickory nut."

"Do you want to interview his beta?"

"You're giving him too much credit. Nothing about this pack screams organized hierarchy. I'm bumping them to the bottom of the list until we get a report that indicates otherwise." Oh, how I wished for hand sanitizer even though I hadn't touched Mendelsohn. "Unless you disagree?"

"This is your show," he deferred. "For what it's worth, I agree with your preliminary assessment."

"I appreciate you letting me handle him."

"Momma would have beat me with her dishtowel if she heard him talk to you that way."

A prickle of unease stiffened my shoulders before I could loosen them. "Why would she beat you?"

"For not breaking him over my knee." He chuckled. "After he apologized to you first, of course."

"Of course," I breathed, reminding myself his mother wasn't like mine.

Sweet as he meant it, I couldn't afford to let a man stand in front of me. Not the POA, and not Ford.

We made it almost back to the truck before a preteen girl, thankfully fully dressed, ran up to us.

"Are you here about Tammy?" She caught me by the arm. "Please, ma'am. Are you?"

A cold stone sank to the bottom of my stomach at the bright hope burning in her eyes.

"I'm here about Shonda Randall. Do you know her?"

Her shoulders slumped, defeated. "No."

"All right." I guided her to the rear of the truck to give us privacy. "Why don't you tell me about Tammy? Why did you think I would be here about her?"

Worrying her bottom lip with her teeth, she checked to make sure no one was paying us any attention, though no one appeared to care how the underage crowd entertained themselves. "Do you mind if I hold your dog while we talk?"

"Snowball, do you mind?"

Butt swishing, she padded right up to the girl and reared on her shin.

"I'm guessing that's a no." I smiled like it was a joke, but it was far from it. "So, who's Tammy?"

"She's my big sister." She glanced up then. "I'm Jessica."

"Nice to meet you, Jessica." I leaned against the tailgate. "Where are your parents?"

"They died."

Must not have been recently based on her matter-of-fact delivery.

"I'm sorry to hear that." I noted her clean face and neat clothes. "Who takes care of you now?"

"The pack."

From what I had read on wargs, most packs shared parenting duties. That must be the case here. She was a healthy weight, showed no physical signs of abuse, though I knew from experience how easily those could be hidden, and gave no indication she was afraid of approaching outsiders. She appeared healthy and well-adjusted, which meant the Mendelsohn pack was doing one thing right.

"When was the last time you saw Tammy?"

"Two days ago." She set her jaw. "Tam's birthday is tomorrow. She'll turn eighteen, and she was worried the alpha might..."

I connected the dots, and my gut twisted. "The alpha wanted her."

"Yeah," she whispered. "Tam didn't have a boyfriend or anything, but she didn't want to...you know."

"No woman should ever be forced to have sex."

"Yeah," she said, stronger this time. "That's what I think too."

Heart breaking, I made a promise to myself that we would find a way to sever her ties with this pack and situate her with a new one. "Do you have access to a phone?"

"Tam bought me a pay-as-you-go cell before she left," she said quietly. "No one knows I have it."

The radio silence between them bothered me given Tammy's forethought in ensuring Jessica could stay in touch. With so many unclaimed bodies from Perkerson waiting on an ID at the morgue, I had to acknowledge there could be a grave excuse for Tammy not contacting her sister to let her know she was okay.

"Keep it that way." I pulled a card from my back pocket. "Here's my number. Call if you hear from Tammy, or if anyone tries to make you do anything you don't want to, okay?"

"Okay."

Our chat had finally drawn notice, so I got her number before she scurried away to where three other girls about her age congregated in a tent too small to hold all the cots lined up in neat rows. Jessica draped her arms over the shoulders of two of the girls and led them inside while the third one closed the flap behind them.

"They're watching each other's backs," I murmured to Ford. "There are empty tents, but they're crammed in together."

"Lee." He placed a hand on my arm. "Violence is not the way to fix this."

Until he touched me, jarred me out of my own head, I hadn't felt the comforting weight of steel in my hand, and that terrified me.

Laughter jarred the shadow unspooling from my feet as Ambrose relished my fear.

Laugh all you want. I rallied before he gained the upper hand. *I go down, you go down with me.*

Thankfully, we didn't share a mental bond, but that didn't mean he couldn't catch the drift of my thoughts or emotions. Hard to miss when he was bound to me. The reminder of just how tight we were tied sobered him into quiet reflection, which I trusted about as much as the aforementioned lion with a steak on my palm.

"You're right." Done playing with Ambrose, I turned my attention back to Ford and set out for the truck. "Let's go." I waited for him to get in the cab before I hit him with my request. "Give me Midas's number." Fine, it was more of a demand. "Please."

"I can't do that." He had the grace to sound sorry about it. "Midas guards his privacy."

"Then take me to him."

"I'm not his PA. She's drooling on your thigh. I have no idea where Midas is tonight."

"Take a wild guess."

"Probably on a date." He shrugged. "The alpha wants him mated sooner rather than later."

The slight hitch in my breath pissed me off that much more. "Where does he take the candidates?"

That's how he would think of them, I was sure. A man who avoided touch, limited his contact with women to self-defense classes hosted at various shelters, wasn't going to view them as mate material. He was going to see them as a duty to be fulfilled, one of the terms of his new position. All he had to do was decide which particular cross he wanted to bear.

"Joelle's."

"I'm hungry. How about you?"

"I could eat," he said with a laugh. "Might as well make it good. Once Tisdale catches wind we invited ourselves to dinner, this could be our last meal."

SEVEN

Midas shredded his buttery roll into pieces so small he would need a toothpick to spear one into his mouth, not that eating was on his mind. He had trouble choking down more than a drink on these dates, and he made a point to keep it nonalcoholic.

"What do you think?"

The voice, as buttery soft as the roll, perked his appetite just as much. "About?"

Forcing a smile, Rebecca took a breath. "Where did I lose you?"

At the beginning.

Then again in the middle.

And, oh yeah. Also there at the end.

A commotion at the front of the restaurant spared him from admitting he hadn't paid attention to her since the moment they sat down except to make sure she ordered whatever she wanted from the menu, regardless of the price, as payment for enduring his company for a painful couple of hours.

A blonde tornado with a brewing storm in her eyes whirled past the startled hostess, all bouncing curls and attitude, and aimed her path of destruction right at him.

For the first time all night, he found his interest piqued, and he regretted that the woman across from him could tell. More than that, he resented she would rather grit her teeth through the interruption than lose her shot at landing him.

He wasn't a damn whale.

Hadley wore jeans with blood crusted on her thigh in a sharp line. She must have cleaned one of the twin blades she often carried on her pants, which made him curious who had pissed her off enough to earn the bite of her swords. Sweat made her tee cling to her, and corgi hair stuck to her like glitter.

Dodging the hostess, who was now calling for security, Hadley cut through the restaurant, ignoring the looks, the whispers, the pointing fingers, and slammed her palms down on his table hard enough to rattle the silverware. "We need to talk."

"I'm on a date," he stated the obvious.

"You haven't touched your food except to play with it. Your water glass is mostly full, and I'm betting it's your first of the night. I don't know why you haven't turned to booze since you're so obviously bored out of your mind, but I get that you can't risk getting drunk without waking up mated to goddess only knows who."

"We're on a date," Rebecca reiterated. "You're interrupting."

"You're not on a date. You're on a recon mission. You're trying him on to see if he fits."

A soft breath punched out of Midas. "That's enough, Hadley."

Fierce hazel eyes captured his and dared him to ignore her. He was half tempted to try just to see what she would do. Add his blood to the mix already coating her was his guess.

A dangerous smile tickled the right corner of his mouth, but he mashed his lips flat again.

"Give me ten minutes, and then you can get back to your mommy-approved evening of staring through the window at the clock tower across the street while you count down an appropriate amount of time before making your excuse to leave."

Head whipping toward the window, Rebecca gawked at the true reason he always asked for this table.

None of his dates had ever noticed the setup, let alone the reason behind it, but Hadley had him figured out in under a minute.

"I'll be right back." He tossed his napkin on his untouched plate and stood. "Where is...Snowball?"

"Outside with Ford." Nose wrinkling at the fancy trappings his mother insisted on, she gave the hostess a withering glare that made the woman shrivel in her stilettos. "This place has no patio. They don't allow dogs. Can you believe that?"

"I'll be sure to leave them a bad Yelp review."

Her eyes lit for an instant, like he had finally hit on a topic that interested her, but she wiped off the expression when they reached the open floor space near the restrooms.

"We have a problem."

Angling his body closer, he ducked his head and lowered his voice. "Another murder?"

"I visited the Mendelsohn pack tonight. One of the Perkerson Park victims may very well be a seventeen-year-old by the name of Tammy, who ran away rather than let Deric touch her. I learned this from a girl named Jessica, who worried I might be bringing them bad news about her big sister. She wants out. We can help her now, or we can let her fall through the cracks. What will it be?"

A knot twisted in his gut that wouldn't release until he fixed this, but curiosity won out, and he acted as unaffected as the alpha herself might. "What are you suggesting I do about it?"

The crackle of righteous fury in her eyes reminded him of the sky before lightning struck.

"Nothing." She met his gaze, held it. "I'll let you get back to tapping your foot, I mean, your *date*."

Hadley turned to go, but he caught her by the arm, the feel of her skin electric.

"You just said this girl is a warg, and that she's underage. I have no claim on her. I can't walk up to Mendelsohn and demand he hand her over, and I can't go around stealing kids in the middle of the night."

"I can't leave her there." She didn't pull away, she leaned in. "You didn't see her. She's sharing a tent with three or four other girls about her age. She's protecting them since she couldn't protect her sister."

"Why didn't you take this to Linus? Your office has the resources to handle witness protection and relocation. You've done the same for other abuse survivors. Why is this girl different?" He didn't mean to, but he tightened his grip, his intrigue stronger than his usual aversion to intimacy in any form. "Why did you come to me?"

"You volunteer at women's shelters. You teach them self-defense. You care."

Uncertain how he felt about her referencing his atonement like a virtue, he asked, "Are you saying Linus doesn't?"

"He cares, probably too much, but this isn't going to be his city forever." Determination burned in her gaze. "Atlanta will be mine one day, and I'm not going to stand for this. Your pack is our office's closest ally. I don't know how to stay on the right side of the law for this, but I also don't think I care."

The last part rattled her. She hadn't meant to say it. But she had. To him. She...trusted him.

"I'll make some calls to shelters with experience dealing with shifter kids." He searched her face. "Mendelsohn can't do a damn thing if those kids leave of their own free will. Runaway is not the same as kidnapped. Prove they're at risk in their home environment, and I'll make sure no one can touch them."

A smile flirted with the corners of her mouth, and she exhaled with relief. "Thanks."

Noticing he still held her arm, he forced his hand open. "Give me your phone."

"I get that you're the alpha-to-be, but you've got to work on your manners."

In danger of returning her smile, he growled, "Please give me your phone."

She handed it over then smirked while he added himself as a contact. "I feel so special."

"Maybe next time you'll call first."

"Next time I'll have your number so I can call first."

Shaking his head, he returned her cell. "I have to get back to dinner."

"Five bucks says you don't remember your date's name."

"Rebecca," he said dryly. "Where's my five bucks?"

"Darn." She snapped her fingers. "I don't have any cash on me."

"Don't gamble with what you don't have."

"Ford wants to come over for a movie night." Wariness pinched her delicate features before she smoothed them. "I could put that five toward a pizza if you're interested in joining us."

Ford was doing the job Midas had recruited him for last year, but all of a sudden it didn't sit well.

Nothing Hadley had said or done since arriving in Atlanta warranted the vague warning Lethe had given him about the POA's new protégé. He had been willing to let it slide at the time, but he couldn't afford to keep handling Hadley blind. He had to think of the pack first. His sister had relished the role of beta, had embraced the role of alpha. Her word carried weight with him, and he trusted her instincts.

"Maybe next time." He glanced toward the table and the impatient woman waiting on him. "Spend that five on Ford. He likes sausage and pepperoni with extra red onions."

"Maybe." She shrugged off his rebuff. "Next time you might not get an invite."

She put a sway in her hips that hadn't been there before and left him staring after her.

Feeling eyes on him, he glanced out the front window and noticed Ford watching him watch her.

Back at his table, Rebecca made it clear she had seen him too.

"You've shown that woman more interest in ten minutes than you've shown me all night." Her hands bunched the tablecloth. "Am I wasting my time?"

"Yes," he answered honestly, making a fist beneath the table to hold on to the feel of Hadley, the sensation as bizarre as his...not attraction. Fascination? "You knew that already."

EIGHT

Out on the street, Ford waited with Bonnie. I wasn't sure how much, if anything, he had overheard from my conversation with Midas, but he studied me with an intensity that left my nape tingling. Or maybe that had more to do with the beta I had left in my dust.

Midas had given me food for thought, and I was chewing over his reservations about us helping the girl. Now that my temper had cooled, I could admit more information was required before any action was taken. Since I had a prime resource who could do the digging for me, I texted Bishop the request for a background check on Jessica.

"We've got time to hit the Clairmonts before we call it a night," I told Ford on my way past. "Let's knock them out of the suspect pool." I shrugged. "Or into it."

Bonnie trotted over, happy to ditch Ford, and I bent to pick up the leash she manifested on the spot. She surprised me by rearing up on my arm to give the place where Midas touched me a good sniff before shooting me a knowing look through narrowed eyes.

"Whatever it is you're thinking, stop right now." I stood under Ford's watchful gaze. "What?"

"I don't get it," he admitted. "This thing between you and Midas."

"What thing?" I felt my palms go damp. "There is no thing."

"You ran straight to him," Ford said, a slight edge in his tone. "And he...let you."

"Kids are in danger. Girls. From what I have no issue calling a sexual predator. What kind of man would Midas be if he shrugged that off?" Aware I had ruffled Ford's feathers, I attempted to smooth them. "If it makes you feel any better, he blew me off when I invited him to our movie night."

Glossing over the fact I had invited another guy in the first place, he grinned from ear to ear. "So, we're on?"

"Looks that way." I scratched behind Bonnie's ear. "How do you feel about pizza?"

Ford shook his head over me treating her like a dog. "Me or her?"

"I meant Bonnie." I straightened. "I already know you like it, and how you like it."

He glanced through the window at Midas, but he didn't say another word, just pointed across the street.

"That's their building?" I hadn't paid attention to the street signs on the way over. "How convenient."

The poshest wargs in the city would want to be close to the poshest restaurants and retailers.

We hit the crosswalk and approached a tasteful entrance guarded by an unobtrusive doorman.

"Ms. Clairmont has been expecting you," he said in a bass rumble. "Check in at the desk, please."

Two out of three doormen found me perfectly tolerable. This was proof, in my opinion, that the nightshift doorman at the Faraday had it out for me. Thank the goddess I would be back to using the window as my front door soon.

"Thank you." I led Bonnie through the door he held for us. I walked straight to the counter where a young man sat with a guest book flipped to a blank page. "Hadley Whitaker for Ayla Clairmont."

"Sign here, please." He indicated the topmost line with a pen more expensive than my shoes. Though, to be fair, odds were his pen didn't have to walk through blood or other bodily fluids. He could afford to invest in something nice while I had to go for practical, borderline disposable. I took it from him, admiring its weight, and made my mark. "Take the elevator on your left to the sixth floor. Those are our office suites. Ms. Clairmont will see you in room 612."

The camera in the elevator was obvious, so neither of us spoke on the ride. The hallway we entered was minimalist but elegant, lots of grays and blacks and whites. A door was open at the far end, and I heard a woman's voice carrying on a one-sided conversation. She hung up the landline phone when she spotted me in the doorway and waved us in.

Ayla was curvy in a way that made men drool, and she dressed like a woman who didn't mind using her breasts to get who or what she wanted out of life.

I glanced down at the uniboob my sports bra gave me under my tee and debated if my job would be easier if I wore leather and flashed cleavage. Probably not. Goddess only knows what I would come home with stuck between and under them.

"Hadley." She gestured me toward a seat opposite hers. "I haven't seen you in months. How's training?"

"I can't complain." I sat and didn't fuss when Ford took point behind me. Bonnie paced in the doorway, giving the impression she was on patrol, which was too cute for words. "How's alphaing?"

Her throaty laugh came off as genuine, a neat trick. "I can't complain either."

"Your doorman informed me I was expected," I said lightly.

"I heard you visited the Loups and Mendelsohn. I assumed I would be next and made Deon aware."

"Where did you hear it from, if you don't mind my asking?"

"Here and there." She spread her hands. "I have my sources."

Most factions had lost interest in me after the first few months, but Ford joining me for this investigation had shoved me back into the spotlight.

There would be those in power looking to pick apart my candidacy over this. I would get spanked for preferential treatment if I didn't spin it right, but I was in too deep to back out now.

"In that case—" I kept my tone friendly, "—I'll make an assumption about what your sources have told you and skip to the point. Do you know a woman named Shonda Randall?"

"Don't you mean *did* I know her?" She leaned forward and folded her hands on her desktop. "It's my understanding she was murdered in a most gruesome fashion." She cut her eyes toward Ford. "She was gwyllgi, I believe."

The Clairmonts, with their downtown location and more urbane outlooks, came off as soft. Compared to the other packs in the area, they were, but there were less obvious downsides to dealing with them than with Mendelsohn or the Loups. The Clairmonts' distance from city center gave information time to find cracks to hide in. Ayla's position made it easy for her to keep eyes and ears all over town.

"All right." I had tried playing dumb, but Ayla was too smart for it. "Let's cut to the chase."

"Don't stop on my account." Her eyes twinkled with mirth. "I enjoy the game. Mr. Lawson does as well."

"You'll have to forgive my ineptitude," I said dryly. "I didn't receive the same home training."

"Did any of us?" Her laughter invited me to join in. "His mother is the single most powerful and influential necromancer alive. Have you ever met her?"

The edges of the room grew as warped and twisted as my memories of Clarice Lawson and her cronies.

"The punishment for summoning is six months imprisonment. She must pay the tithe and serve her time."

"If she is unable to pay the tithe at the end of six months, her bond will be made available for purchase."

"*She will remain a detainee of the Society until her debts are absolved.*"

Then, out of the darkness, walked...salvation.

"*There's no hope of her paying the tithe. Let's not pretend otherwise.*" Linus folded his hands behind his back. "*She has no priors, her record is spotless, and she has pursued an education tailored to providing valuable services to our community. All things considered, I propose a lucrative compromise that will please us all.*"

He hadn't done it for me, not back then. Thinking who had inspired him to stand against his mother made me heartsick for a friend, a life, that was best forgotten, and I promised myself once he moved to Savannah full-time it would be.

"No," I said hoarsely. "I haven't had the pleasure."

"Probably for the best," she decided. "You don't want to end up on her bad side, or his for that matter."

Salvation is a rope you use to climb out of despair. Darkness presses in on all sides, leaves your arms shaking and your chest heaving. Every inch you gain is a battle won, but still, below you yawns the void. Every inch gained can also be lost. Your arms can shake until they falter, and your chest can heave until it quits. Salvation doesn't walk, it pokes and prods and demands you put in the work.

Cast in that light, the POA hadn't saved me so much as he had given me the tools to save myself.

"The truth is," Ayla started, "we're missing three pack members. All disappeared over the last week. All female. A chef, a realtor, and an artist. All were last seen in the company of a man." She angled her head toward me. "We knew you visited Mendelsohn because we have friends there who mentioned your visit."

More like spies, paid to keep tabs on the pack and report interesting tidbits to Ayla.

Prepared to be impressed if she said yes, I asked, "You infiltrated the Loups too?"

"Infiltration wasn't required." Her smile turned coy. "I pay a flat rate for information pertinent to me."

Yet another reason why I doubted Garou or his Loups were involved. He received money to perform heinous acts, but he would sell out the previous buyer if a new one with deeper pockets came along. He was a businessman, and he would always take the better deal, loyalties be damned.

"We crosschecked the dates our missing persons were reported against Mendelsohn's schedule. They're a match. They coincide with visits he made to the city."

Aware she was dragging it out, turning it into a power play, I asked, "What was he doing in the city?"

"Parties." Her lips pursed. "He disappeared for hours at a time at each."

That jibed with Mendelsohn asking me if he met Shonda at a party, not that I wanted to give him even that much credit. He was the alpha, born and raised in that pack, and couldn't tell one woman from another, let alone put a name to a face.

"Let me guess." I saw where this was going. "He vanished into a back room with his harem?"

"His harem wasn't in attendance, but yes. He took several non-warg women into a back room."

The man's sex drive was not normal, but that wasn't a crime. He could be on pills, charms, or any number of things to keep him hard as the rocks tumbling around in his head.

"Does your friend have names? Can we track the women down, question them?"

"She wasn't invited. She got this secondhand from partygoers as they left."

Hearsay wasn't good enough. I had a second source, the kid, Jessica, but all she could vouch for was the fact Mendelsohn partied in the city often. That wasn't a crime, as long as he put on pants first.

Mind racing over the possibilities, I regretted not coming here first. "I wish you had reached out to me."

"Do you really care?" She studied me. "You've been here barely a year, and gossip abounds about you and that shadow of yours."

Ford tensed on my periphery, not much, but enough. She had been fishing, and she caught his reaction too.

"I'm here." I leaned forward, ignoring Ambrose's sudden interest in the alpha, who had mentioned his favorite topic, himself, and mirrored her posture. "What does that tell you?"

"Many things," she murmured. "Have a care that those with fewer resources than I have at my disposal don't start to imply your man here is simply the hand up a puppet's back."

Gritting my teeth, I kept my tone polite. "No man currently has his hand up my back or elsewhere."

"You're bold." An appreciative glimmer brightened her eyes. "I like it."

"No woman currently has her hand up my back or elsewhere either."

She bit her lush bottom lip to hold in her grin. "You're using your own hand these days?"

A flush attempted to climb into my cheeks, but I crushed it. "Let's say I'm self-sufficient."

To cover glancing away first, I faked checking on Bonnie. I didn't spot her right off, so she must have extended her patrol to the hall in front of Ayla's office.

Chuckling under her breath, she pulled herself together. "Will you keep me informed of your progress?"

"I'll do that if you do the same." I mulled over the consequences but then decided involving Ayla directly might save us time. "Reach out to the cleaners. Eight bodies were found in Perkerson Park this morning. The preliminary reports aren't available yet, but they should be within the next twenty-four hours. Some might belong to your people."

The humor fled her expression, and grief tightened the skin around her eyes. "We haven't been contacted..."

"The condition of the bodies means it might take a while for the cleaners to match all the pieces. They'll be running DNA to determine species and identities, but the process would go faster and smoother with your help."

"Of course." She closed her eyes. "I'll make the arrangements."

"Our killer is a warg, according to saliva samples found in the wounds. Once we have names to go with the other victims, I'll need to be in contact with their families. Or, if you feel that's too invasive, I would appreciate updates from you."

"Grief is a private thing. I can keep you informed, but I must request you not approach my people. If you uncover any evidence that leads you to believe a member of my pack is involved in these murders, bring them to me. I will exact my own justice."

Given that was the typical party line with supernaturals, I didn't have a leg to stand on. "All right."

"I would like to be alone now," she said, lowering her head. "You can see yourselves out."

The familiar refrain of *I'm sorry for your loss* almost tripped over my tongue, but it felt premature.

Hope was a fragile thing, and one wrong word from me would shatter it for her forever.

Ford and I left, Bonnie on our heels, and we didn't speak again until we were all situated in his truck.

"You didn't tell me Ayla has a crush on you."

"Really?" I twisted toward Ford. "That was your takeaway?"

"I am a man."

"You were also horrified by our visit to the Forest of Nipples and Peen earlier."

"I can't believe you said that." He dropped his face into his hands. "The mental picture..."

"Consider it payback for letting Ayla's flirting with me distract you."

"I'm going to talk to Midas about dissolving our partnership."

"What?" Blood rushed in my ears, deafening me. "Over one little peen joke?"

"You don't need me. You handled yourself today, very well, without my help."

"Please tell me you're not implying Midas paired us up because he's afraid a woman can't do the job."

"You didn't let me finish." He flicked me a quick glance. "You're working your ass off for Shonda. There's nothing I can do for her that you're not already doing."

"You're just feeling guilty after Ayla threw our partnership in my face."

"That too." He angled his chin toward me. "I'm not saying he'll go for it, but I'll try."

"I appreciate the vote of confidence."

The prospect of going back to working alone wasn't as welcome as I expected, but I wrote it off as missing the bonus of having a partner with his own wheels. Maybe Bishop was right, and I needed to buy a car.

Ford tapped my hand where it rested on the seat. "You're not off the hook for movie night, though."

"It's a date, as soon as I close this case."

"Do my ears deceive me, or did you just ask me out, darlin'?"

"It's a turn of phrase." I snorted. "Don't think my using it makes you special."

"Ouch." He placed a hand over his heart. "You are as cruel as you are beautiful."

"Save all those lines to use on your dream girl." I adjusted my seat belt as I faced forward. "Don't throw them away on me."

Ducking his head, he rubbed his jaw. "Who's to say you're not one and the same?"

"I says." I fidgeted with the buckle. "The next twelve months of my life are spoken for."

Eyebrow cocked, he challenged me. "What about after that?"

"You're not going to wait a year for a date." I scoffed. "You're a shameless flirt."

"Have you considered I'm only flirting with you?"

"Have you considered you're only flirting with me because it makes your job easier?"

"You don't trust easy, Lee."

"Once bitten and all that." I stroked Bonnie's coarse fur for comfort. "You don't want me, Ford. You want an all-access pass to my life so you can nose around in it. Let's not pretend otherwise."

"Are you qualified to dispense dating advice? How long have you been single?" He cocked an eyebrow. "Besides, I saw the way you looked at—"

"Are you seriously dragging Midas into this conversation?"

"I'm not blind, Lee."

"You could have fooled me," I tossed back. "Clearly you have something in your eye."

"There's something between you. Midas—"

"Goddess." I flung up my hands. "Why don't you two get married already?"

"Mated," he corrected. "I can't bear him children to carry on the family name, so our love was doomed from the start."

I really wish I hadn't laughed, but he had made me snicker more in the past forty-eight hours than I had in months. I could see why he coped through flirting and laughter. He was good at both. "Take me home?"

"Sure." He cut the wheel. "Working the mall tonight?"

"That's usually the first four hours of my night, not the last."

Shopping centers are great places for overhearing gossip and shutting down stalking behaviors before they escalated in the parking lot.

They're called *malls*, not *mauls*.

Where I rented my kiosk was owned by a Society family, and it kept Society hours, but the daily dish was hottest and freshest at sundown. Miss that first rush of nocturnal shoppers, and you might as well call in sick. Unless you were one of those weirdoes who actually hawked their wares instead of eavesdropping on passersby. I hear some folks are into that. Earning a livable wage.

The trill of my phone had me digging around in my pocket, and I swallowed when I read the ID. "Hadley."

"Meet me at the H.E. Holmes MARTA station."

"Do we—?"

Midas ended the call.

"—have another one?" I thumped my cell against my forehead. "I'm guessing you heard that."

With less than a foot of space between us, Ford likely heard every word as clear or clearer than me.

"Guess that answers my question," he said as he cut the wheel.

"Yeah." I sank my fingers into Bonnie's fur. "I guess it does."

NINE

The cleaners arrived as Ford threw his truck into park, telling me that Midas had placed his calls back to back, and they started squawking about contamination before their bootied feet hit the ground. I didn't have to look far to find Midas. He stood beneath a tow-away sign in front of the rear entrance, the one directly off I-20 West, dressed in the same clothes he had worn on his date.

The outfit was carefully bland and a size too large. I could see Midas hanging the stiff khaki pants and saggy button-down shirt in his closet on a hanger labeled *Mate Repellant* for the nights his mom set him up with women. If he hoped the drab outfit detracted from his looks, he was out of luck.

The man was beautiful. Physically perfect. As long as you didn't look in his eyes. That's where his truth lived, and it was stark, a silent scream that I alone seemed to hear.

"Wait here," I told Bonnie, who was alibied for this murder. "You don't want to see what's out there."

The corgi, who had seen worse, seeing as how she had scouted Perkerson Park, disagreed with me.

"I can't draw attention to myself, or to you, by bringing a pet on-scene."

Ears pinned to her skull, Bonnie bit my hand just shy of breaking skin, and I yelped.

"She's right." Ford attempted to reason with her. "You need to stay put for this."

When she turned her head to look out the window, ignoring us, I took it on faith that she would behave.

We hit the asphalt in the parking lot, but Ford kept glancing over his shoulder as we crossed to Midas.

"Are you scared she'll pee on your seats?" I elbowed him in the ribs. "Or worse?"

"Definitely *or worse*." He threw a companionable arm around my shoulders. "You should have seen her tackle the elevator doors. Her teeth and jaws are like fu—, I mean, freaking can openers. Bonnie will get to you if she decides she needs to, truck or no truck."

"You can curse in front of me. I've heard worse." I had a big brother with a big mouth, not that I could admit it to Ford. "I won't clutch my pearls or swoon or do anything girly."

Not that there was anything wrong with acting feminine, but *girly* was shorthand that encompassed a set of behaviors men auto-matically understood thanks to a lifetime of societal programming.

Midas stood with his hands in his pockets, and his gaze traced the curve of Ford's arm where it wrapped around my shoulders.

"Another tip?" I shrugged off Ford and approached Midas. "Did you speak to the caller directly this time?"

"Yes." He craned his neck. "Where's Snowball?"

"In the truck." I hauled him back on track. "Tip? Caller?"

"The caller was male. He dialed the den's landline and asked for me. Dispatch doesn't hand out our numbers, but they did transfer him to my cell. He sounded young, Southern, and he told me that he stumbled over a packmate on his way to the parking lot. I asked for his name, he refused. I asked for the victim's name, which he must have known to identify her as pack, and he broke character. He ditched the accent, laughed once, and hung up the phone."

"He's taunting us." I studied the parking lot filled with the curious. I examined each of their faces for signs the killer was here, watching. "He's escalating."

This particular MARTA station was one of the busiest in the city thanks to its easy access to I-20 and Douglas and Cobb County. The parking lot held something like fifteen hundred vehicles, and it employed its own police force. There were cameras mounted everywhere and plenty of people moving through the station toward the buses and the train.

"Give me a second." I walked away from the gwyllgi while I dialed Bishop. "We've got another body."

"Fuck."

"Pretty much." I rattled off the address and our exact location. "Pull surveillance, and let's find this guy."

"Do you need me to act as your aide?"

"Ford is here. So is Midas. I need you at HQ more than I need you on-scene."

"Small hiccup on the background you requested."

"What kind of hiccup?"

"The cleaners have their database locked down while they run their checks. Those usually don't last but a few hours. I can wait, or I can check my pocket for keys, if you catch my drift."

The call was a tough one, but I had to prioritize. "Wait it out."

"I'll pull in Reece and Anca." He hesitated. "Make no apologies."

The sign-off was one our team had adapted from the Woolworth family motto passed down to Linus from his aunt, Maud Woolworth, his fiancée's adoptive mother.

"Survive," I agreed and ended the call.

I shot the POA an update along with a promise I could handle the job, and I prayed I wasn't lying.

With that done, I rejoined the guys, who had been discussing notification of the victim's family.

Confirmation the victim was gwyllgi, that the killer had told that much truth at least, had to hurt them. "You've got a name?"

"Tilda Wainwright," Midas said. "She's a nurse." His mouth pulled tight. "She was a nurse."

"I don't get it. The pattern makes no sense." A richer darkness rippled beneath me, eager for a taste, so I flicked my fingers and sent Ambrose to investigate. "No attempt was made to conceal Shonda's body. She was left in public, in plain sight. The killer wanted her found quickly."

"The cache was old," Ford said, understanding. "It could have gone undetected for days or weeks longer."

"There was no reason for him to give up his hunting grounds." He had a sweet spot here, and he had gone undetected so far. "Unless he didn't plan to return there. Even then, it's risky giving us that much evidence to work with. It will put us closer to IDing him."

"This location promised Tilda would be found immediately," Midas said, picking up where we left off. "Does that mean he'll call with the location of another cache next?"

"Goddess, I hope not." That was a pattern I did not want to see emerge. "I need to see the body and speak with the cleaners." Ambrose too. "Bishop is expecting my report."

Thankfully, the man who provoked Bonnie into her gwyllgi form wasn't present to hassle me. However, I grimaced at the quick efficiency with which they processed the scene to clear it up before humans could document more of it with their phones. There would be no sweeping this under the rug. Money and favors would have to exchange hands to erase this.

"Hadley Whitaker, right?" A tall redhead flagged me down. "I'm Siobhan."

"This your scene?" I took the hand she offered, shook. "I have questions."

"I have no answers—yet—but this is my scene."

"I meant on the Perkerson Park case." I ought to be looking at the body, but a connection inside the cleaners could prove useful. They weren't a social bunch, so I chose to take it as a good sign that she had singled me out of her own volition. "When will those reports be available?"

"Tomorrow." The blood drained from her cheeks. "We've been working overtime to get all the evidence catalogued."

Catalogued was a sanitary description for the work of piecing together so many bodies.

"Thank you." I couldn't put off viewing the body any longer. They were prepping it for transportation to their private morgue. "I need all the help I can get stopping this guy."

"Reece knows how to get in touch with me," she said softly. "I'll send over the files the second they go live on our server."

Well, that explained how he got his samples.

One of her underlings appeared at her elbow with a baggie and a question, and I left them to their work.

Tilda Wainwright lay curled facing the wall with her arms covering her head. She wore maroon scrubs, so she had been murdered on her way to or from work at the hospital. Her blonde hair was streaked with crimson highlights, and her shoes were bright white Crocs spattered with gruesome polka dots.

From this angle, the pinkish-white bone of her spine was visible. Whoever had done this had eaten the meat between her shoulder blades and her pelvis. They had gnawed her ribs, which had splintered and cracked until they snapped off under the pressure of the killer's jaws.

I jumped when a hand landed on my shoulder and spun to find Ford. "What's up?"

"Just wanted to check on you." He gave me a reassuring squeeze. "Midas is talking to Bonnie."

"I think I'll join them." I had a few questions for him. "Are you coming with?"

"Not yet." He let his focus slide to the body. "I need a moment."

"How rude is it for me to ask you to compare the scents from the previous scenes with this one?"

"Pretty damn rude," he groused, "but I'll try."

"Thanks."

Cutting through the crowd to Ford's pickup, I reached it as Midas was shutting the door on his conversation with Bonnie.

"Can we talk?" I ignored the corgi pressing her nose to the glass. "Privately?"

He started walking, and I fell in beside him.

"Bishop has a theory I didn't want to believe, but I think he's on to something."

"Bonnie," he said simply.

"Where did you find her? Specifically? What do you know about her?"

"At the shelter on University Drive Northeast." He guided us down a well-lit but mostly empty sidewalk. "I was teaching a women's self-defense class there, and she watched. She wouldn't participate, and I didn't push her. The room got hot, and I scented her on the way to get a drink of water."

"How did you know what she was so fast?"

"She's not the first of her kind I've come across, and that's all I'll say about that."

So much for teasing out information on how many of their fae cousins they were hiding.

Twisting the interrogation, I chose a less prickly course. "You're three for three in the tip department."

"I've only spoken to him once."

"That doesn't change the fact our killer is contacting the den each time he kills. He asked for you this time. Did he request you for the others as well?"

"Yes," he said softly, and I could tell I had gotten him thinking.

"We can't discount the fact the killer wants you personally informed of his accomplishments." I took a half step to catch up with his longer strides. "You found Bonnie. You brought her home. A week later, bodies started piling up." I kept going, hashing it out. "There must be a connection."

"He's a warg." Midas puckered his brow. "I'm gwyllgi, and so is Bonnie."

"You're descended from gwyllgi and wargs, so your species are compatible."

Midas slowed his pace. "Do you think Bonnie was in a relationship with the killer?"

Magic aside, she would hardly be the first woman to run from an abusive boyfriend or husband.

"We have to question her." There was no easy way to ask, so I spit it out. "Can you alpha mojo her into shifting?" The color washed from his face, and he glanced away from me. "I've heard pack can't disobey a direct order from their alpha...or their beta. Bonnie is new, and she's fae. I'm not sure if those things cancel out one another."

"I'll talk to her."

"Midas..."

"I don't use my influence that way." A dangerous thread wound through his voice, an edge that would garrote me if I kept pushing against it. "Don't ask me to again."

Holding up my hands in a peacemaking gesture, I let it go. "All right, all right."

"You're not what I expected in a successor for Linus."

"I could behead you with my swords. Then you might see the resemblance."

His dark laughter enticed as much as it repelled. "You're fire. He's ice. You're passion. He's calculation."

"You can call me hotheaded. It's okay. I get that a lot."

Passion as a descriptor made me uncomfortable.

"You're opposites."

"Don't worry, we don't attract."

Midas stared at me, right in the eyes, and I could tell I had shocked and/or horrified him.

Too bad I couldn't manifest the fire he accused me of having to burn the look off his face.

"Humor is my preferred coping mechanism too." I cleared my throat. "I'm sorry I subjected you to it."

"Linus would never cheat on Grier."

"I'm not suggesting—" I groaned long and low. "I don't have a thing for the POA." Thinking of him as *Linus*, even if we did sort of grow up together, made our working relationship too personal. "It was a joke. Obviously a bad one. A terrible one. One I will never make again if you could only please stop staring at me like I drowned a bag of puppies in front of you." I bit my tongue until it hurt. "That wasn't a dig at you being gwyllgi. The puppy thing. Goddess. I'm going to shut up now."

We walked another five minutes before he broke the silence, with a laugh of all things.

"You're not very funny."

"I'm not the one laughing." I risked a glance at him from the corner of my eye. "I owned up to it being a bad joke, but you're over there snickering. What does that say about you?"

"That I'm laughing at you and not at your warped sense of humor?"

"That's just cold," I grumped, relieved he didn't actually think I wanted to get horizontal with the POA.

A shiver rippled through me as my brain supplied an image of how that would go, not with the man, because that would be mildly appealing, but with the embodiment of the wraiths he commanded, which almost made me wet my pants.

"You can't be cold."

"What?" I shivered again. "Oh, no. I gave myself a fright is all."

"You were thinking about Linus," he surmised. "About how it might go if you did attract."

Busted.

A flash of heat blasted into my cheeks. "You have no proof."

"Your scent changed," he observed, "but you weren't aroused. You were...afraid."

The heat in my face seeped into a biting chill.

"So, as I was saying—" I laid the cheer on thick, "—you need to coax Bonnie into shifting back and answering a few questions. I'll talk to her when we get home, soften her up, get her primed for you, but you'll have to convince her cooperating is in her best interest."

Fae magic and necromantic magic weren't compatible on a lot of levels, but I could convince Ambrose to help me smash through her block if she wouldn't relinquish it otherwise. I would hate to do it, and we would be the opposite of friends afterward, if that's what we were now, but potential victims outweighed potential friendship every time.

"He hurt you," he said slowly.

Clearly, he was having trouble picturing a world where his buddy Linus went around hurting innocent women to get his jollies. Problem being, I wasn't innocent. The POA ran on order, and I had been a creature of chaos. He was right to put me down when he did. The miracle was that he helped me back up, gave me a second chance. Miracle wasn't the right word. I knew that, and I knew why he had done it, but it still humbled me.

Bent, not broken. That was me. I hoped it was me. I wanted it to be.

"The POA has never raised a hand against me unless it was warranted." I spotted Midas's temper rising in the crimson flicker of his eyes. "Women aren't inherently good. My gender doesn't mean I can't do evil. It doesn't mean I'm worthier than a man. It only means I can lactate and reproduce."

Once again, my sense of humor had robbed him of speech.

"You're right," he admitted after he recovered. "I have trouble..."

He didn't finish the sentence, and it made me doubt that was all he'd meant to say in the first place.

"You have a thing for abuse survivors." I did *not* look at the scarring up his arms, but he must have sensed my thoughts sway in that direction, because he rubbed a hand over them. "I can respect that. Careful it doesn't blind you to the bigger picture. The abused can be abusers too."

The statistics for abuse survivors repeating what was done to them was stark.

I would never have kids. Never. Not in a million years, and not for a million dollars.

I was too afraid.

Midas was right. I had fire, I had passion. I had a temper.

That didn't make me a monster, but my mother had been one. Was one. I worried how much of my mother's daughter I was after all those years of tiny pinches, hard slaps, and kicks delivered when I was already down.

I had proven I was capable of committing evil. I didn't want to prove I was capable of birthing it too.

"Hadley."

"I should get back." I turned and started walking away, from him and those grim thoughts. "Ford is my ride home."

"I'll stop by your apartment at dusk," he called to my retreating back.

I raised a hand to show I heard and would be ready, but I was halfway to running to put distance between myself and thoughts of *her*.

Maybe the POA was nuts for letting me step into his shoes, or at least try them on.

Then again, who better to hunt monsters than one of their own?

Ahead of me, my shadow walked backward across the pavement, craning his neck to stare at Midas.

"Shut up." I stomped past him. "No one asked you."

TEN

Midas kept walking after Hadley fled, eventually breaking into a punishing jog. The predator in him was affronted she had discovered his weakness after knowing him for such a short time. The primal urge to dominate heated his blood, but she wasn't pack, she wasn't gwyllgi. She owed him no allegiance and no submission.

Part of him worried that might be the reason he kept dropping in where he wasn't needed when he had already tasked Ford with acting in the pack's best interest.

"Midas."

Eyes closing, he had no choice but to stop and listen. "Yes?"

Ford was out of breath from running flat out to catch him, his chest heaving and his hair damp with sweat. "You didn't have to come tonight. I could have handled it."

"I know that."

"Tell me it's not Lee."

Lee.

The familiar ring of it itched the far corners of his brain, but he couldn't quite scratch it.

Yet.

The question shot out of his mouth without permission. "Are you pursuing her?"

"I... Hell. I like her." He rolled his shoulders. "That's hardly breaking news."

Ford had developed a dangerous crush on her, and Midas had hoped working together would cure him. So far, exposure therapy was only deepening his infatuation.

"Damn it." Ford cursed under his breath. "I can still do the job."

"You can't keep her in check if you're dating her, Ford. You're good, but you're not that good."

"Lee is a smart woman. This investigation is an excuse for me to get a read on her, and she knows it." Amusement bounced in his shoulders. "She's called me out more than once."

Midas grunted, expecting nothing less. Linus wouldn't have trained her if she wasn't diamond sharp. The past year had done nothing but polish what was there.

"I don't think she's into me," Ford admitted. "That doesn't mean I won't try, with your blessing."

"You two seemed chummy enough when you arrived." He wished he could blame the growl roughening his voice on the scarring, but Ford knew him too well. "You have a date set, right? A movie night?"

"Yeah, but it's not a real date. She knows I want to snoop around her place." He laughed a little to diffuse the tension. "I wouldn't be surprised if she turned up at my place with a DVD—or, god forbid, a VHS—with some black-and-white cheesefest to avoid having me in her space."

"I thought you liked science fiction."

"I enjoy the futuristic aspect of it, the looking forward. Her tastes run toward looking back."

There was comfort in the soft lines of black-and-white movies, where the good guys always won, and death never happened on screen. How she swallowed the shrinking violets so often cast as heroines, he had no clue. Lately he'd found himself watching movies he thought she might enjoy, curious what she saw in them, what comfort she found in them, and why she needed comfort in the first place.

But he couldn't ask without reciprocating.

Show me yours, and I'll show you mine.

His past was written in the crosshatch scars marring his forearms. He didn't cover them, didn't hide them. They were a warning sign, an indicator that he was broken. Not bent. Broken. It was easier for everyone if they got that sorted upfront without him having to say a word.

"She ran to you." Ford ruffled a hand through his hair. "She didn't gut-check herself against her team, or Bishop, or Lawson. Or me. We visited Mendelsohn, and she wanted you after."

"You just finished telling me she's smart. Hadley saw I have a soft spot for abuse cases, and she brought me one. End of story."

"Your mother would rip out her throat before she let Hadley steal her heir," Ford said quietly.

"She would try." Midas almost found a smile for the mental picture of his mother going toe-to-toe with Hadley. "There's more to Hadley than meets the eye." He shook his head. "That's why I keep turning up, why I keep getting involved. There's something about her. She's dangerous, more dangerous than a well-trained woman with swords ought to be."

"Tonight Ayla mentioned Lee's shadow. Do you know what that's about?"

Midas tugged on his ear, thinking. "Are you sure she wasn't talking about you?"

"I don't think so." He shrugged. "No one else is following her that I can tell."

"Bishop might be the face of the POA's team, but there are more of them. Some who patrol the streets the same as Hadley." Midas gave up on shaking loose whatever thought was slowly forming and left it to simmer in the back of his mind. "Do you think Ayla meant one of them? Linus might want tabs kept on her while he's out of town. Who better than one of their own?"

"Maybe," Ford allowed. "I'll pay closer attention, see if I can figure it out one way or another."

"You should go." Midas checked the time on his phone. "She's ready to call it a night."

"I won't ask her out if you don't want me to, for whatever reason." Ford glanced back the way he'd come but hesitated before turning. "Any reason at all."

"Try your luck." Midas ignored the vibration tickling the back of his throat. "Just let me know if you need to step down from your position. I need an impartial witness, not rose-colored updates."

"I'll do that." Ford reached for the keys in his pocket. "You've got time, if you change your mind."

"I won't." Midas pivoted on his heel and walked away before Ford made him an offer he couldn't refuse.

ELEVEN

I gave Ford fifteen minutes, and when he still didn't show, I collected the grumpy corgi and left him a note pinned under a windshield wiper explaining I had called for a Swyft. I was tired of waiting, tired in general, and all I wanted to do was sleep for a few years and wake to find the case had been solved while I was unconscious.

The Swyft driver, who rolled up in a bland white sedan and not the racy lime-green number I hoped to continue avoiding, didn't speak a word to me, even when I asked permission to bring my dog, so that was nice.

Less nice was how the doorman ran his eyes over us as we entered through the front door of the Faraday, his attention lingering on Bonnie then jerking back to me when he felt my stare.

"What?" I stopped on the threshold. "Do I have something stuck in my teeth?"

Maybe I was a tad irked Ford had ghosted on me, or maybe this confrontation had been a long time coming.

"Midas asked me to let him know when you got home. Just checking to see if you're intact."

"Oh." All my righteous anger evaporated in a blink. "Well, here I am. Two arms, two legs, so forth. Unless you count the dog. Then it's six legs—or maybe six arms? Either way, all limbs are accounted for."

At least he waited until I was through the door before reaching for his phone to tattle.

Goddess knows, I had enough keepers. What was one more? Midas must be worried about Bonnie. As soon as she got herself unstuck, she would be out of my hair, and so would he.

The elevator had been repaired since Bonnie took a bite out of it, but that was magic for you.

Since I refused to carry her up the stairs, we stepped into the booth and rode it up to my floor.

A tiny part of me expected Midas to be standing there, waiting to spark our next argument.

I wasn't sorry to be wrong.

Rubbing a hand over my breastbone, I let us into the apartment and hit the lights.

Bonnie shimmered on the edge of my vision before exploding into her gwyllgi form. The appearance of a pony where a corgi had been knocked me out of the doorway, into the hall, and onto my butt.

"What's gotten into you?" I got to my feet and leaned around her. "Oh no."

The canopy over the bed, shredded to ribbons. The fabric draping the walls, ripped down. The futon was flipped over, stuffing everywhere, the TV—goddess, the TV—was torn clean off the wall and smashed to bits.

Sinking onto the floor in the carpeted hallway, I pulled out my phone and dialed Bishop.

"No luck with the surveillance so far. Whatever did this tricks the eye. I'm cleaning up the footage. I ought to have something by dusk."

"I need a room for tonight." I cut into his update. "Which base is empty?"

"Base One and Six," he said automatically. "What's wrong?"

"Call the cleaners for me, will you? Send them to my apartment at the Faraday. Someone tossed it while I was out. We need to find out if that person is our killer."

"I'll be right there."

"You don't have to—"

"Shut the hell up," he snapped. "I'm not leaving you to deal with this alone."

He ended the call, and I just sat there while Bonnie reapplied her glamour and crawled into my lap.

THE RESPONSE TIME for cleaners never ceased to amaze me. I discovered five minutes after hanging up with Bishop that a few lived in the building next door, as they were first to arrive. I didn't have to wait much longer for Bishop himself to storm through the door. I expected him to keep going until he shoved through the cleaners to see what had been done, but he gathered me in his arms.

The offer of unsolicited comfort caused my brain to skip and my knees to go weak with gratitude.

"Thank the old gods," he breathed into my hair. "I'm glad you're all right."

I hadn't realized how much I needed a hug until he offered one to me, and I clung to him. "Me too."

Though, if this was the work of our killer, he would have saved us all a lot of hassle by dropping in on me while I was home and letting me lop off his head.

Maybe it ought to worry me that decapitation as a punishment fit most any capital offense among paranormals, but I had learned from the best, and he was *really* into the neck-and-head-separation deal.

"Do you need anything?" Bishop released me, making a point to ignore the corgi. "Clothes? Toothbrush? Deodorant? Woman stuff?"

"They'll need to process all that, and I don't want to hang around to watch. I'll just borrow sweats from HQ for today. I can make do with samples from the shelter supply cabinet for the rest."

"What about that?" Bishop recoiled when Bonnie wagged her butt at him. "Does it need anything?"

"The shelter kitchens are always stocked, so she's good to go."

On our way out, we ran into Ford waiting for the elevator we were exiting.

"Lee." He breathed a sigh of relief. "You all right, darlin'?"

News traveled fast when you lived in a building run by pack. No doubt the doorman had dialed up Midas for clearance when the cleaners showed up on the Faraday's doorstep. Ford would have been his next logical call.

"I'm not great," I admitted, "but it comes with the territory."

"We'll find out who did this," he said, keeping up with us as we crossed the lobby. "We'll find out how they did it."

"Keep me updated on anything you spot on the security feeds." I lifted a hand. "Later, Ford."

The doorman was on his phone, but he spared me and then Bonnie a lingering glance as we passed him. Probably updating Midas. Bishop led me to the ride he must have ordered for my sake on the way down.

After we got settled, Bishop gave me a look. "You were joking back there, right?"

"About the security feeds?" I snorted. "I have to at least *pretend* we don't have access to the entire city's network."

"Reece will have the footage ready for viewing by the time we get where we're going."

A thought occurred to me, and I was only half teasing when I asked, "Who will send us fifty-billion strings of text to guide us through the city without you there?"

"It's automated," he said blandly. "I'm a genius, but the evil part is debatable."

"That's not evil, that's lazy. Automated? Really?"

"Do you know how old it gets passing those codes back and forth manually?"

"Um, yeah." I cuddled Bonnie on my lap. "I do."

Scooching closer to the door, he gave me plenty of space. "You shouldn't cuddle that thing."

"It's not a thing." I scratched her pointy ears. "Besides, she's adorable."

"Until she bites your face off," he muttered, then noticed the car slowing. "This is our stop."

"You sure you want to get out here?" The driver frowned at us in his rearview mirror. "This ain't exactly a safe place to go walking at night."

"It's all right," I assured him. "I brought my dog with me."

His expression told me what he thought about that, but I was only a fare, and he was ready to move on to the next one.

Once Bishop and I were alone, we started following the automated codes to HQ. I wanted to shake him, point out since he was here, he could lead me there, but he was big on protocol, and protocol demanded we jump through hoops until our knees wobbled before we got where we were going.

Ten minutes later, I spotted the parking garage that led to Base Six.

About the time I cleared the first landing, I got a text from Midas.

>>*Sorry about your apartment.*

Me too.

>>*I'm overseeing the cleaners personally.*

The fact he was there in an official capacity, not as the heir, but as building security, meant he could rifle through my things without anyone batting an eye since he had a vested interest in bringing the culprit to justice.

You don't have to do that.

>> *Where are you staying tonight?*

At one of our shelters.

>>*Do you need anything?*

We keep them stocked. I'll be fine for a day.

>>Tell me where to meet you at dusk. We'll talk to Bonnie and get your answers.

My apartment. I'll kill two birds with one stone. You'll talk to her, I'll start cleaning.

What a truly depressing thought. I wasn't out much money for the trashed décor, but it had taken me hours and hours and hours to do that much sewing and crafting, enough to style a cohesive look.

Bishop waited for me on the landing. "Midas?"

Throttling a flush before it surfaced, I did my best to sound casual. "How could you tell?"

"He called me when he heard the news about your apartment. I expected he would reach out to you eventually."

After glaring at it, I pocketed the phone. "Why call you and not me in the first place?"

"I got the impression he wanted to know if you were okay, and he wanted an answer other than *I'm fine.*" He entered the code to access the base. "He must have figured I would rat you out."

The door opened, and I followed him inside. "Did you?"

"I told him, and I quote, 'She's fine.'" His chuckles did, now that I thought about it, sound a bit evil. "He's an ally, but that doesn't make him one of us. He's not entitled to stick his nose in your business. If he's got a question for you or about you, he's got your number."

A warm, fuzzy sensation spread through my limbs as he locked us in. "I didn't think you cared."

"You're too busy pretending you don't care about anyone to think anyone else might care about you."

"I care about plenty of people," I protested. "A whole city's worth of them."

"They're numbers, Hadley. They're not friends. That sounds harsh, but there you go. You can't know or protect every one of them. All you can do is try. But me? Our team? We're rooting for you, not waiting on you to screw up and get sent home."

The room wavered behind a sheen of tears. "Why is everyone hitting me over the head with a friendship stick lately?"

"This job will chew you up and spit you out if you go it alone, that's true for all of us. That's why the POA created a team. He knew it, and he planned ahead to avoid burnout. You think we're loyal to him, and we are, but the office comes first. You're on track to become the next POA, and that means our loyalty—and friendship—belongs to you too."

"Thanks," I said thickly, then cleared my throat before facing the monitors. "Reece, what have you got for me?"

"A blur," he mumbled, distracted. "I can't get the stills I took any clearer than this."

A series of photos lined up on the lower screens, but they didn't illuminate the killer's identity.

"Tall, male, and a para of some kind is all I can promise you." Reece highlighted a portion of footage. "Magic and technology don't always play nice, but this is one of two things. A charm that's covering his tracks, or a power that's covering his tracks. Either way, his tracks are covered. I've dug through footage taken at the Faraday as well. Same problem. Our MARTA murderer, or someone like him, was in your apartment."

"Any idea how he got in?"

"He didn't walk in through the front door or use the fire escape." Intrigue mingled with frustration in his voice. "He stepped out from a blind spot."

"Meaning he knew the location of the cameras." Bishop worked his jaw. "The last breach at the Faraday was an inside job. Stands to reason this one was too. The previous leak has since been plugged. This is an all-new drip."

"Great." I blew out a tired breath. "I'm living in a sinking ship."

Reece grumbled about rats, and his screen went dark.

"We'll keep digging," Bishop promised me. "Get some rest."

"A girl can dream."

I let myself into a large room stacked with enough bunk beds to sleep a dozen people. One en suite bathroom opened off to the right, but it was meant for sharing, with two enclosed toilet stalls. A kitchen meant no one staying here ever went hungry. The dining area had fold-down tables, and it doubled as a living room. The only TV in the space was mounted on the back wall so anyone eating could watch.

Each of our bases contained the exact same housing facilities, and sadly, most were kept full.

This job wasn't all hunting serial killers and visiting nudist colonies. Most nights I saw no action. Others I busted up drunken/drugged brawls or domestic disputes. The latter often required additional resources to prevent recurrence. That's when we stepped in and provided for the victims. It was safer for them, and humans, for supernaturals to be kept separate while they healed.

Cornered predators lashed out, and a warning that another supernatural could shrug off might kill a human.

When a base had guests, we partitioned off its adjacent command center, containing them in the residence area. That gave them access to the bunkroom, the bathroom, the kitchen, and the dining room while keeping them out of HQ itself. There was a lockbox Bishop could activate for remote entry as well. That way, we didn't see them, and they didn't see us.

"Do you need anything?" Bishop lingered in the doorway. "I'll leave the seal unlocked for you in case you need computer access."

"I'm good." I chose a cot at random and climbed in. "I'm too tired for a shower. I'll grab one tomorrow and do laundry on my way out."

"These sheets have seen worse. Trust me."

"Believe it or not, that's not the most comforting thing you can tell a person who's too tired to worry about fleas, ticks, or bedbugs."

"Sweet dreams." He flipped off the light. "There was one weird thing. Midas asked me the brand name of your sewing machine. Yours had rubbed off."

"That is weird. What does my sewing machine have to do with anything?" May it rest in peace. "It was a thrift store find. Ten bucks. It paid for itself ten times over."

"That's more or less what I told him."

While I turned the odd question over in my mind, Bishop left, his footsteps tapering into silence.

I wasn't sure what he was, or how he traveled the city so quickly without transportation, or why he managed the bases, or much of anything else, honestly. I hadn't noticed the creeping burnout until he mentioned it, but I was tired, and I had been for a long time before coming to Atlanta.

Maybe I had gotten it wrong, and a social life was just what the doctor ordered.

TWELVE

I woke at dusk, thanks to Bonnie's snoring, and hit the kitchen to whip us up breakfast. We kept staples in all the pantries, so I was able to treat myself to a double café mocha made with a couple pieces of bribery chocolate, along with eggs, bacon, and toast. I made her a plate of the same and left it on the floor for her while I took a quick shower then dressed in a pair of gray sweats and a white tee. We kept a ton of them, in all sizes, in the closet for guests who left their homes with only the clothes on their backs.

Most people respected the system and only used or took what they needed, which was fine, but one time a full set showed up on eBay with the POA's forged signature...

Sadly, we didn't provide hair goop, so I had to leave my curls to their own devices.

"Ready?" I called to Bonnie as I exited the bunkroom with our dirties balled up for the laundry service. "Midas is expecting us at the Faraday." I dumped the sheets down the chute then prayed she wasn't not answering because she'd had an accident she didn't want me to find. "Bonnie?"

A faint squeak perked my ears, and I jumped as a mouse ran over my foot.

A *white* mouse.

"What do you think you're doing?"

As I watched, she scurried from corner to corner, searching for a way out. I could have told her there was none.

Maybe I shouldn't have mentioned Midas. He must have said something last night that spooked her. Too bad for her, fear and guilt provoked similar fight-or-flight responses. The former was regrettable. No one wanted to further traumatize a victim. The latter was inescapable. I had to do my job, even when it meant adorable creatures and/or potential friends took their turn in the hot seat.

"This is for your own good." I caught her in my cupped hands and dumped her into a tall glass before slapping a coaster over the top. "You can't run away from this. Lives are at stake."

Too many of them had already been lost.

I had a theory, based on nothing much, that she couldn't change glamour from mouse to dog again unless she had room for the dog to fit. She would shatter the glass if she tried, which she could shrug off, but I got the feeling there was more to it. That her projected mass required appropriate space to manifest, not just the will to change.

Basically, I had a mouse in a cup. A corgi wouldn't fit in a cup. Therefore, she was stuck as a mouse until I let her out, giving her room to glamour herself into a larger form.

Thanks to her escape attempt, I didn't feel too bad about holding her hostage. I would, however, need a ride if I wanted to keep her from giving me the slip before I was ready. I pulled out my phone, thumb hovering over the Swyft icon, but I dialed Ford in the end.

"Hey."

"Hey back," I said briskly. "Can you give me a lift to my place?"

"Sure thing." The *tick-tick-tick* of his blinker told me he was already in his truck. "Where are you?"

"Head to Dickerson's Seafood. I'll meet you out front."

Onto my tricks, he pressed his luck. "Sure you don't want me to take the direct route?"

"I don't know what you're talking about, *darlin'*." I hung up with his laughter in my ear. "You heard the man." Mouse-sized or not, gwyllgi senses were superb. "Let's go."

Balancing my hostage, I backed out the exit door then locked up behind us. I got a few weird looks from folks on the street. Okay, I got a *lot* of weird looks, carrying a mouse around in a glass in the city. Most people trapped them or tossed them, but here I was, taking mine for a walk.

The corgi glamour had definitely been less conspicuous, even if it still got us noticed because who didn't love corgis? People would remember exactly that—they saw a super-cute doggo. They wouldn't remember me. I was just the person at the other end of the leash. With a mouse? I was transformed into That Crazy Lady with a Mouse in a Cup. The mouse was overlooked, except for the initial double take to see if they really saw what they thought the first time, but I got noticed in a way that told me people were measuring me for a straitjacket.

Mr. Dickerson himself came out carrying a broom when he spotted me loitering in his parking lot.

"Girl, what you doing?" He adjusted his wire-rimmed glasses. "That a mouse in a cup?"

"I caught it in my apartment."

"Didn't have no heart to kill it?" He clucked his tongue. "Dump it here, right here. I'll do it for you."

Thankfully, I was saved by Ford pulling in the spot beside me.

"That's my boyfriend," I lied to the nice old man. "I called him to kill it for me."

"That's fine." He lowered his broom. "Next time, maybe have him come to your place? Don't look good for me to have a mouse near my store. People get ideas about raisins in their food."

"I apologize." I held up the mouse. "It scared me is all. I wasn't thinking."

"You have a good night now." He pointed the broom at me. "Remember, don't run no more after dark."

"Yes, sir."

Mr. Dickerson let himself back in his store, and I passed the hostage to Ford through the window he had lowered to better hear me lying like a rug.

"Do I want to know?" He took a sniff, and his eyes widened. "Snowball?"

"Yes, indeed." I rounded the truck and hauled myself onto the seat. "She's in time-out."

"I guess so." He handed her back. "I'm your boyfriend, huh?"

"Don't get a big head." I settled in for the short ride. "Mr. Dickerson is human. He caught me on patrol one night and offered me a ride home. I told him I run this neighborhood for exercise, and he almost had a heart attack. I make a point to swing by once a week so he knows I'm still alive."

"You figured it would put his mind at ease if you had a big, strong, handsome man in your life."

"As old-fashioned as he is, only one part of that sentence matters."

"Ouch."

"It's just a flesh wound." I patted his arm. "Your ego will survive. You apparently go around telling people you're big, strong, and handsome. Pretty sure that means you've got plenty to spare."

"I try, and I try." He nosed the truck up to the curb in front of the Faraday. "You shoot me down at every opportunity."

"I'm not actually your girlfriend, Ford. I don't have to stroke your ego."

The mottled red blossoming in his cheeks inspired pity in me, and I didn't tack on *or anything else.*

But I was thinking it.

"The cleaners finished up three hours after you left. There's a log of all the personal items they took for testing. If you're missing anything that's not listed, let the Faraday know, and they will arrange for replacements."

"I have renter's insurance."

"The Faraday has only been breached once since our pack took over security," he told me. "It happened almost two years ago. To Linus." He threw the truck in park and got out with me. "It sets a bad precedent, makes it look like we can't protect high-profile clients. Our alpha will not be pleased about this."

"These things happen." I led the way past the doorman, who was too busy perfecting his statue impersonation to notice what I held. "Hazards of the job."

I had used that line more in the past twelve hours than in the past twelve months.

"It's okay to be upset," he said once the elevator doors closed behind us. "It's okay to be afraid."

"Oh, don't worry," I was quick to assure him. "I'm plenty pissed."

Fear had no place in my life. Not anymore.

The hall stood empty, but I didn't think too much about it. I had probably beat Midas here.

"Do you hear that?" Ford cocked his head. "Are you expecting someone?"

"No, and yes." I passed him the mouse cup. "Stand back."

Adrenaline dumped in my veins as I gripped the knob and found my apartment unlocked. A quick twist of my wrist opened the door, and I rushed the figure who spun around with a gleaming weapon in hand.

By the time my brain put a name to the face (Midas) and I had ID'd the weapon (staple gun), it was too late. I hit him center mass with my shoulder and knocked him backward, right onto the futon. Momentum got the best of me, though, and I tumbled after him. He landed in a seated position, and I landed between his thighs, on my knees, with my arms loosely wrapped around his waist.

"Um..."

Midas flattened his spine against the fabric. I wasn't sure he was breathing, but his eyes sparked crimson.

"I wasn't expecting you." Slowly, slowly, I kept going until I sat on the floor, but I didn't pull back before I got a nose full of his scent, cedar and amber. "I didn't mean to tackle you. I don't even like football. Except for tailgating, which is worth the crowd and the noise if you do it right."

He closed his eyes, fisting his hands where they rested on the futon, but I never thought for a minute he might hurt me, and not just because of my gender.

Folding my legs into lotus position, I gave him space. "Are you all right?"

"I wanted to surprise you."

The frustrated tone convinced me he wasn't going to rip out my throat if I took my eyes off him, and when I did, I goggled at the transformation my apartment had undergone since I left it in shambles.

"You fixed it." I got to my feet and ran a hand along the walls, draped in the same material and colors. "Where did you find so many top sheets?"

"You're not the only franchise in the city."

"You bought from a competitor?" Clutching the material, I gasped out, "How dare you?"

A smile twisted the right side of his mouth, but he kept his eyes shut. "You were closed."

I wandered through the space he had so carefully reconstructed without ever having been my guest.

The sewing machine, new with a user manual pinned underneath, almost brought tears to my eyes.

This was why he called Bishop. He was piecing my life back together after it had been shattered on his watch. Maybe that's all it was, just professional courtesy. Or, like Ford said, part of the Faraday package. When I spotted the TV on the wall, the screen a few inches bigger, the fancy mount capable of hiding the DVD player I saw peeking out from behind it, I couldn't stop my eyes from leaking. He even hid the cords in the walls, something I had been too cheap to do at the time I had the original installed and had regretted not doing ever since.

New futon, new dining room table, new dishes, new...everything.

"You got it all right." Afraid of giving him too much credit, I had to ask. "How?"

"Bishop."

Who knew his routine checks on my living space would serve a purpose down the line?

After I completed a dazzled circuit of the room, I found myself standing in front of Midas again, subject to the full weight of his stare.

I hadn't owned much to start with, so he didn't have to source but a few things to set my apartment back to rights. Even for him, the biggest investment had been time. That still didn't explain why he did it.

"Thank you." I wiped my face dry with the back of my hands. "You don't strike me as a hugger, so that's all I've got." I laughed wetly. "I don't know what else to say. Just, thank you."

Slowly, slowly, as I had done, he leaned forward, eyes never leaving my face. "You're welcome."

We remained that way for a long moment, him in a submissive pose, me in a dominant position, before he exhaled through his teeth, unable to stand it any longer. "There's something we need to get out of the way."

Unsure where this was heading, I hooked a thumb over my shoulder. "Ford and Bonnie are in the hall."

"I'm aware."

I swallowed once to wet my throat. "You're not going to bite me, are you?"

"Hadley," he said on a sigh, a wrinkle gathering across his forehead. "Kneel."

"I just got off my knees," I pointed out, but lowered myself without hesitation, which made me question what the heck I was doing taking orders from him. "Now what?"

"Look in my—" He sighed. "You're already looking in my eyes."

"I can't help it." I started to rise, but he caught me gently by the wrist. "Ford told me it was as much your fault as it is mine. That means you're in as much trouble as I am. So whatever you're thinking of doing to me, you should do to yourself first."

"Hadley Whitaker," he said, smoothing his thumb over my pulse, "you are an equal in my eyes. You may look upon me without fear. You may hold my gaze and not be punished for the offense. You are absolved, here and now, for any prior trespass, and no insult can henceforth be taken."

A few seconds lapsed where I waited for tingles to spread through my limbs or for magic to caress me. Neither happened, and that left me more confused than ever. "What did that accomplish?"

"His inner beast won't force you to submit," Ford said from the doorway. "That's what it accomplishes. You're a dominant personality, a predator, and it's hard for the same to be around you. The oath, for lack of a better word, he swore allows you to look freely upon him, to maintain eye contact with him, and not be punished for either by anyone—including him."

"That will come in handy."

Though it would have been less dramatic if he had just told me *I won't growl at you for looking me in the eye from now on.*

The tension in Midas eased several degrees as I watched, and he openly looked at me now, inviting me to do the same. I'm embarrassed over how long I sat there, drinking him in. I would have felt worse if he hadn't been doing the same. I felt like both an animal in an exhibit at the zoo and the person admiring it.

Ford was right. Midas was starved for contact. Not physical, but... I don't know how to describe it.

Once he noticed he still held me, he frowned at his palm, which had grown damp, and broke his grip.

"Now that we have the formalities out of the way, we have a

small problem." I pinched my pointer and thumb together to illustrate. "About the size of a lab mouse if you want to get technical." I waved Ford over, but his gait was stiff when he crossed to me. "Bonnie tried to escape this morning."

"Shut the door," Midas told Ford. "We need privacy for this."

Ford handed Bonnie off to me then did as he was told and took up a position there.

"Release her." Midas eased onto the floor with me. "She won't run."

Trusting him that she wouldn't bolt for the gap under the door like a runner sliding into home, I removed the coaster and tipped the glass gently on its side where she could scurry out onto the polished concrete.

"You're under no obligation to answer my questions," he began, and I choked on an instinctive rebuke. "Refuse to cooperate, continue to endanger my pack, and I will turn you out. You have made no effort to socialize, and you refuse to live at the den. I didn't push you because I thought you weren't ready. Do you want a new life as a member of the Atlanta pack, or are you only using our resources to escape your old one?"

The two weren't mutually exclusive, and Midas had a right to want an answer. I had no doubt he would do all he could to help her in any case, but there was no reason to shelter her at the Faraday, or employ her as his PA, if she had no interest in either long-term.

The mouse flexed its whiskers, jerked its head to glance back at me, then whipped its tail.

"No one is going to hurt you," I reassured her. "We just want answers."

The air around her shimmered, standing her fur on end, and she began to grow until I had to scoot back to make room for Bonnie the human to sit between Midas and me.

Dressed in the same outfit she wore to Perkerson, with the same damp hem, she inched away from Midas until she sat beside me.

Reading into her body language, Midas held my stare to convey this was my show.

As much as her posture begged for it, I didn't touch her or comfort her. "Did you know Shonda Randall?"

"No," she rasped. "I might have seen her in passing, but we were never introduced."

New to the pack, living separately, I could buy that. "You were acting as Midas's personal assistant."

"Yes."

"Did you intercept the call about Shonda's death?"

"Y-y-yes." She twisted her hands in the fabric of her skirt. "I took a message and gave it to Midas."

Unlike my first exposure to her, where her fragility called to my protective instincts, I had trouble swallowing the act this time. I had spent too much time around her while she was glamoured to believe the stark differences in her personalities were genuine. A gwyllgi form could definitely boost her confidence. I had no trouble with that. But a corgi? A mouse?

A slim chance existed that she had blossomed under my care, but that smacked of an inflated ego, and I tried to keep mine squashed flat. Hubris had landed me with Ambrose, after all.

An edge crept into my voice I didn't try to dull. "Did you recognize the caller's voice?"

Bonnie wilted on the spot, and a sob escaped her. "Yes."

"Who is it, Bonnie?" Unable to resist the misery pouring off her, I rested a hand on her shoulder. "Who are we dealing with here?"

"My son," she whispered. "He's my son."

Pity softened my tone, but I wasn't done yet. "That's why you investigated Perkerson Park alone."

"Siemen asked me to meet him, and I thought I could reason with him, so I went alone, but he wasn't there." A tremor shook her fragile limbs, and I tightened my grip. "Once I saw what he had done, I knew there was no saving him. That's when I told Midas what I found, and then he called you."

"You've been able to shift for a while now, haven't you?"

"I wasn't tricking you that first morning. I was terrified, so afraid Siemen was watching, waiting for me, I couldn't switch back. I'm safer as my other self, and I didn't want to face him like this."

"I need some air." Midas rose in a fluid motion and strode for the door. "Ford—"

"—keep an eye on her," I finished for him. "I need to confer with Midas."

As Ford stepped aside to let us pass, he flared his nostrils and swore under his breath, but I didn't have time to stop and grill him if I wanted to catch Midas.

"Go back in and finish your interrogation," he ordered, like his title meant boo to me. "You're not done yet."

"I'm done when I say I'm done, and I'm not pack. Your Jedi mind trick doesn't allow you to boss me around, Goldilocks."

The jaw I had admired earlier began grinding. Audibly. "You overstep."

"Pretty sure the vow you made means not only can I say whatever I want, I can look you in the eye while I do it." I bet he was regretting that decision in record time. "What is your problem?"

"I found her," he said coldly. "I welcomed her into my pack, into our den."

"I welcomed her into my home, into HQ." Thank the goddess for her magical gag order. "So what?"

"This whole fiasco is—"

"Tell me it's your fault, and I'm going online to purchase the world's smallest violin to play for you."

"She knew she was being hunted and said nothing. Thanks to me, a killer is—"

"—in Atlanta?" I folded my arms across my chest. "Try again. You found her here. Her son, if that's who we're dealing with, was always going to come after her. Atlanta was always going to suffer. It stands to reason that since she's gwyllgi, and our initial tests show he's warg, half warg anyway, he was always going to target the same demographic."

"You told me yourself it was personal. That he was calling me to—"

"—brag? In light of what we've just learned, I better understand why the calls were placed to you. He watched her, found out you had taken her in, given her a job, and he discovered how to get in touch with her through her capacity as your PA." I stepped closer. "This is not your fault. All you did was show kindness to a woman in need. There's no shame in that. There's no blame either."

Midas speared his fingers through his hair and tugged on the ends. "Can I talk now?"

"The floor is yours."

He stared at me, but he didn't say anything.

"Well?" I cupped a hand to my ear. "I'm waiting."

"You derailed my entire argument."

"You're new to the leadership thing. I am too. Believe me, I get it. It's easy to accept the blame for every little thing that goes wrong. The thing is— We're only human." I snorted when he arched an eyebrow. "It sounds better than *we're only a necromancer and a gwyllgi*, okay?" I sliced my hand through the air. "My point is this. We're going to make good calls, and we're going to make bad ones. We're going to help some people, and we're going to hurt others. We're going to do our jobs to the best of our abilities, and there's no room for looking back. The past is past. Chin up, eyes forward, head in the game."

"The decisions you make don't impact—"

"—a large group of people I'm sworn to protect?" I tapped my chin. "Hmm. It's almost like being the POA means every heartbeat in the city is your responsibility."

"Can you please stop—?"

"—cutting you off?"

"You are the most frustrating woman I have ever met," he told me, not unkindly.

"The feeling is mutual," I assured him. "Except the woman part. I'm, ah, pretty sure you don't qualify."

"Pretty sure?"

"I'm not a booster seat for the male ego. Ask Ford."

Mentioning Ford struck a chord with him, and his expression shuttered. "Finish questioning her."

"Yeah, okay."

He took the elevator down, and I walked back to my apartment, knocked on the door, and let myself in.

Ford kept his eyes averted, and it gave me the creeps. "What crawled up your butt and died?"

"He can no longer hold your gaze," Bonnie said to the vicinity of my navel.

"We'll sort this out later." He brushed his fingers down my arm. "Work, don't worry about me."

Bonnie had moved to the futon while I was out yelling at Midas, so I joined her there and almost moaned as I sank into the new mattress. If my old one had been cloudlike, this one deserved its own angelic choir.

"I didn't mean for this to happen." She stared at the slender fingers twined on her lap. "I ran away when I couldn't take it any longer. I didn't expect Midas to find me, to be found at all, but that doesn't excuse what I did. I should have turned him down. I should have stayed at the shelter. Or maybe I shouldn't have left the pack in the first place."

"You had every right to leave a situation that made you unhappy or put you at risk." I ran an absent hand over the velvety-soft fabric, forcing my thoughts away from brooding beta gwyllgi. "Where you went wrong was in assuming trouble wouldn't follow you. You should have told Midas where you came from and why you left. He could have protected you, and his pack, better with that information."

"I heard what you said to him in the hall."

Gwyllgi hearing made keeping secrets hard, so I wasn't surprised given our volume. "And?"

"Do you believe that?" Voice a bare whisper, she asked, "Would Siemen have done this to these people with or without me here?"

"Yes." Of that I had no doubt. "He targeted the warg packs as well as the gwyllgi. There's no reason to believe he wouldn't have done the same whether you went to one of them for help or stayed in the shelter instead of going with Midas."

"It's my fault." Her fingers went lax. "I am responsible."

Blame was easy to cast but harder to cast off. She was doing a fine job of piling it on, so I didn't add to her burden.

"Talk to me about your son." I offered her a pillow to hold to give her hands something to do. "Why is he hunting you? Why is he killing to get to you?"

That poor lavender pillow would have begged for mercy had it a voice. As it was, I worried she might squeeze the stuffing right out of it. It did the job, though. Gave her something to hold on to when her world must feel like it was crumbling all over again.

"I was given to a warg pack a century ago, and they used me to…" She wet her lips. "I have many children." She squished the pillow tighter. "None of them came out right."

Dread whispered up my spine, and I didn't want to know but had to ask, "What do you mean?"

"Lore on both sides of the veil between Earth and Faerie claims gwyllgi who interbred with wargs became creatures of this world. Their children were born with half the magic of their parents, but they were born free of Faerie rule, and that was what mattered."

"That's the version I was told too."

"Lore is a story passed from one generation to the next, embellished as it flows in one ear and out another's mouth."

"You think there was more to it?"

"All my children were born feral, more warg than gwyllgi. Their forms were warg in appearance, but they were twisted, horrible things that made the earth weep to behold them. Their madness prevents them from holding their shifted form. It wasn't uncommon for them to take down deer and other large prey in one form but eat their kill in another."

That fit with how Reece interpreted the data. "Are there more like your son still out there?"

"No," she whispered. "I killed them. All but the last." She wet her lips. "I would have done the same to him if his father had given me half a chance, and Siemen knows it. That's why I fled the pack. Their punishment couldn't be worse than what my son was devising for me."

"He wanted to kill you before you could kill him."

Head down, she nodded. "Yes."

"We'll need a name, description, and any other information you can give us."

"I will help in any way I can."

"I'll hold you to that." I got to my feet. "Give me your word you won't leave this room."

"I will not leave this room," she repeated, elaborating more. "I will not attempt another escape."

Fae couldn't lie, but they could twist and bend the truth until they got what they wanted out of the deal. The question was, what did she want? Protection? Shelter? Or something else?

"Ford?" I ushered him into the hall and shut her in. "Can you draft someone to keep an eye on her?"

"Yeah." He took out his phone and sent a text. "Ares will be up in a minute."

"Are you sure leaving her with a man is wise?"

"Ares is a woman."

"Well alrighty then." I led him to the elevator to wait on our relief and pitched my voice low. "How much of what she just said do you believe?"

"I can believe a warg pack thought bringing gwyllgi blood into their line was a good idea, but she didn't say exactly how or why she ended up with them." He mashed the button for the lobby again, but the car didn't rise any faster. "There are packs who still drown babies who are born with deformities or with other imperfections. Psychological issues don't always present themselves until the child is older. It's not common anymore, but culling does happen when a pack member shows signs of madness."

"The world is too small these days, thanks to technology, to risk exposure."

"The world has always been too small to risk exposure."

Me and my measly twenty-seven years couldn't argue with him there.

"You think she was right to cull her children?"

Cull had a nicer ring to it than *murder*.

"We might look human at times, but we're animals too. There will always be those among us who are more tame than wild, just as there will always be those who heed the whisper of instinct and do as it demands."

"That was a long-winded way of saying you see where she's coming from," I pointed out.

"I wanted to avoid you looking at me the way you are now. A mentally ill human teen might turn a gun on their classmates at school, a mentally ill paranormal teen can slaughter entire towns before they're caught. You can't measure them with the same stick. Not if the true measure is protecting innocents—paranormal and normal."

The elevator doors slid open, and a muscular woman with choppy brown hair joined us in the hall.

"Ares," Ford greeted her. "We need you to keep an eye on Bonnie while we're gone."

"Sure thing." She popped a bright pink bubble. "In or out?"

Seeing as it was my home, Ford let me decide, and I chose house arrest. "In."

Ares blinked as if she hadn't noticed me standing there until I spoke, and when she did look at me, she dropped her gaze to the carpet. "Apologies."

"Not this again." I rubbed my forehead. "You can look me in the eye. I don't mind."

"I can't," she said, and I could tell it irked her. "I would have to get Midas's permission."

"I'm confused." I pinned Ford with a scowl. "How did she know? You witnessed, so I get that, but she just looked at me."

"He marked you," Ares answered. "I can smell it."

Ford studied the wallpaper like the pattern contained the mysteries of the universe explained.

"He didn't mark me." I would remember that. "He looked me in the eye, recited some words, and left."

Ares was less subtle. "Did he touch you at all?"

The imprint of his fingers was a heated memory on my skin, but I didn't want to confess that to them.

"I touched him," I admitted, remembering the futon incident. "With most of my upper body. I heard him moving around in my apartment and tackled him."

"You tackled *Midas*? Midas Kinase?"

"Blue eyes, blond hair?" I held a hand high in the air. "About this tall." I replayed it in my head. "I didn't touch skin, though. Just his shirt. And his jeans. I was between his legs, so...maybe his boots?"

"Ford," Ares blurted, shock plain in her tone.

"I know," he said, hurt plain in his.

"Well, I don't know." I cornered Ares. "What are you talking about?"

"Gwyllgi take after wargs in a lot of ways." Her posture screamed she wanted to run, but she stood her ground. "Wargs believe in soul mates, fated mates, life mates, whatever you want to call them. Not all gwyllgi do because fae are long-lived, and some prefer to find a soul mate per century versus one for eternity."

"I'm not liking the direction this conversation is going." I stepped back, bumping into Ford. "She's not saying what I think she's saying, is she?"

"Are you sure he didn't touch you?" She dipped her head, breathing in. "Skin to skin? At all?"

Giving up on privacy, I told them the rest. "He grabbed me when I lost my temper."

The only bodily fluid we had swapped was sweat, and that was more of a transference from him to me. After working in my apartment for hours, I wasn't going to call the guy out for a damp palm. It would have been weirder if he hadn't been hot after all he'd done, and in a cramped space too.

"Midas didn't mate you." Ford reached out, but he let his arm fall to his side. "If that worries you."

"Oh, thank the goddess." I slumped against him, and I didn't miss his flinch. "I'm not ready for that level of commitment to anything with less than seventy-five percent cacao."

Ares eyed me with pity, like she knew more than she let on. "Other gwyllgi can scent his interest in you."

"He's not interested in me," I assured her. "It's got to be some residual magic from the Care Bear Stare he used to activate my eye-contact powers."

"Care Bear...Stare?" Ares burst into laughter. "I have got to remember that one."

I might not have received a classic education as far as Bishop was concerned, but I wasn't totally pop culture ignorant in the realm of cartoons.

She walked to my apartment, amusement still bright in her face, and let herself in.

"Did you notice the smell?" I lifted my arm to my nose. "I don't smell anything."

Alone in the hall, Ford stared at the recessed lighting until I questioned if his mother had warned him about the dangers of staring into the sun. "He didn't mean to do it."

"That's good news then." I brightened, ready to hunt him down. "He can undo it."

"Not exactly." He rubbed his neck until I was amazed it didn't pop off his shoulders. "You can wait it out, let it fade. As long as he doesn't renew it, it will go away on its own."

Eyeing my door with longing, I considered postponing our next stop. "Will a shower help?"

"No."

"I have some Goo Gone."

"That won't work on this."

"Gojo?"

"That won't help either."

"Frak." I hit the button to summon the elevator. "This is going to make for an awkward few days."

"You can say that again," he murmured and followed me into the car.

Down in the lobby, I got a taste of how lonely it must be for Midas.

No one held my gaze. No one even tried. Though I felt their attention in the prickling between my shoulder blades as I strode past. It was like I'd donned an invisibility cloak. Even the doorman kept his eyes fixed high above my head.

I would have to start any conversation, and I bet an ounce of Vintage 2014 Andean Alder To'ak chocolate they would speak to my chin.

"I see why Midas hates the royal treatment." I shuddered on the sidewalk. "That was downright creepy."

"He grew up with it, a witness to it, I mean. Not a recipient. He's got a higher tolerance than you do."

After we climbed in his truck, I hit him with the question that had been on my mind since I plowed into Midas upstairs. "Did you know what he was doing? Not the marking thing, the redecorating thing?"

"The Faraday is responsible for any lost or damaged property that's the result of failed security measures." He cranked up and pulled into traffic. "They can afford to offer that insurance since it's only been cashed in once prior to this."

"Replacing everything I own wouldn't cost as much as the POA's couch," I agreed, unashamed of my cheap digs. They were mine. Bought with my sweat and effort, all tokens of my new life. "Honestly, I imagine if a thief stole an embroidered hand towel out of his bathroom, that would still cost more than my whole apartment's worth of furnishings."

"I heard a rumor he orders toilet paper printed with dollar bills."

"No, the rumor is he pays someone to tape dollar bills end to end then rolls them and uses that for toilet paper." As the person who started the rumor, accuracy was important to me. "Have you ever seen his apartment?"

"Not since he moved in, no."

"Trust me, the toilet paper is plush enough I can believe nuns handstitch it in convents in the Alps or something, but it's plain white."

Head shaking, he pulled into the slow lane. "Where are we going?"

"Perkerson Park." I checked the darkened floorboard and found Ambrose coiled there. "The killer—" calling him Siemen felt premature, "—used that cache for days, if not weeks. I want to have a look around the area now that the cleaners are done with the site."

The trip over was short, but it felt longer without Bonnie's soft ears to rub between my fingers.

Maybe I didn't need a friend. Maybe I needed a nice, uncomplicated dog. A real one. Not a fae one.

We stepped out into the parking lot, empty since the park closed at dusk. I found my way back to where I first spotted Bonnie standing near the creek and barely resisted the urge to ask Ford to sniff around to see if he could identify the trail and follow it.

"I'll save us time and tell you I can't track worth a damn," Ford said from behind me.

"Really, Ford?" I noticed a narrow footpath, possibly a deer trail, and decided to explore it. "Did I say anything?"

"I could feel you thinking it at me."

One thing necromancers had in common, whether Low or High Society, was excellent night vision. The waning crescent moon gave me enough light to pick my way through the woods without stumbling. I don't know what I hoped to find. I wasn't sure the killer had gone this way, but I had to do something. I was tired of sitting around, waiting for another tip that came too late.

"Scat."

"As in poop?" I checked my soles, hoping I hadn't stepped in any. "Or as in *scat you cat*?"

"The first one." He pointed off the beaten path. "Definitely warg."

"No guarantee it's our guy, though." I debated how badly I wanted to poke around in stale droppings and decided I would rather continue on, see where the trail ended. I took out my phone and pulled up the GPS app, adding a pin on the map to identify the scat. "Let's keep going."

Ford didn't mention smelling anything else, and I didn't notice much worth commenting on. We walked until we hit another parking lot. Apartment buildings hugged the corner of the street, and a subdivision ate up space too.

"He can't be this obvious." I searched for any indication of where he might have gone, but the trail was cold, and it was wishful thinking to expect otherwise. "What are the odds the killer lives here? He could have leased an apartment, rented a house." A thought was slowly forming. "Have we crosschecked the victims' addresses against this location?"

"Shonda lived near Piedmont Park." Ford scratched his head. "Far as I know, the cleaners have only ID'd two of the eight victims found here. I doubt the addresses have been run considering the limited data pool."

"I'll get Bishop on it." I sent him a text. "He'll have those results to us soon."

"Did you crash with him last night?" Ford studied my chin,

which I hoped hadn't sprouted any black hairs to warrant that kind of attention. "You left with him, so I wondered."

"I have no idea where Bishop lives, so no. I didn't crash with him. He's a coworker, a glorified babysitter more than anything." I took one last look around and started back the way we'd come. "Please don't tell me that Midas marking me requires you to stick your nose into my nonexistent personal life."

"Just the opposite." He hesitated a moment. "Any man with half a brain would leave you the hell alone."

"What does that make you?"

The corners of his mouth twitched. "Half as smart as I thought I was."

THIRTEEN

I n his childhood room, deep within the den, Midas sprawled across a twin bed and laughed until his ribs hurt while his niece, Evangeline "Trouble" Kinase, climbed his sister like a tree during their video chat.

"Unca Midas lets me braid his hair," she whined. "Momma, *pleassse.*"

Blue was Lethe's favorite color, and she hadn't stopped dyeing her hair various shades since she was old enough to defy a direct order from their mother. However, bright hues attracted clever little fingers. That might explain why the shoulder-length bob his sister preferred was gone. A pompadour with an undercut had taken its place. There wasn't much left to braid, except on top.

"Yeah, Momma." Midas wiped tears off his cheeks. "*Pleassse.*"

"I will end you," Lethe snarled. "Do you see my hair? *Do you see it?*"

"It's robin's-egg blue. Hard to miss."

"She climbed in bed with me last week and cut all the hair off one side of my head before I woke up and caught her." Lethe lifted her daughter by the scruff, like she was a puppy, and set her on the floor.

"No, Eva. Go play with Daddy. I bet he would *love* you to style his hair."

Her mate, Hood, kept his sandy-blond hair in dreadlocks that brushed his spine.

He would not, in fact, love his daughter to style his hair. However, Midas kept his mouth shut.

Watching Eva skip off, he hated to be missing out on so much. "How is the little tyrant otherwise?"

"She's fifteen months old. Developmentally, she's a six-year-old."

While Lethe was pregnant, a dominance fight would have cost her the child had her best friend, Grier Woolworth, not stepped in and performed healing magic on them both. Grier was a special type of necromancer. Her Society called her goddess-touched, and her father had been the heritor of an ancient vampire. The resulting combination was a powerful woman with uncharted powers she was doing her best to navigate without guidance from her estranged family.

When Grier saved Eva, she accelerated her growth. Eva had developed faster in the womb, been born premature, and had grown like a weed since she drew her first breath. Right now, she showed no signs of slowing down. One of the reasons Linus spent so much time in Savannah was to help Grier monitor Eva.

His current working theory was that she would plateau at puberty and mature normally from there, the way some fae did.

Midas hoped he was right. Gwyllgi enjoyed long lives, but he didn't want Eva's to speed past on fast-forward.

"How are you?" Lethe held the screen up to her face. "You look pale."

"I'm sitting in my room, in the dark, with a tablet lighting my face. Of course I look pale."

"Whatever." She muttered *storyteller* under her breath. "How are things then?"

Liar was one of Eva's favorite words to shout at strangers. Her mom and dad were busy trying to reprogram her, but no luck yet.

"A serial killer followed our newest packmate home from the women's shelter where I found her."

"What?"

"The POA is on it," he reassured her.

"No, he isn't. He's making goo-goo eyes at his fiancée. I can see them from here. It's disgusting, and it blocks my view of the chocolate raspberry mousse cake he baked last night."

"You're at home. How are you seeing them? Did they come for a visit? Am I interrupting?"

"I bought a telescope," she said primly. "I'm a mother now. I can't be over there all the time, and you know how Grier is. She's always being kidnapped or attempted-murdered."

Midas bit his tongue to keep from asking if Linus and Grier knew they were tonight's entertainment. Lethe's maternal instincts had been in overdrive since Eva was born, and her best friend would just have to deal with how she coped with the fact they were neighbors instead of roommates these days.

For the sake of keeping the peace, he said, "Hadley is on it."

"Hadley Whitaker." Lethe said the name like it was dirt she couldn't wait to spit out of her mouth.

"Yes."

"Do you trust her to get our pack justice?"

"Not *our* pack," he reminded her, a spark of temper flaring. "*My* pack. And yes, I do."

"Huh." Mashing her eye to the screen, she squinted at him. "That's interesting."

Choosing to misinterpret her, he agreed. "Looking at your face right now is like viewing abstract art."

"I'll assume you mean art done by an abstract master and take that as a compliment." Not to be deterred, she held her device at arm's length. "You like her."

"I respect her," he said a beat too late to be believable. "To either of them.

"Hmm."

"What does that mean?"

"Nothing." She looked away, a glint in her eye. "Nothing at all."

"You warned me about her. Why? What do you know that I don't?"

"Unca Midas has a girlfriend?" a small voice squealed then ripped the screen from her mother. "Can I meet her? Is she pretty? Does she like kids? She'll like me. Momma says I look just like you, and she's your girlfriend..."

The rest of what Eva had to say blended into a string of incoherency, she chattered at him so fast.

"Give me that, you little imp." Lethe reclaimed the screen. "Did you hear that? Daddy is calling for his big helper to make Mommy a BBB sandwich."

"BBB?" He thought about it for a second. "Bacon, bacon, bacon?"

"Who in their right mind would sully a bacon sandwich with lettuce and tomato? I mean, really."

"Hood is going to catch on eventually," Midas warned her. "He's going to realize it's Mommy who wants alone time, not Eva who wants Daddy time."

"Oh, he knows." A glimmer of pride brightened her smile. "She's dominant. She's stuck to me like glue, just like I was to Mom. She has her nose in all the pack business, and routinely makes patrols around the property. It's *precious*. She issued a citation to Mila Reed for not sharing her ice cream with her sister."

"A citation?"

"Um, well, Eva is *dominant*-dominant. Grier almost had a heart attack when Eva got into a brawl with Theodore Posy. The little imp was gnawing on his throat, trying to rip it out, when Grier intervened. After that, Grier suggested the citations. Even bought her a flipbook from an online cop supply store."

Theodore Posy.

Three hundred pounds of scarred-up, pissed-off gwyllgi who hated everyone and everything except for the angora rabbits he bred for their silky wool. He also enjoyed knitting and had stabbed more than one person with a knitting needle for laughing at him for either or both. He tried to teach Lethe once, but her temper was worse than his, and she had less patience.

Their mother hadn't been sad when he gave up the Atlanta pack to move to Savannah.

"Does she have all her teeth?" Unfamiliar with the stages of child development, he had no clue.

"Yes." She held up her left arm, which was covered in pinkish half-moon-shaped grooves. "She's a biter."

Already challenging her mother. "You must be proud."

"I'm grateful every time I get the chance to tell her not to eat the neighbor's familiar's kittens, which are living under our porch, or to put my bacon down or I'll eat her instead." Tears glimmered in her eyes. "I'm thankful I got to be a mom. Whatever comes next, I'm glad I got to know Eva."

That right there, love for her child, was what had outweighed her already thin patience. Eva's condition tipped the scales for Lethe. Living in Savannah meant easy access to Grier, and to Linus. With a miracle child, they had expected the miraculous developmental progress, but it was one thing to have an emergency and bundle your kid up for a three-hour drive from Atlanta to Savannah and another to scoop her up and run next door to the only person who could help.

Reminding himself of that, that Lethe's ambition wasn't to blame for his current predicament, he made a bit more peace with his situation. He loved Eva too, and he would do anything for her. Even give up his best friend and take on her role to free Lethe up to walk her own path for the sake of her child.

"I'm glad too." He spotted the imp stalking her mother in the background but didn't say a word. "I should let you get back to mothering."

"She's behind me, isn't she?"

"Yep."

Lethe exhaled and counted softly under her breath, a habit he had picked up from her. "I have to go."

Her finger slipped off the button, and the call continued as she set down the tablet. He heard her roar at Eva and stomp off bellowing about monsters who ate little girls who interrupted sibling bonding time.

Midas listened until the room went quiet then ended the call with a sigh when he realized Lethe hadn't told him why Hadley required a warning label. She had used his adorable niece against him, and he fell for it.

He wasn't brooding in the quiet for long before the bedroom door swung open and his mother swept in.

"I heard the most peculiar thing," she said, flipping on the lights and joining him on the bed. "It can't be true, but I thought I would ask."

Midas no longer indulged in any of the activities that might cause a mother to enter her adult son's room with caution. The worst she expected was to wake him from a nap. He flushed, embarrassed for no good reason, annoyed with himself when it had never bothered him before.

"Ask away." He set aside his tablet. "What have you heard?"

So far, there had been no fallout from his botched date with Rebecca. Granted, his mother hadn't expected it to go well, so she might simply be relieved it didn't go worse. Or Rebecca might have been too ashamed to admit how badly she had been treated and decided to edit the details.

"That you granted Hadley Whitaker certain privileges."

"Where did you hear that?"

"Ares mentioned you performing a Care Bear Stare on Hadley. She could barely keep it together long enough to explain what in god's name she meant."

"A Care Bear..." Midas rested his head against the wall. "Hadley called it that?"

His mother's lips pursed. "Apparently."

"I didn't see the harm."

His inner beast wouldn't quiet until it could look its fill, and for that to happen, she had to be his.

No.

He quelled that primal urge before it could rise. She had to be... given certain allowances.

"Your professional relationship with her is whatever you choose it to be." An elegant shrug lifted one dainty shoulder. "Linus and I shaped ours how it suited us, and it's between you two how you go forward as the next generation."

"But?"

"Ares also mentioned you marked her."

"No." Shock propelled him onto his feet. "She's wrong."

Damn you, he thought at his wilder half. *What have you done?*

The feral beast that lived under his skin was unable to articulate words, but it managed to project smugness at him.

"So I thought until now." She watched him pace. "What has gotten into you?"

"This role doesn't suit me." He struck up an old argument to give him time to deal with what he might have done unawares. "Lethe was allowed to work security details, she held down a position at the Faraday, and she traveled." Dragging his sister into their conversation made him feel like a child, but this was their mother. "Why is it you keep me inside the city limits? You won't even assign me a job. The only schedule I'm given involves the women you expect me to wine and dine that week."

The rest of his time was devoted to his personal cause and had nothing to do with the pack.

"When Lethe was heir, she had more freedom because I still had you." His mother sighed. "She is an alpha now, and you are my sole heir. Until you have children, I must keep you close. We protect too many old ones to allow the leadership of this pack to be decided by brute strength. We need brains, not brawn, in order to protect the haven we have created."

"A killer is hunting our people—"

"You appointed Ford as your proxy to aid Hadley in whatever capacity she needs. It's called delegation, and it's key to avoiding burnout when you're in a leadership role. Particularly when you're new to shouldering so much responsibility."

"Are you telling me you never want to put down your planner and step out on the street?"

"When I was your age? Yes. Now? I've settled into my role and embrace all the battles and challenges that come along with it. They may not be physical, but they're just as strenuous."

He quit pacing and faced her. "I'm doing my best to adapt."

"I know." She rose and crossed to him. "I can tell it's hard on you. Hard for you. You'll get there."

"I appreciate the vote of confidence."

"That's what mothers are for." Noticing the tablet, she beamed. "You were talking to Lethe? How's our little Eva?"

The rest of her visit fell on safe conversational grounds. They talked about Lethe, about Eva, about everything but the dark cloud hanging suspended over the city.

In her mind, Ford was on the job. She let it go without a backward glance, but Midas struggled. Beyond the first crime scene, he shouldn't have appeared at a single other. He should have left Hadley and Ford to handle the matter, but he had trouble taking a step back, watching from the sidelines. It wasn't in his nature to sit and wait.

After his mother left, when he had a moment alone, he looked at his hand, knew if he rubbed his fingers together, he could recall how soft and warm Hadley's skin felt under his.

"I didn't mark her," he reassured himself. "I wouldn't do that to her."

Or to himself.

Reclining on his mattress, he fell asleep and did not dream of hazel eyes or wild blonde hair.

Neither did he touch the scraps of pastel fabric tucked under his mattress that somehow still smelled like her.

FOURTEEN

The absolute best thing about my cover as a Peachy Keen Sheets franchise owner working out of a mall kiosk was having no boss to rap my knuckles when I brought a laptop with me and dismissed the ebb and flow of humans out looking for a quick bite and to incur a little debt. Veteran shoppers and locals cut a wide path around most vendors. Your odds of being approached increased exponentially when you actively ignored potential customers. It lulled them into a false sense of security.

Some gadget peddlers got downright aggressive with their sales tactics, and it was entirely possible to walk out of a store and into the arms of a man or woman who gooped product on your face before you could escape then dragged you to their kiosk where you could rinse off before they moved in for the kill.

Doesn't your skin feel softer? See how well the product works? Wouldn't you like to achieve this effect in your own home? How many jars should I put you down for? Oh! Did you know we sell lotion as well? And lip balm? And eye cream? And, and, and.

Tourists and out-of-towners were the easy marks, and phew boy had I seen some spectacular takedowns in my time working this corner.

The four hours I warmed my stool earned me enough pocket change to purchase special edition DVDs no sane person would ever watch with me and allowed me to mingle with humans and supernaturals alike.

While I counted down my last thirty minutes, I reread the preliminary report on what the cleaners were calling the Perkerson Eight.

Thanks to Reece, I knew the saliva in the bite wounds matched those found on Shonda. So did the bite imprints. Not that it surprised me considering their middles had been scooped out like ice cream. Tying the cases together gave me a firmer grip on them, but I was still trying to catch smoke with my hands.

The timer on my phone beeped, and I shut my laptop before locking up my merchandise for the night. It wasn't hard for me to sell the product. I didn't have to lie or wheedle. I honestly liked the sheets. They were soft, almost fuzzy—like peaches. Tonight I couldn't work up the enthusiasm to snag innocent shoppers and beat them over the head with our color of the month. I had too much else on my mind.

Thankfully, my stipend from the Office of the Potentate covered my bills. Otherwise, I would have had to hustle to make ends meet.

Even with the OPA covering my rent, I had utilities, groceries, and Swyft bills. Living downtown was *expensive.*

Then again, I had always lived with my folks. Maybe the cost of living wasn't high so much as I just wasn't used to paying it. Back home, I'd had a job at a Southern belle-themed ghost tour company and been a full-time student. The only expenses I'd had were clothes, fun, and gourmet chocolate.

Taking the path that promised the least amount of exposure to my fellow kioskers, who were a cannibalistic species willing to snatch a dollar from another entrepreneur as quickly as from a tourist, I sought out the bright station papered with intricate henna designs and other temporary tattoos.

"Hey." I walked right up to the artist. "Saanvi, right?"

"And you're Hadley." She set aside the brush she was cleaning. "How can I help you?"

"I have a design I'd like you to look at, if you don't mind." I opened my laptop then showed her the cropped image of the foot bearing a henna tattoo. "Do you recognize this pattern?"

"No." A frown gathered between her eyes. "This isn't one of mine."

The expected response, but it still sucked to hear it confirmed. "Does it hold any special significance?"

"Feet connect the mind, body, and spirit to the earth." She pointed out a circular flowerlike design. "That's a mandala. They signify success, courage, prosperity, and wealth." She traced the border with a fingertip. "The rest is mostly paisley, for fertility." She withdrew, as if the photo unsettled her but she couldn't pinpoint why. "These are common patterns. You see them at weddings or stalls like mine."

"Thanks." I passed her a twenty for her time. "I appreciate your insight."

On my way out, I hit one of the food court restaurants for dinner. Bourbon chicken, fried potatoes, and glazed noodles confused about their nationality were my go-to fave, but I was open to suggestions.

It wasn't lost on me that several gwyllgi cut me looks out of the corners of their eyes once they caught scent of me. Bathing in perfume had worked about as well as Ford promised it would, but I still had to try.

"What do you want?"

Distracted by the tone, I glanced down from the overhead menu and blinked. "You?"

The pixie-haired Swyft driver stared back, spatula in hand. "Me."

"You work here too?"

"Bills." She rubbed her fingers together. "I got 'em."

For her to be so money hungry, she must be paying for her car out of her own pocket.

That or she had an addiction costing her a small fortune and leaving her no time to indulge it.

"I'll take the bourbon chicken, fried potatoes, and noodles."

"Combo?"

"Sure."

"What do you want to drink?" She snapped her fingers. "Come on, corpse-raiser. You had to know that was coming."

"Sweet tea," I blurted, reaching for my debit card. "Here."

"Hey, look at that." Since she hadn't asked for it yet, she winked. "You're learning."

"How many jobs do you have?"

"A few." The girl dished up food as fast as she drove. "You haven't dialed me up all week."

Thankfully, I didn't have to lie. "I'm working a case with someone. He's got a truck."

Her rapid-fire motions slowed. "Midas?"

"What is your deal with him?"

"Exactly that." She snapped the lid shut with a click. "*My* deal."

"Just making conversation." I caught the takeout box she tossed at me. "Got a fork?"

"In the bag." She poured my drink and slid it across the counter like a barkeep slinging a shot. "Napkins too, so don't waste your breath or my time."

Backing away slowly, I took my food and headed for the parking lot. About to pull out my phone to call for a Swyft, I saw a familiar truck rumble to the curb in front of me. The window lowered to reveal a grinning Ford.

"Hey, darlin'." His gaze dipped to the container. "I hit the BBQ joint on Dekalb. Wanna go halfsies?"

"I don't know." I cradled the food against my chest. "What did you get?"

"Burnt ends, pulled pork, ribs, fries, and banana pudding for dessert."

A rumble in my stomach betrayed me. "Are you sure you can spare any for me?"

"I offered a trade." His smile widened. "That bourbon chicken smells mighty good."

"How did...?" I would have palmed my forehead if my hands weren't full. "Gwyllgi."

"I was the last time I checked."

"Can you take this for me?" I reached up, almost putting my hands over my head, and passed over my food and drink before climbing in his pickup. "Goddess, did you have to jack it up so high?"

"Yes." He winked. "One day, maybe I'll show you why."

"Hey, you nearly made eye contact." I hauled myself in. "I call that progress."

Twelve hours had made a dent in the mark at least, that was progress in my book.

The second my butt hit the seat, he sneezed. "Excuse me."

"Bless you." I took the food back and got settled. "Did you see the Perkerson report?"

"I did." He sneezed again, louder this time. "Sorry about that."

"I bathed in perfume," I confessed. "It didn't help."

"I can tell, and I told you it wouldn't."

"Let's go back to my place, and I'll shower before we eat."

Relief filtered through his voice. "Bonnie still there?"

"No." I had gone to bed alone, staring up at the canopy. It was a touch more lopsided than the original, with staples in the fabric where Midas had given up on sewing and run out of hot glue, but he had hidden them well. That counted for something. "Guess she figured since the gig was up, she might as well go back to her place. Ares was with her the last time I saw her."

Ford sneezed three times in a row, his eyes closing a smidgen, and the truck swerved a hair.

"That reminds me." I retied the knot on top of my takeout container. "As much as I hate to encourage you to talk about your man crush, do any factions have a beef with Midas?"

Tension ratcheted through his shoulders before he forced his muscles to relax. "Not that I'm aware of."

"Hmm. That's weird. Maybe it's personal then."

"What's personal? You're losing me."

"The Swyft driver who dropped me off at Shonda's crime scene was weird about Midas. I saw her again today, working in the food court, and she got hostile when I mentioned him." I shifted my attention out the window. "She's an odd duck, but people—women in particular—seem to like him well enough. It struck me as odd that she's laser focused on him is all."

"He's never had trouble with the ladies," Ford agreed, "for better or worse."

The pixie, or whatever she was, held a grudge. I'm not saying Midas couldn't take care of himself, but I might be willing to dig around after I closed this case and see if she was a problem waiting to happen or if she had her braces in a twist over nothing.

"Just thought I would ask." I happily dropped that topic and picked up another. "I didn't think I would like having a dog, but now I miss it."

"She was never a dog," he reminded me. "I don't think you miss what you think you do."

"Enlighten me, Oz the Great and Powerful."

"Such a geek," he muttered. "You're starved for human contact. A dog was a handy conduit for the touch and conversation you've been denying yourself." He cut his eyes toward me. "Tell me I'm wrong."

"I'd be happy to."

"Mean it."

"Maybe there's a kernel of truth in all that somewhere," I

allowed. "I like Bonnie, liked her, whatever, but I don't know who she is, really."

Glass house, meet stone.

"You'll still have me." He smiled out at the road. "The end of the case doesn't have to be the end of...us."

A twisty feeling in my gut made it hard to decide if that was a good thing or a bad one. I liked Ford. I felt like we could genuinely be friends, despite the fact I was pretty sure his alpha had him spying on me. Considering all my *friends* were spying on me, and for good reason, I couldn't find it in me to hold that against him. I also felt like he wanted more, and I didn't know if I had it in me to offer. There was no spark. Not like with...

Don't think it, don't think it, don't think it.

Not like it should be when you're considering an entanglement. That initial zing is what kicks off a relationship and makes you ponder if you should, if you want to, if you dare. You don't fade into the mostly comfortable friendship Ford and I enjoyed until after the whirlwind romance part, right?

"I'm onto you." I scoffed, turning his offer into a joke to avoid it getting serious. "You just like me for my swords."

"I do like women with claws."

"Have you considered dating a cat shifter?" I managed to keep a straight face. "I hear they're quite..."

"Feral is the word you're looking for." He blasted air out his nose. "I dated one when I was in high school. We thought we'd do the whole Romeo/Juliet thing. Us against the world. By the end of senior year, I was ready to fake my death."

"That was Juliet, not Romeo."

"I never said which of us was which." He grinned. "I'm not the die-for-love type."

"Who is?" I drew in a deep breath perfumed with mouthwatering food. "Fried potatoes, on the other hand, those are worth a fight to the death."

"You can have them." He rested a protective hand over his mountain of takeout boxes. "Now ribs..."

We debated life versus food on the way back to the Faraday and all the way up to my apartment.

I left him parked on the couch with the holy grail of remotes while I showered and changed.

When I got out, a quick ten minutes later, he was dictating an email to his mom, directions on how to use the new pressure cooker he bought her for her birthday, and I forced my heart not to melt.

"I'm starving." I headed to the kitchen. "Let's eat."

The space, small as it was, felt empty without Bonnie. Maybe Ford was right. Maybe I was lonely. Or maybe it was the slight strangeness of the new items, similar to my old ones but not quite, that made the place feel less like home as I set the sewing machine on the kitchen counter to clear up the dining table.

"Are we discussing the case over lunch?" Ford made himself at home, bringing plates and glasses out of the cupboards. With so few cabinets, it didn't take much to figure out where I kept what. "Or are you squeamish?"

"We can talk shop." I took ice and bottled water from the fridge. "I'm good."

After we sat down and divvied up the food, we got down to the business of eating.

"Bishop is searching through records to determine if our killer has moved into the area near Perkerson." As I licked sauce off my fingers from the ribs, I decided I needed the name of his BBQ joint. "Bonnie was able to narrow the window of time she spent in the city before Midas found her. That helps with searching for records. Her son followed her from Mississippi, but she's lived all over the country."

"Still a needle in a haystack." He slurped up a noodle. "Have you considered the time-honored tradition of using bait?"

I would be lying if I said I hadn't considered it. "Do you think Midas would sign off on that?"

"On using a submissive woman, suffering obvious trauma, to lure out her abuser?"

"You could have just said *no*."

"Ask him." He put it mildly. "You might persuade him where others would fail."

"You want me to present your idea to him so he growls at me and not you. That's what I'm hearing."

"Then you listen very well."

"We have to do something." I stabbed a hunk of pulled pork that melted in my mouth. "We can't sit on our hands and wait for the next call."

A hard knock on the door twisted my gut until I regretted stuffing my face with so much enthusiasm.

"Come in," I yelled. "Door's unlocked."

Maybe it was rude, but wise people didn't leave a gwyllgi seated at a table full of food and expect to come back to more than empty plates.

Ford cranked his head around to see who was calling on me, but he had to have known. He must have sensed it was Midas.

"I didn't realize you had company." Midas stood in the doorway, hand on the knob. "I can come back."

"It's just Ford," I said too quickly, and regretted his flinch. "Hungry? We've got plenty."

"Talk about swimming against the current," Ford said on a sigh. "Hadley wanted to talk to you anyway." He gave me a pointed look. "Remember?"

"I remember." I didn't miss the tension growing between the men. "I'll text you when I'm ready to go."

"I'll be down in the lobby catching up with Roe and Giada," Ford said. "Take your time."

The names were unfamiliar, but it's not like I had made an attempt to learn the pack roster. More than likely they were the two sisters who had given him their number. I warned him not to toss their note, that he would piece it back together at a low point, but men never listened.

That I found this scenario amusing told me I wasn't serious about Ford.

Frak. Frak. Frak.

"You didn't say if you were hungry." I cleared Ford's place and set another one for Midas. "Since you're gwyllgi, I'll assume the answer is yes."

Midas didn't move past the front door Ford shut behind him. "I came to apologize."

"For the marking thing?" I waved it away. "Ford told me it was accidental."

"That doesn't mean I don't owe you an apology."

"Sit." I pulled out a chair. "Eat."

He did as he was told, tucking a lock of golden hair behind his ear.

"You're new to the heir gig, so I get it." I sat back down and dumped mounds of food onto his plate when he made no move to select for himself. "There are a lot of things I'm still learning too. I'm not mad."

He lifted his fork, studied his plate, turned it in his hand, speared the pulled pork, but still didn't dig in.

I braced my elbow on the table then cupped my chin in my palm. "Please tell me this isn't a caveman thing where Ford bought the food, and you can't eat it because of man cooties or some silly thing."

"Pack etiquette is not some silly thing." His lips thinned. "Our instincts are what keep us alive."

"What's the deal with the food?"

He set down his fork. "I'm not sure."

"I hope it's not poisoned." I sniffed the leftovers, praying the pixie girl didn't take revenge on those who shunned her car services. "Ford and I ate enough to ensure we'll both kick the bucket. Maybe even a few of them." I shoved back from the table and opened my freezer since my fridge was empty. "I froze single servings of spaghetti last week for when I'm craving meatballs but too lazy to cook. I can heat one up for you?"

"You don't mind?"

"Nah." I selected one of the storage containers and popped it in the microwave. "Won't take but a minute." I mashed in the time. "Well, technically I guess it will take four minutes and forty-five seconds, but who's counting?" I checked my fridge before asking about sides. "You want toast? I can do garlic butter or garlic butter and cheese?"

"Plain toast is fine."

"You're not putting me out." I leaned my hip against the open door. "I offered."

"Can I have the cheese version?"

"Sure." I got out what I needed and set to work. "Who told you about the mark thing?"

"Mom."

"Ouch." I winced in sympathy. "I bet that went over like a lead balloon."

"Why do you say that?"

"I saw you on your *date*, Goldilocks." Yes, I made air quotes. Big ones. Really threw my whole body into it. "Your mom probably alphabetized the entire pack's list of eligible females then checks them off as you burn through them."

"Necromancers believe in arranged marriages," he pointed out, sounding tired. "How is this any different?"

"From where I'm standing, it's no different at all." I might have slammed the oven door on the toast. The butter on my hands made it slip through my fingers. "I'm not saying they're all bad. Some of them work out okay. Grier and Linus, for example. I've seen it go bad just as often. More often. My parents..."

I worried my bottom lip with my teeth until it bled, a habit from childhood, from the times when I had to bite down to keep from talking back, to keep from screaming, to keep from *telling*, and the taste brought stinging heat to my left cheek. Surprised when my reflection in the silvery toaster didn't show the familiar handprint, I touched the skin and felt the distant throb through my memories.

"My parents," I tried again, remembering my role, "my father, actually, had good luck securing Boaz Pritchard for my sister. Adelaide seems to like him. Maybe like can grow into love over time."

For both of them.

The spot between my shoulder blades tingled with the force of his stare. "Will they marry you off?"

"No." I wasn't a true blood relation, so Mr. Whitaker couldn't sell me off. Besides, his daughter's sacrifice had secured his family's financial stability. He had no need to bother with me, the reminder of his dead daughter, and no wish to, I was sure. "I'm off the hook."

"You don't sound happy about it."

"There's security in knowing you will marry, even without effort on your part. You can focus on your own pursuits until it's time to form a partnership and divide your energies. I don't have that. If I want to marry, I would have to...try." I felt my lips puckering. "The odds of that happening are slim."

"You don't want a mate?"

A person who loved me? All of me? Accepted the dark shadow I would forever cast?

Did such a person exist? Did I want to find them? Only a saint could overlook my past, and I would never outgrow the fear I would fall short of their expectations. I was done living that way. No mate was worth my walking on eggshells for the rest of my life.

"I'll have plenty of time to worry about a mate after I'm POA."

"Yes," he agreed dryly. "You'll have so much more time when you're personally responsible for the running of an entire city for your faction."

Chuckling, I pulled his toast out of the oven and his food out of the microwave. It was nice serving another person a meal I had prepared—granted, last week—rather than eating straight from the takeout box in front of the TV.

"Let me get you a clean glass." I reached for the one Ford had been using, and Midas caught me by the same wrist. "Oh crap." Though his grip was light, I couldn't seem to move. "Ford said not to let you touch me again."

Midas dropped his arm, flexing his fingers as he tucked his hand back on his lap. "Sorry."

Figuring the damage had already been done, if that's how it even worked, I palmed his shoulder. "What's a few more days?"

Once this case closed, I might not cross paths with him for another year, and all this would be forgotten.

That would be ideal. Yeah. It would be for the best. Definitely. Much less complicated that way.

The muscles beneath my hand clenched, and his breath punched out hard.

I leaned around him. "Are you okay?"

"Touch is...difficult for me."

"Then it's my turn to apologize." I started to withdraw my hand, but he covered it with his. "You don't have to prove you can endure it." Feeling his palm go damp, just like last time, I jerked back but had a feeling he had repeated his mistake. "Don't make yourself uncomfortable on my account."

Lips parting like he meant to argue, he shut his mouth and nodded agreement, though he didn't look very happy about it. Not that he ever really looked happy. He looked...sad. Tired. Like he needed a hug when that much physical contact might overload his circuits.

While I swapped out the glasses, he started eating. This time, there was no hesitation. He had shoveled half of it down his throat by the time I rejoined him with a fresh drink.

"It's good," he said between bites. "You made it from scratch?"

"Thank you, and yes. I've been experimenting this last year. I used to live on takeout. Now I'm trying to be more self-sufficient." I had only set off the smoke alarm four or five times. "I don't mind saving the money either. I would cook all my meals if my hours permitted it, but it's just not practical."

Curious why this food and not the other passed inspection, I was forced to conclude it did have to do with some male nonsense. Probably the marking issue too. I was no pro on gwyllgi courtship or mating rituals, though I was starting to think I should change that for my own protection. The issue here appeared to be that another male gwyllgi had bought the food to share with me. Therefore, the food was repugnant to Midas.

Thinking it over, I picked up a cold rib and nibbled even as my stomach cut into the button on my jeans.

The shift in Midas's focus from his plate to my hands startled a flinch out of me.

"Do I have sauce on my chin?" I collected a paper napkin out of the bag and started blotting. "Cheeks? Nose? Cleavage?"

"No." He resumed eating, but he kept glaring at the bone I set down from the corner of his eye.

Yep.

Definitely male nonsense.

Figuring this was as good a time as any, I made Ford's pitch. "We need to get ahead of the killer instead of always playing catch-up."

He lowered his fork. "How do you propose we do that?"

"We need to draw out the killer."

His very sharp teeth made short work of his toast. "You're not acting as bait."

Tapping the rib bone with my fingertip just to watch him scowl, I said, "I was thinking of Bonnie."

"Oh." He sipped his water. "She's not acting as bait either."

"Why would I be bait?" I licked the sauce off my finger, pretending not to notice him watch the motion with painful intensity, an almost tangible curiosity. "Bonnie is who he wants."

"He's following her, which means he's noticed you. He's seen you two travel together the past few days, and he's aware you've been rooming together, which is likely why he broke into your apartment. He wants to know what you are to her. Odds are good he wanted to determine if you're leverage that can be used against her."

"Classic *meet me at the woodshed near the stump with an ax sticking out of it or your friend gets it?*"

Midas set the last corner of his toast aside. "You watch horror movies too, don't you?"

"Oh, come on." I stole another napkin. "Everyone knows there are ax murderers in the woods. That's why people leave axes in stumps, ripe for the plucking, in the first place. They're feeding the local wildlife."

"I wouldn't worry about the mark." Midas wiped his hands clean. "No one will smell it over your geek."

"I see you've been talking to Ford about me." I wrinkled my nose. "Did he braid your hair while you gossiped?"

Midas self-consciously raked his fingers through the wavy length. "No?"

The only thing that stopped me from teasing him more was the fact his hair was obviously a hot-button topic for him. Looking the way he did, I wondered if he got challenged more often than others in his position might. I wondered if packmates mistook his reserve for weakness. Then I wondered how, if they noticed his arms, and all of them must have, they could ever think he was less than a survivor.

Whatever happened to him, he wore the experience in silvery scars down his forearms. Just because they didn't put the story into actual words on his skin, it didn't silence the message. If anything, it amplified his mystique. He hadn't snapped under pressure. That much was evident. He was still functional, still able to laugh, to enjoy friendships, to...

I don't know what he was doing with me. Not flirting, not courting, not anything I could put a name to, but it was something all the same. Otherwise, he would have left me under Ford's supervision. Midas didn't strike me as the micromanaging type. He didn't appear to be the managing type at all.

Power and leadership abilities weren't the same thing. Plenty of gwyllgi were formidable. That didn't mean they needed to be in a position where they made decisions that affected their smallest and weakest members. Midas, through his concern for the latter, might cripple the growth of the pack if he led unchecked. He would forever be looking behind him, circling back, when it was up to the alpha to forge new paths, blaze new trails.

"You're staring." Midas shifted in his chair. "Do *you* want to braid my hair?"

Gears in my head ground and crunched, but it didn't compute. "Are you offering?"

"No." A smile lifted the right corner of his mouth. "I'm not."

"Meanie."

"Watch your language." He gathered his dishes and stood. "What if there were children nearby?"

"They would laugh at a woman my age name-calling like I'm still in kindergarten."

A text chime prompted me to check my phone, and I did to make sure Ford wasn't nudging me.

"Bishop got a hit on a rental house on Braddock Street Southwest." I read down to what flagged his attention. "The agent in charge of the listing disappeared two weeks ago." I kept going, expecting what I found. "Alisha Brown." I held my screen where he could see her picture. "She was one of Clairmont's."

There were times when I hated being right about a hunch, and this was one of them.

"Let's go." Midas scraped his plate clean then tucked it in the dishwasher. "He might still be there."

"The last time he called to brag, he got you and not her. Depending on how closely he's watching us, he'll notice his mom isn't tagging along for a change. He might go to ground if he thinks we've moved her into witness protection. He may already be gone."

As much as I hated wasting food, the rest was picked over, and I couldn't stand the sight of it after I had eaten so much the first time around. I would feed it to the stray cats the next alley over after I got home.

Not that I would ever admit to gwyllgi that I was occasionally a feline sympathizer.

Midas held the door and locked up behind me, which was weird on every level. That I had gone out the front door, that I hadn't thought to check it but he had, that he was here, after eating with me. Just—all of it. Very weird. Very strange. There was no time to think about why, but it felt so...nice.

Ford stood in the lobby with two older women, obviously a couple, and a cute one at that, and allowed them to each kiss him on the cheek before he broke away to join us.

The moment he realized Midas had marked me again, he did an almost comical double take, like it could be seen as well as smelled, and he looked Midas in the eye long enough Midas had to choke back the rumble building in his chest.

"We've got a lead." I eased between them, forcing Ford to shift his focus onto me. "Can you give us a lift?"

"He's coming with us?"

Muscle bulged in his jaw, and I didn't miss the slightest emphasis on *us*. "Yeah, he is."

"Midas?" Ford made his friend's name sound like an accusation. "You're coming with us?"

"You heard her." Midas stepped up behind me, not touching me, barely breaching my personal space. From what I had observed from him, it was the same as him humping my leg in public. There were audible gasps from the peanut gallery. "Do you have a problem with that?"

"Not at all," Ford said breezily. "Your chariot awaits."

However, the charioteer was quick to leave us in his dust.

"He wouldn't be so pissy if you'd let him braid your hair," I muttered. "This is all your fault."

Midas chuckled, and that attracted even more eyes from residents in the lobby.

"Nothing to see here." Doing my best princess impersonation, I offered a royal wave. "Go back to your lives, citizens."

Yet another one-liner from a cartoon. Who doesn't love *Toy Story*? I should make a list of cartoons I've actually watched for Bishop. There were more in my repertoire than I realized when he shamed me for not watching *Peter Pan*.

"Are you done?" Midas shackled my wrist, his fingers light and warm and seemingly drawn like magnets to that exact spot, and hauled me out of the lobby. "Or should I bring you a ladder and a fresh box of sixty watts?"

"That you know what I was doing tells me two things." I stumbled after him. "You definitely had a sister, and you're definitely royalty."

"What it tells me is you were murmuring *unscrew the lightbulb* under your breath."

"Pageant kid, hello?"

On the circuit, I had heard it called *screw in the lightbulb* or *elbow, elbow, wrist, wrist,* or even just *the rodeo wave* or *the royal wave*. The first instructor I had was British, and she liked us to twist that bulb for all it was worth. Hers was the one that stuck with me.

"You did pageants?"

For the span of a heartbeat, I swore I could smell hairspray. Entire noxious clouds of the stuff. It made my eyes water, and my mother had always jabbed my scalp with a bobby pin and recited her favorite line in my ear.

"Stop whining, or I'll give you something to cry about."

You would think the trophies and crowns would have made her happy, or validated me, but all they did was shine a light on my inadequacies as far as she was concerned.

Those performances gave her the perfect excuse to critique me, to correct me. To tell me every wrong thing I said or did in great detail, to highlight every mistake I made in my routine, to point out every misstep on stage, to make sure I understood that even if I came home crowned, I hadn't won a thing. Not her love, not her respect, not her happiness.

Not enough, not enough, not enough.

I might have continued on after middle school, but once I started winning, I attracted too much attention. I was a rough-and-tumble girl, but bruises shaped like fingerprints were hard to blame on falls, and she enjoyed my tears too much to curb her growing appetite for punishment.

Eager for a distraction, I jerked a thumb toward the lobby. "I think that lady fainted." I made my eyes wide with concern. "Do you think we should check on her?"

Midas whipped his head around. "What lady...?"

"Made you look." I beamed at him. "No one fainted, probably, but a few looked primed and ready." I didn't attempt to remove myself from his grip, but I offered more resistance to let him know he was still holding on. "You shocked a lot of people back there. You marked me, for what I now suspect is the second time in two days, you laughed at a joke like a normal person, and you—goddess forbid—touched a woman of your own free will."

"I don't understand why I act the way I do around you."

"I don't understand why I act the way I do around you, either."

He snorted but held on. "You mean like a five-year-old?"

"That was prepubescent humor, I'll have you know." I harrumphed, broke free, and climbed in the truck. Mostly so I could sit in the middle and provide a physical barrier between the two friends who seemed to be struggling for civility lately. "Give me your seat belt clicky thing."

After Midas sat, he frowned at me. "Why?"

"There are noses pressed to the glass in there. I doubt they can see us clearly, since the windows are fogging, but I want to make it obvious you didn't touch my butt to reach the clasp. They almost hit the floor when you latched onto my wrist. I can't imagine what would happen if they thought you had touched lower."

"Lee," Ford sighed. "Leave the man alone."

"Where's the fun in that?" I grinned when Midas let me fasten him in. "There. Your dignity is preserved."

Midas dragged a hand down his face, but he didn't wipe off his smile fast enough.

He might not want to, but he thought I was funny, and that was all the encouragement I required to dial it up to ten.

"How do you put up with her night in and night out?" he asked Ford over my head. "She doesn't drive you crazy?"

There was a rumble in his voice when Ford answered, "She drives me crazy, all right."

I decided to take it as a compliment.

FIFTEEN

As soon as Ford pulled into the driveway of the suspect's house, Midas cracked his window and filled his lungs, filtering out the mundane to focus on the hint of musk that told him a warg lived, or had lived, here.

The brush of Hadley's hand against his hip as she hit the release on his seat belt he ignored. The smell of her shampoo, the tang of barbecue sauce staining the hem of her tee, which reminded him of how she held his gaze while she licked her fingers clean, he ignored too.

He tried damn hard to, anyway.

"What do you smell?" She leaned over, invading his space, flaring her delicate nostrils like she might catch the scent. "All I smell is the neighbor cooking out down the street who must have marinated his hamburgers in lighter fluid."

"A warg lives here." He almost bumped noses with her, she had gotten so close. "I can tell the species, so that might eliminate our killer."

"Bonnie used magic to conceal her scent," she reminded him. "Her son probably knows the same tricks."

"I'll take the back," Ford said, expression all business. "You take the front."

"All right." Hadley withdrew. "Coming?" Challenge glinted in her eyes. "Or are you waiting here?"

Mom was going to skin him. If he was lucky, he would be dead before she got started.

"I didn't come along just for the ride," he said to earn one of her wicked smiles.

He got out, turned back for Hadley, but she jumped down before he could stress about if he ought to offer her help. After working with Ford for the past few days, she had clearly learned her way around his truck.

That shouldn't have bothered him as much as it did, but he was here, wasn't he? Sticking his nose where it didn't belong yet again.

All those years where Lethe chafed under Mom's rule, he never understood her problem. He was starting to grasp it now. The urge to make Mom see things his way, to let him do things his way, to let him run things his way began to itch beneath his skin. It wasn't a reflection on her or her ruling style. He had no complaints about how she ran the pack. As it was thriving, no one had cause to question her methods.

Still, he couldn't help he believed he was wasted as a figurehead, that he ought to be securing the pack's future in a way that didn't involve him selecting a mate who wanted the same thing from him that he wanted from her: nothing.

For the first time since he took his place as heir, he felt...good. Right. Like he had taken a step down his own path.

"What do you think you're doing?" Hadley fisted the back of his shirt, yanking him to a stop with a strength he hadn't expected from her small frame. "You're backup, Goldilocks."

The beast in him bared its teeth, but he didn't have a leg to stand on. This was her case, and he had been the one to hand it to her.

"Fine," he growled, and saw the crimson in his eyes reflected in hers.

As though the night itself scabbarded her blade, she drew it from darkness.

Tension thrummed in the tense lines of her body as she tested the doorbell, then knocked on the door.

With neighbors on either side, most of them human, she didn't risk announcing herself. She took a measured step back and braced. Soft words passed her lips, too faint for even his ears to catch, a prayer to Hecate, maybe? Then she kicked in the door. She flipped on the lights with the tip of her sword, though he knew her night vision was as sharp as her weapon of choice.

"He's not here," she said with certainty that made him curious how she could tell so quickly.

Pulling in long breaths, he filtered the scents and decided they were hours old. "I agree."

A door creaked open in the rear of the house, and Hadley was off like a shot, chasing after danger.

Midas's heart almost stopped as he followed, but it kicked back into gear when Ford entered the living room.

"You're not subtle, are you, darlin'?" he teased Hadley. "Do I need to teach you how to pick a lock?"

"Pardon me for not carrying a set of lock picks with me everywhere I go," she bit back. "Who does that?"

"I believe in emergency preparedness," he said primly. "You never know what might come in handy."

"True." She eyed the silver picks in his hands with avarice. "You'll have to teach me sometime."

"It's a date." His smile was as big as Midas had ever seen it. "That will put us at two, after our movie night."

"I will call your momma and tell her you tried taking me out on a lock-picking date," she threatened, "and you won't be able to sit for a week."

Hadley hadn't said their movie night wasn't a date, and she hadn't set Ford straight about them being two for two after he taught her to pick locks.

Ford laughed, delighted, and Midas literally saw red, had to glance away until the glow faded.

"There's a trail out back." Ford jerked his chin toward Midas. "Ask him to play bloodhound. God knows you're not shy when it comes to asking me."

Hadley turned hazel eyes on him, the dare in them clear. "Well?"

Midas glowered at Ford. "Thanks for throwing me under the bus."

"Hey, she's the one driving." He pointed at her. "You got a problem, take it up with her."

"Beep, beep." She mimed honking the horn. "Get on board or get left behind, Goldilocks."

Thanks to the freshness of the warg's scent, Midas didn't have to lower himself to sniffing couch cushions to get a lock on their suspect. Walking past both of them into the backyard, he identified the well-worn path leading into Perkerson Park.

"He went this way." Midas crouched where the scent would be closer. "Often."

Hadley was a warm presence at his back. "Did he take it tonight?"

"No." He shook his head. "The scent in the front yard is stronger than this."

Her gaze swept the bare dirt and crushed grass. "Is it the same?"

"Warg," he answered. "Not what I noticed on the first or third scenes."

"Ford?" She gave him room to join them. "You've been on all the scenes. Can you link what you smelled there to here?"

Casting her a flat stare, he squatted farther down the path.

Midas rose to his full height when Hadley remained by his side, and they waited together.

SIXTEEN

The soul-deep tether binding me to Ambrose tautened as he stretched its farthest limits, and he yanked me a step forward before I dug in my heels. The scent of magic had him salivating, far more power than a warg possessed naturally, but I had to play this the right way or risk exposing us both.

As nice as it had been to expand my social circle beyond Bishop and the POA, I was ready to get back to working solo. Had Ford and Midas not been here, I could have ordered Ambrose to search the premises without first using the cover of breaking down the door to muffle my voice. I could have eliminated the house without stepping foot inside and found the trail then followed it instead of ignoring the hard tug in my chest where the hungry bastard twisted and clawed to go after his prey.

Only the knowledge the killer wasn't in our immediate vicinity kept me from saying to hell with it, outing myself, and going hunting alone.

"The scent is richer here, different." Ford rubbed a hand over his nose. "I'll try again farther down."

"Different is good." I shifted on my feet, restless. "Different puts us one step closer to nailing him."

Midas, hair gilded under a motion light, turned to me. "You trust gwyllgi noses that much?"

They might not be as accurate as Ambrose when tracking magic, but they picked up scent trails just fine. "Don't you?"

Frustration clear in his voice, Ford yelled, "I need a second opinion here."

"That's my cue." Midas strode off, leaving me behind to observe.

Bishop called a few seconds later, and I answered, knowing he expected an update.

"Well?" He slurped. Loudly. "Did you find him?"

"The jury is still out," I admitted. "A warg lives here." I repeated to him what I had reminded Midas. "Bonnie used a charm to alter her scent. He might be doing the same."

A niggling doubt surfaced, but I couldn't put my finger on what about that bothered me.

"Jury?" He slurped a second time to make sure I got the mental picture of him drinking blood hot from the microwave. "What jury?"

"Midas and Ford. They're sniffing around to see if the scents match up."

Spluttering commenced and then coughing and then wheezing. "You've got Midas Kinase playing bloodhound for you?"

The bloodhound comparison was either used so often because it was accurate, or because it was an insult. I really ought to ask before I went there again. I was also starting to assume Midas was a far more common name than I realized since everyone identified him as *Midas Kinase*. "Yes?"

"Midas goes out of his way to avoid women with the exception of the classes he teaches. The work he does at shelters is timed like clockwork. I'm not saying his desire to help isn't genuine. You only have to see him in action to know it is, but he's like a kid choking down a pill he doesn't want to take but knows is good for him." He kept clearing his throat but recovered his composure. "What have you done to him?"

"Nothing." Delighting in tormenting Bishop, I couldn't resist adding, "*Yet.*"

Midas snapped his head up and fastened his impossibly blue eyes on me.

I wished then I was like Ambrose, that I could swirl away into nothingness.

"So," I said, turning my back until I got my heart to slow its pounding, "we're checking out a trail leading into the park. I'll give you an update when I have one."

"Stick to yanking Ford's tail," Bishop advised, as if he could see the trouble I had gotten into thanks to my big mouth. "He's less likely to bite you for it."

"Har har."

"I got sidetracked by the deluge of surveillance footage, but I see the block is off the cleaners' database. I'll start digging around on your warg kid and get that background info on Jessica to you ASAP."

I ended the call and pocketed the phone to give me a few extra seconds before turning.

A refusal to show weakness was the only reason I didn't scream or jump back when I found Midas standing inches away from me.

"You need to see this." He waved me on. "We found another cache."

Already dreading what he had to show me, I made myself follow, and then I breathed out, "Animals."

A few cats, a dog, a possum, and small furry bodies that might have once been squirrels decomposed in a hole worn smooth around the edges. He'd had the presence of mind to dig under a bush to conceal them, but he hadn't bothered to cover them with dirt, and other animals had been feasting, as evidenced by the various pawprints from the local wildlife.

"Why switch from animals to people?" That was a big leap.

Huge. "These appear to be older kills, but they're smaller. Decomposition would be faster. What do you think?"

"I agree." Midas stepped up beside me. "These predate the bodies from the park. The ground kept them cooler, and the bush kept them out of direct sunlight, slowing down the process."

"Practice or simple hunger?"

"Hunger," Midas decided. "Animals store food this way. It's natural."

I didn't say a word, but I felt my face rearranging its expression.

"Natural for us," he clarified. "It's nothing I haven't seen in gwyllgi whose beasts are ascendant."

"He left his cache of victims in water." I recalled the bizarre factoid about raccoons washing their food that had popped into my head when I first saw them. "Statement or preservative?"

"The water is too warm this time of year for it to preserve meat." Midas flinched when he said it, but I knew what he meant. A layer of distance helped more than the mild insult to the dead hurt. "He meant for those bodies to be found. He left them in a public park, stacked them like a cord of wood. Eventually, if he hadn't called us himself, someone would have investigated the blockage."

"I agree." I mulled it over. "Okay, the animals came first, as food. He likely hunted them while he was learning the area. He wouldn't have wanted to draw too much attention to himself until he was certain his mother was here."

"Once he had confirmation," Midas continued for me, "he started enacting his plan."

"He's been taunting her." I could almost hear him. *Look what you made me do.*

"He wants to turn her conscience against her."

"He wants her to surrender to him." An oily sensation writhed in my gut. "He could have taken her from the shelter. The age of this cache proves he was already in the area when you brought her home with you. He was playing with her, letting her think she had gotten away. When you showed interest, offered her a support network, he set his plan in motion. He couldn't risk her revealing herself. He would assume your pack would covet her for her gwyllgi blood and double down on protecting her."

"You're good at that," he remarked. "Getting in his head."

I wasn't in his head, but I had Ambrose in mine, and his thought process had given me keen insight into the criminal mind. "Bonnie filled in a lot of blanks for us. It's hard not to draw a mental picture."

"I can see why Linus felt confident enough to leave you alone in the city with this case."

Pleasure at the compliment unfurled through my chest, but motion caught my eye, and it drained away just as fast.

Ford stood with his back to us, gazing in the direction of the house, or maybe he was looking at his truck. He had a hand in his pocket, and he was jingling his keys like he was ready to go or wondered why he was here at all.

Midas caught the drift of my stare and remembered Ford too. I could tell by the way he took a large step away from me and refused to meet my eyes, no matter how long I stared at him.

As much as I wanted to point out I was single and could talk to whomever I wanted, I read the building tension between the two men and hated I was the cause. The fact Midas wanted me to be aware I was hurting Ford by not paying him my full attention stung. Fine. If that's how he wanted it, I could shut down this... Crush? Fixation? Infatuation?

After all, I wasn't the one who marked him. Accidental or not, *he* had marked *me*.

"I want to make sure there are no more surprises waiting for us out there," I told them. "I'm going to follow the path, see where it ends, mark his likely points of entry into the section of the park where he made his cache."

Tired of the puffed chests and grumpy faces, I didn't wait to see if either or both decided to tag along. It was easier this way, I assured myself. Working alone meant I wasn't distracted, my attention wasn't divided. It also meant I could utilize Ambrose to his full potential.

"Follow the magic," I told my stalking shadow, who leapt from tree to tree. "There must be remnants."

There was no reason for the killer to hunt animals as anything other than himself. There were no laws, well, no supernatural laws, against the killing of prey animals in the city for the purpose of feeding yourself or your family. That included feral animals but excluded pets. Not that tossing a collar in the dumpster after you got the midnight munchies was hard. Charms of all kinds were expensive, an education I had recently received. They also had a limited shelf life. There was no reason for him to burn magic hunting deer when he would need it hunting his own kind.

The shadow reshaped himself into an arrow pointing off the beaten path, and I followed his directions with only a slight hesitation. Ambrose had tried to kill me once to be free of me and move on to a new host. As much as I wanted to believe those days were behind us, I knew in my bones the reason he acted charming was to con me into lowering my guard.

A tattoo in red ink that glimmered black when it caught the light marked my ankle, one of Linus's own designs, a riff on a triquetra, and it bound me to Ambrose. He wasn't getting free of me without killing himself, and Ambrose was far too canny for that, but I had learned the hard way to never underestimate his hunger for freedom, or magic.

"Hmm." A hollow tree was the only eye-catching landmark nearby, so I went to explore it. Rot had eaten a hole in the front, near the ground, giving the bark the appearance of having been curled aside and pinned back against the trunk. "I'm going to be pissed if I stick my bare hand in there and come out covered in bees or worse."

Mimed laughter was his response, and if I felt the tickle of his amusement, I stamped it out fast.

Fabric, not fuzzy insect bodies, greeted my fingertips, and I hooked a nylon strap. Tugging as gently as I could, I dislodged what appeared to be a backpack. A go-bag was my guess. My suspicions were confirmed when, after Ambrose examined it for magical traps, I opened it to find several thousand dollars in cash along with three fake IDs, a change of clothes, shoes, water, protein bars, and...charms.

I fanned the IDs across the ground and snapped pictures of them, front and back, then forwarded them to Bishop. The names, addresses, and other identifying information were different on each, and none of them matched the rental address, meaning these weren't in the name he was currently exploiting.

"There's not much cash here." I fanned through it again, thinking. "He would need more than what I've got to dump this identity and pick up the next." I crammed it back into the pack. "There are more of these, there must be, but I don't see the point in tracking them down."

In this area, kids would probably find the others one day while playing in the woods and shock their parents stupid with a stack of bills no one would ever claim.

"Tell me about these charms." I counted three, each a different size and shape. "What do they do?"

Happy to oblige, the shadow dipped its fingers into the center of each then licked them clean.

A flutter of panic filled my chest when he sharpened himself into a spear and hurled himself at my heart.

Agony pierced me, and for the second time tonight, I imagined I heard his mocking laughter.

The information trickled into my thoughts as I massaged my chest, thinking on what he had discovered.

"One to hide his scent, one to change his appearance, and one to...?" Fresh pain twisted my heart like an orange on a juicer, but I got the message. "Amplify?"

The shadow took a mocking bow, his outline more defined than I would like, given the magic he had skimmed off the charms.

Rubbing the last one through my fingers, I admired its design. "What does it amplify?"

A combination of charms this potent would punch up the magic on the user enough to knock out electronics, like video cameras, but a person wearing this combination was in hiding deeper than I was, and that was saying something.

"You talk to yourself a lot."

Tension strung my spine taut, and I could have kicked Ambrose for letting Ford sneak up on me. High on magic, my shadow self was skirting a dangerous line.

"Only when I need expert advice." I stuffed the charms in the pack then held it out to him, eyebrows raised. "Would you mind?"

"I had no idea when Midas volunteered me for this detail that I was undergoing K9 training." He took the pack, sniffed it, and recoiled. "That's it. This is his. No doubt."

"Not the warg scent?" I made sure I understood. "You can match this to a scene?"

"Yeah." He grimaced. "He's used this bag or restocked it recently. I smell decay on the fabric."

I was staring back toward the path, debating how to convey what I had learned, when he cleared his throat. "Hmm?"

"If you're looking for Midas, or a second opinion from a gwyllgi, you're out of luck on both counts."

"He left?"

"He called for a Swyft."

A distant zing of concern struck me. "Everything okay?"

"Fine," he rushed to assure me. "Don't worry."

There was more. I could see it, almost taste it, but I had a job to do. That job didn't involve ferreting out what could be more important to a future alpha than protecting his pack from a killer.

Focused on the job, I didn't leave room for distraction. "I want to see where this trail goes."

Ford turned a slow circle, jostling the bag on its strap. "What trail?"

Frak. Frak. Frak.

I was slipping.

I hadn't meant to let Midas's defection get under my skin, but it wedged there like a splinter.

"I assumed you could track the killer since both his scents overlap at this point," I lied with ease that made my gut churn. "Did I get ahead of myself?"

"You aren't shy about asking for what you want," he said. "I'll give you that."

No, I wasn't. An old habit, and a bad one. It had gotten me into more trouble than it was worth.

"Fine." I sighed dramatically. "I'll buy wings to go with the pizza on our movie night."

Honest shock lit his features. "You're still inviting me over?"

"I told you I would." I moved past him, nudging Ambrose along with a discreet wave of my fingers. "I try not to lie more than necessary. It's too hard to remember them all after a while."

"You sound like an expert on the topic." An edge crept into his tone, making it easier to remember that no matter how much he might like me, and I felt he genuinely did, he had ulterior motives for palling around with me. "Trip over your tongue much?"

Every time I opened my mouth, I risked forgetting myself and telling the truth instead of the lies I was supposed to recite on cue. It got old fast, having to pause and think before answering the simplest questions. That hesitation might convince him I was dreaming up a lie, but I was holding back the truth.

"Believe me when I say my mouth does nothing but get me in trouble."

He grunted, a masculine sound that was neither agreement nor disagreement, and let it go.

When my cell rang, I hated that my first thought was Midas had called to apologize for leaving without saying goodbye. It wasn't Midas, it was Bishop. "That was fast."

"Not really." A keyboard clacked in the background. "I'm not calling about the IDs you found. I'm calling about an ID on a body in relation to your request."

"Okay." I held up a finger to stall Ford. "What did you find?"

"Tammy Burns."

"Damn it." I pinched the bridge of my nose. "I figured, but it still sucks hearing it."

"I did a quick search to locate her parents, and that's where it gets interesting. They're both deceased."

"That's not the word I would have used. More like tragic. Besides, I already told you the parents were out of the picture."

"That's not the interesting part. This is." He let a beat pass. "She has no siblings."

"That can't be right." I dropped my arm. "I spoke to her sister."

"You spoke to someone, but she wasn't Tammy Burns's sister, and her name wasn't Jessica."

The world dropped out from under my feet. "I don't follow."

"I checked the pack roster, the official one that must be updated biannually with the wolf king."

There was no wolf king, Bishop was just being an ass. There was an alpha of alphas among the wargs, and he didn't play when it came to controlling what information on his people got leaked. That meant he kept strict tabs on alphas throughout the country, and their packs. He wanted names, matings, births, all of it. Fail to comply, and he killed the alpha and redistributed their pack to more responsible ones.

For Bishop to say there was no record *of* Jessica Burns in the Mendelsohn pack meant there was no Jessica Burns *in* the Mendelsohn pack.

"Who did I talk to then?" I started toward the house in earnest. "She had a small circle of girls around the same age with her. She might have been using Tammy to fish for information, scared they might be next."

"Did she say or do anything unusual?"

"She was the only pack member who approached me." The sister angle won me over, no questions asked. "Nothing she said or did sent up any red flags. She was a normal kid. She spent most of the time..."

"Most of the time doing what?"

"Playing with Snowball." I picked up speed. "Any kid would have done the same. I didn't give it a second thought."

"Lee?" Ford kept pace with me. "What's wrong?"

"We need to go back to see Mendelsohn." I reached his truck first and yanked on the handle until he let me in with a fumbled mash of his key fob. "Bishop, I'm going to track down Jessica. Keep me updated."

"Make no apologies," he said, and I heard the warning.

"Survive," I agreed.

Ford joined me in the cab as I ended one call and placed another.

Jessica didn't answer.

The phone rang and rang and rang.

Strapping in, I confronted him. "How much did you hear?"

"Enough to know we're going to see Mendelsohn. Something about the girl? Is she missing?"

Already redialing Jessica, I waited, but she never answered. "Bishop says she doesn't exist."

SEVENTEEN

The Mendelsohn pack was cooking out when we arrived, cheddar brats and hotdogs mostly, which seemed downright dangerous considering the amount of sausage already swinging in the wind, but that was their problem and not mine.

The first person I bumped into—thankfully not literally—was a man old enough to be my grandfather.

"Can you tell me where to find Jessica Burns?" I waited a beat. "Sir?"

"He's deaf as a stump," a warm feminine voice said from behind us. "I'm Gayle, his granddaughter. How can I help you?"

Lucky me, she had on a flowy dress that quit mid-thigh. "I'm looking for Jessica Burns."

"We don't have any Jessicas in the pack." She lifted a hand to the topmost button, and she worried it between her fingers. "Do you mean Tammy? Tammy Burns? She's been missing eight—no, nine —days."

"Jessica is about ten. I met her right over there." I pointed where Ford had parked the first time. "She claimed Tammy was her big sister."

"That's not right." Gayle shook her head. "Tam was an only child. Her parents died a few years back, and she came to live with Deric. He's her second cousin. He's all the family she's got left now."

Unease squirmed through my gut. "Jessica told me Tammy was about to turn eighteen, that she left because she was afraid Deric wanted to add her to his harem."

Her laughter was a bright, sharp zing through the air. "Deric is hedonistic, but he would never lay a finger on that girl. All his partners are twenty-one years or older. They're very much consenting adults."

"The girl who introduced herself to me as Jessica went into a tent with other girls her age. Where are they? Can I talk to them?"

"The girls had a sleepover a few days ago. That must be when you saw them together. They jealously guard their private rituals from the boys and from outsiders. I'm amazed they would have included another child without a fuss." She scanned the crowd. "Come on. I'll take you to the heathens."

Ford met my gaze, which was nice, considering he had been unwilling or unable to do so earlier, and I read my own concern reflected back at me.

Gayle led us to a tent that might have been the one I remembered seeing last time, but now there were only two cots, and one of them held a fuming preteen girl.

"Lyssa," Gayle called, "can you come here a minute?"

"I'm grounded," she snarled. "I can't go anywhere but this dumb bed."

With an attitude like that, I had to wonder what the little angel had done to get herself in trouble.

"Where's your mom?" Gayle peered through the flap. "We have a guest who would like to speak to you."

The girl slanted me a look, and her eyes widened. "I remember you."

I checked with Gayle. "Okay to go ahead?"

"Sure, sure. I'll stay so she's not alone while she's being questioned. Danica won't mind."

Danica must be the mom, but right now all that mattered was Lyssa. "Do you have any friends named Jessica?"

Her gaze slid around the room before touching on the exit. "No."

The kid was lying, but calling them out never worked. "Do you know Tammy?"

"She's nice. She paid me in French fries to braid her hair once."

"Does Tammy have a younger sister?"

"No." Lyssa scrunched up her face. "Deric is like her brother. Does that count?"

"Who was the girl you were playing with the day you saw me?"

She stuck out her leg, wiggled her toes. "Just a friend from next door."

"Do you remember the last time you saw Tammy?"

"More than a week. I wanted to ask if she would buy me fries again, but I couldn't find her."

"What color is Tammy's hair?"

"It's yellow." She glanced up, smiled. "It's soft, and it smells *so* good."

"What color hair does Jessica have?"

"Yellow," she answered and then sucked in a breath.

"It's okay." I sat on the cot opposite hers. "You can talk to me about her. You won't get in any trouble. I promise." I leaned in closer and lowered my voice to a whisper. "I might even buy you fries if you help me find her."

Lyssa licked her lips, but she held firm.

"Do you like chicken nuggets?" I rubbed my stomach. "I like barbeque sauce with mine."

"I do too," she gushed. "Mom says it's too sugary, but I would bathe in it if she let me."

The kid slapped her hands over her mouth, even though she hadn't said anything incriminating.

"How about this?" I pretended to consider her. "I'll have a chat with your mom. If she agrees, and you tell me everything you know about Jessica, I'll buy you a gift card so you can have fries and nuggets every Friday for a whole month. Deal?"

To her credit, Lyssa didn't rat out her friend immediately.

It took about ninety seconds.

"Jessica is weird," Lyssa said haltingly, "but she had fries, so I didn't mind playing with her."

So far, other than the species of the victims, we had made no connections between them otherwise. The murders had pointed toward random acts of violence against female shifters. If the killer knew Lyssa, and likely her circle of friends, then it stood to reason he had stalked his victims. Fries were a generic bribe for girls in their age group, and living a more naturalistic life meant less access to processed foods, but still.

Lucky guess? Or careful research?

"Where is she from?" I asked carefully. "Did she say?"

"Her parents live in one of the trailers over there." She pointed vaguely across the road. "She wanted to make friends with us, but she was so...weird."

"How was she weird?"

"She wanted to play really dumb games like haircut, except she wouldn't let us throw away the hair. She put the pieces in plastic bags and made us write our names on them."

Not in years had I wanted to use my second favorite *F* word so much.

"Thanks, Lyssa." I stood. "I have to go, but I'll talk to your mom about our deal, okay?"

"Sure." She made big eyes at me. "Do you think, since I helped you, and I heard you tell Deric you're gonna be the potentate some day, you could maybe tell her I don't need to be grounded anymore?"

Giving her a wink, I smiled. "I'll try."

Flopping on her back, she resumed counting the stitches in the peak over her head.

Gayle followed us out, and I put enough distance between us and Lyssa to ensure little ears didn't hear big problems.

"Don't let her or any other kid play in the woods without adult supervision. Don't let them out of your sight. Make sure the women pair up, but groups would be better."

"What's going on?" Her hand returned to the top button of her dress. "What happened to Tammy?"

"Tammy was murdered," I told her softly. "We believe a rogue warg killed her."

"What does that have to do with the girls?"

The truth, that it appeared he had inherited enough of his mother's magic to give him a knack for crafting charms, was classified information that would out Bonnie. Based on what Lyssa had told me and what I found in that backpack, I had no doubt the killer had used magic to appear as a girl to appeal to the girls. It gave me a bad feeling about where he got the lock of hair for Jessica.

The cell hadn't been a gift from a concerned older sister. It had been a burner phone, a tripwire for me to stumble over. A concerned call from me would tip him off when the gig was up, and I fell for it. I had called, several times, clanging the frakking alarm bell until his ears must be ringing.

"That information is classified." I hated I couldn't give her more. "Trust me when I say those girls are in danger. They've had contact with a person of interest in multiple homicides, one who preys on women and girls."

These had interacted with him, and that made them potential targets.

Ford, who had hung back while I questioned the girl, escorted me to the truck while I texted Bishop with my suspicions about Jessica.

"Bonnie didn't tell us her son inherited her magic." I chewed my bottom lip. "She's protecting him."

Gwyllgi born this side of Faerie didn't have more than transformational magic. Crossbreeding them with wargs neutralized most of their gifts. Granted, I had never come across a first-generation hybrid.

They might inherit more power, abilities that got bred out of their descendants as more warg blood joined the mix.

"Victims protect their abusers all the time." Ford let a bit of growl enter his voice. "Doesn't make it right, but it doesn't make it uncommon either."

"She took the first and second calls." I drummed my fingers on my thigh. "She was playing corgi when the third call came in." I replayed that sequence of events in my mind. "You and I were in the meeting with Ayla. She was pacing the doorway like a guard dog. I remember thinking it was cute. She ghosted once, but it couldn't have been longer than a few minutes."

"We would have heard if she shifted and had a conversation in the hall."

"I didn't keep an eye on her the whole time, did you?" I had been too focused on Ayla, on the danger her loose tongue represented to me. "Bonnie could have ducked into another office, made the call on their landline, and resumed her post."

"You're reaching."

"Maybe," I allowed, "but it's possible."

"The caller was male," he reminded me. "Bonnie is..."

A fae, maybe. A shifter, definitely.

She had changed forms—and scents—multiple times. Right in front of us.

I was missing something, something vital. Jessica had cuddled Snowball, but Bonnie hadn't said a word. She could have ended it there, right then, but she chose to play along. Maybe because she had played us all along.

Bishop couldn't *I told you so* me with this just yet.

About to call Midas and warn him, I remembered why he wasn't here. "Where did you say Midas went?"

"Fuck." Ford punched the gas. "He's with Bonnie."

The reason why the charm Bonnie wore the day Midas found her bothered me so much hit me in a cold rush of understanding. Once again, I hadn't been smart enough, fast enough, or clever enough to pull the big picture into focus in time.

Story of my life.

I had been so eager to derail the scent-charm conversation to protect my own hide, I missed the big picture. I let myself get hung up on how Midas knew she was an albino without following that lead to its logical conclusion—that he shouldn't have known she was gwyllgi at all.

Midas discovered Bonnie while she was in her human form, but the charm she wore was meant to disguise her fae nature. Meaning she put herself in that hot room, guaranteeing he would smell her. She hadn't slipped up, she had baited her hook and wiggled it in front of his nose until he bit.

No wonder Ambrose wanted to eat Bonnie up with a spoon. Charms as subtle as hers were top drawer.

"I'll see what Bishop can do for us." I dialed him up, explained the problem. "Well?"

"Give me a second."

Multiple voices conversed in the background, the team pulling together to help us locate Midas.

"I see him," Bishop said. "He took a Swyft to Historic Fourth Ward Park."

Chest winding tighter, I gripped the phone. "*See* him or *saw* him?"

"*Saw* him, damn it. I'm hopping from camera to camera during the given timeframe."

An apology threatened to pop out, but so did my lunch. "Anything?"

"Midas will be okay," Bishop grated out between orders he hurled at the rest of the team. "He's the next best thing to an alpha."

Ford touched my thigh, and I nearly jumped out of my skin. "What?"

"He's right." He patted me. "Midas will be fine."

"I don't need soothing," I snarled at them. "I need his location."

"Got him," Reece said into my ear, having been patched in by Bishop. "He's still in the park. A woman is with him on the bridge. Someone is walking toward them, but I can't make them out. They're short, really short. Kid short. They must be wearing a charm that causes interference."

That was one mystery explained. "Same as the footage of Tilda Wainwright's killer?"

"Same as the culprit who broke into your apartment too," he confirmed. "Midas is injured." He paused a beat. "I see blood."

"Text me updates." I ended the call then turned on Ford. "Can't you go any faster?"

I almost, *almost* wished for the pixie girl with her green hair and green car to speed me there, but that wasn't much different than a death wish.

"Hold on." A wild light sparked in his eyes, and he started driving like he meant it, like the road had personally offended him and traffic was prey for him to mow down. "One more turn."

There should have been more than one. He cut across lanes, bowled over orange cones, and spun out in the opposite direction to a chorus of honking horns. I didn't care. I was pounding on the dash with my palm like it was a button and wings might pop out if I hit it hard enough.

Tires screeched when he swung into the parking lot, and I didn't wait for him to stop before I flung open my door and leapt onto the asphalt, landing in a puddle of darkness that kept me from shredding my skin during the high-speed dismount.

"Thanks," I gasped at Ambrose. "Now help me find him."

I sprinted toward the pond, toward the bridge, toward the last place Reece saw Midas.

Flexing and curling, Ambrose sliced through the night as he raced by my side, pointing a damning finger at a swirl of blond hair in the water.

"Watch my back," I ordered him then leapt into the pond and swam for Midas.

The water feature wasn't large or deep. I didn't have to go far or work hard to reach him, but it was obvious drowning was a secondary concern. Teeth and claws had ripped open his abdomen, and his blood darkened the water.

A kid. They had used a kid. The shape of one anyway. That and a cowering woman.

Goddessdamn them for turning his weakness—his goodness—against him.

"Midas." I gripped his shoulders and flipped him onto his back. "Can you hear me?"

A snarl rent the night as Jessica sprinted down the bridge, a meld of warg and nightmares bursting from her skin.

There was nothing childlike about her now.

"Lee," Ford bellowed from the grass. "Watch out."

Impact dunked me under the water, and claws slashed at me, going for my throat.

Midas was knocked aside, pushed under with me, and I fought like a demon to shake off my attacker before it was too late.

Razor-sharp teeth sank into my forearm, and the beast slung its head, tearing flesh.

Bubbles tickled my nose as I screamed under the water, and then metal touched my other palm.

Ambrose was offering me a blade for my good arm, and I took it.

Shoving upward with all the force I could muster, I pierced the creature pinning me with steel, and it recoiled, allowing me to surface and gulp oxygen.

Midas was nowhere in sight.

More company had arrived while I was fighting for my life. A second figure burst from the trees, this one slight and female, aiming for the bridge. Magic shimmered in the air around her, crimson and bright, and a bestial cry ripped from her throat as a massive gwyllgi with snow-white fur took her place.

Without his handy Hadley-shaped float, Siemen was at a disadvantage. I sliced at him in the water, doubting the blade would do much damage through his thick pelt, but I had to try. I swept my injured arm back and forth to keep me afloat while I searched for Midas.

From the corner of my eye, I spotted Ford and exhaled with relief. He could find Midas while I—

Snarling and snapping, the gwyllgi leapt from the bridge onto Ford, dunking him.

There was no sugarcoating it. Not anymore. It was Bonnie. I could see her clearly.

Goddess, please, this one time, let me be enough.

Going still, I let Siemen think he had me, let him paddle close enough his rank breath made my gut clench, and then I pulled on Ambrose's strength to help me sheathe my blade in his heart. The creature gurgled and splashed, fighting to escape, but it was too late. He was dead. His brain just had to play catch-up.

While he fought a losing battle with the water closing over his head, I swam to assist Ford.

"I got this," he yelled. "Find Midas."

Permission granted, I dove in the last place I saw him. I had excellent night vision, but it was too dark to see with vegetation blocking light from the surface. I swam and raked my hands through the murky depths, heart a drumbeat in my ears, until my fingertips snagged on damp fabric.

Fisting my hand in the material, I jerked and was rewarded with a masculine body colliding with mine.

Relief built in my chest until the pressure threatened to burst my lungs.

I kicked as hard as I could, propelling us both to the surface where Ford was waiting with helping hands and a bloody face.

Together, we dragged Midas onto land, and I started CPR.

"Come on," I grunted, keeping my chest compressions precise. "Wake up, Goldilocks."

Water burbled from the corner of his mouth, and his breath caught.

"That's it." I kept going. "You're too pretty to die waterlogged. All that beautiful hair? Forget it. You look like a drowned rat." Only when he coughed and spluttered did I dare quit. "I knew it." I wiped the soft blond waves out of his eyes and off his face. "You really are that vain. Guess I can't complain, though. Vanity just saved your life."

"No," he rasped, reaching for my hand. "You..."

A curious shadow sniffed his side, and I remembered why he needed a rescue in the first place.

"Pardon me." I gripped the tattered remains of his shirt and ripped it down the middle. "I need to see what we're dealing with here." The visual was...not great. "Ford?"

"I already called for a healer."

"Good." I used the soggy and generally useless tee to apply pressure to the gaping wound on his side. "Eyes open, Goldilocks. No sweet dreams just yet."

"You..."

"Whatever it is, save it." I stroked his hair with one hand while keeping the other on his abdomen, telling myself it was to comfort him and not me. "You can tell me later."

"...saved...me."

"Did you not hear me?" I tugged on his ear. "Hush."

The right corner of his mouth twitched in a smile it couldn't quite manage.

The healer arrived with his retinue in tow, and I stepped aside to give him room to work. Judging by the reverence shown to him by Ford, he must be a fae gwyllgi.

Midas's blood stained my hands, and I wanted nothing more than to wash them clean, but I wasn't done yet.

"Siemen is dead." I examined Ford, his face a mess of claw marks. "Where's Bonnie?"

"I got in a few good hits." He wiped blood off his forehead. "She went down and didn't come up again."

"Are you sure?" A niggling doubt prodded the back of my mind. "Are you one hundred percent certain?"

Stabbing pain gave me an insta-migraine as Ambrose poked at me.

Ah.

That would be the source of the persistent doubt I was experiencing.

"Stay here." I touched Ford's arm. "You need to be seen by the healer too."

"What about you?" He cupped my cheek in his wide, warm palm. "Your arm..."

"It won't fall off." I gave him greater incentive. "You need to protect the healer."

"He brought guards." Ford was onto my tricks. "No healer leaves the den without them these days."

"They don't know what they're up against." I was out of time to argue. "I do." Hating to pull rank, I did it for his own good. "This is my job. Let me do it. You stay here with Midas."

"Search the perimeter of the pond," I told Ambrose once we were safely out of range of the others. "If by some miracle either of them survived their bath, I need to know if I should rinse and repeat."

The stubborn shadow didn't budge an inch, but he did hold out his hand.

"For pity's sake." I dug in my pocket for the handful of chocolates I kept there for him and tossed one into the void. "Are you serious?" I tossed a second. "Lives are at stake." A third. "Get your ass in gear."

Six ganache squares later, Ambrose shot like an arrow across the pond to sniff down any fresh magic. That left me performing a visual sweep of the area while canvassing its edge.

"I thought you would understand," a soft voice came from the darkness. "Of all people, you should have understood the thirst for power, the craving for more and better things."

Slowly, I turned toward the speaker, yanking as hard as I could on the tether binding me to Ambrose. "Hey, Bon-Bon."

"Hadley."

No signs of grief marred her pale face, and another piece of the puzzle clicked into place. "Siemen wasn't your son, was he?"

"I didn't have to know you long to catch on to how broken your relationship is with your mother. She abused you. I can tell. Mothers are vicious in ways fathers can only dream about. I wasn't certain the reverse would move you, a son threatening his mother with harm, but it did. You'll stand for anyone with the right push, won't you?"

"What do you mean, the right push?"

"Didn't you wonder what the amplifier charm does? They're marvelous things, subtle, and potent when used on the right mark." Her smile soured my stomach. "I crafted the Bonnie persona for Midas. She fit his profile to a T. Though I made tweaks here and there to appeal to your protective instincts as well." The air glimmered around her, sparking in her hair. "Midas saw a wounded bird and returned with her to his nest, and you? You couldn't tuck me under your wing fast enough."

Anger warmed my cheeks at having my past turned against me, the old shame rising like a tidal wave, like bile up the back of my throat.

The scars my childhood left on me hadn't prompted me to perform outreach programs the way it had Midas. He wore his scars boldly, where anyone could see them. I hoarded mine, kept them hidden. He might be willing to bear the cross of his past, but I wanted to break the shackles chaining me to mine.

However we chose to cope, it was our choice, and she had no right to turn our struggles against us.

"Your resilience was laudable, but Midas? He's so broken his mother won't let him out of her sight for fear he might shatter. He's the heir to a dynasty, and he will be its downfall." Bonnie, whoever she was, strolled out to greet me with none of the cowering timidity that had roused my protective instincts. "Why do you think she wants him mated so badly? The pack won't follow weakness, and she wants him paired with a strong leader who can step into her role."

"Compassion isn't weakness."

"Yes," she said without blinking. "It is."

"Midas is a good man."

"Good men aren't fit to rule."

"Agree to disagree."

"He's marked you, several times now." A cruel smile flirted with her lips. "Have you asked yourself why? What about you, more than any other, appeals to him?" She dipped a hand in her shirt and came up with an amplifier charm identical to the one I found in the backpack in the woods. "He doesn't care about you, Hadley. All he feels or thinks he feels is a result of this. You'll see that soon enough. You can't believe what you see reflected back at you in those pretty blue eyes. Magic took his kernel of fascination with you and expanded it tenfold. Without this amping him up, he'll lose interest in you within the day."

The sudden, wrenching hurt made me question if she had ripped out my heart and stomped on it.

How stupid was that? He already confessed he hadn't meant to mark me. Now I knew why he had.

Closure was supposed to make you feel better and not worse, right?

"Who are you?" I gritted my teeth, tugging harder on Ambrose. "What are you?"

"I am Iliana." Her lean features plumped before my eyes, her brittle hair growing softer and darker, until nothing remained of Bonnie Diaz except for her scars. "I'm a witchborn fae, as was Siemen."

"What the hell does that mean?"

"It means..." She snapped her fingers, and the doorman from the Faraday, the one who hated me, stood before me. "I can be anyone." Another snap, and she was Jessica. "I can be anything." Snap, and she was the white gwyllgi no pack in its right mind would pass on. "We collect identities like clothes to fill our covens' closets." *Snap.* The nightshift doorman at the Faraday. *Snap.* A gorgeous Indian woman with henna covering her bare feet and hands. *Snap*. Back to where she started. "We have a suit for every occasion."

"Witchborn fae is starting to sound a whole lot like a skinwalker."

"We are *not* so lowborn." Her hands curled into fists at her sides. "Parading around in another's flesh is a cheap parlor trick any fool with an ounce of magic and a corpse can perform. We capture the essence, the magic. We preserve the soul."

"You kill people to assume their lives."

Talk about the ultimate identity theft.

"Sacrifices must be made."

Ambrose was nearby, which meant my swords were close, but he wasn't here yet. So help me, if he was dragging his heels to get more chocolate out of me, I was going to shove my stash down his throat and hope he choked on them. I had to keep the killer chameleon talking until he arrived. "That explains how Siemen got into my apartment."

Talk about the ultimate inside job. No wonder he knew where the cameras were located. He killed the nightshift doorman to infiltrate the staff, which gained him full access to the building, to my schedule, and to Bonnie. The position put him outside, which proved he thought along the same lines as me in regards to allowing Mother Nature to cover his tracks.

More troubling was learning they had killed the doorman to take his place, meaning the choice of victims shown to us was a statement, not a predilection. They had tailored their dead to hurt Midas, yes, but I was still missing the purpose of dragging the warg packs into the fray. "Why bother with the charade?"

"Atlanta has belonged to the dogs for long enough."

"There's plenty of room for a new faction. There are already dozens."

"Share with them?" She touched her ruined cheek. "Never."

"Your people can share, or they can leave."

"Who are you to issue orders to me? You're a parasite. You share your life essence with a being of pure darkness."

The truth hurt, but that wasn't my whole truth anymore. "I'm the future POA."

"You won't survive on your own."

"I'm still standing. That's more than Siemen can say."

"This city will be mine." Her irises flared blue with power as her temper spiked. "You can't hold it, not against me."

"I can hold plenty against you." A patch of velvet shadow darker than the rest brushed against the back of my hand. "Starting with this." I dipped my hand into his icy core and wrapped my fingers around the hilt of my right-hand blade. "You killed almost a dozen women for no reason but to further your own agenda."

"The mongrels were meant to turn on themselves."

"You wanted to pit the gwyllgi against the wargs."

That explained the diversity of the victims' species. The coven had been ensuring every pack in the area had a stake in the outcome of this investigation. Had Siemen not made a mistake with Jessica, he would have kept killing until tempers boiled over and fights broke out between grieving gwyllgi and wargs. Once that happened, turning them against each other would be as simple as donning a new identity.

"The gwyllgi are the power in this city. They are the ones who must stumble before the others will fall. All Midas needs is a little push."

Interesting that the OPA didn't rate a mention. "Did you think I would sit back and let that happen?"

"I didn't expect them to involve you. This was a pack matter. It should have stayed a pack matter. The gwyllgi would have taken one look at the cleaners' reports and demanded justice." Her lip curled over her teeth. "Mendelsohn is an incompetent alpha, and the Loups will run their course once Garou's heir is in power. Clairmont is sly, but she's too cautious. She would let a crime go unpunished before she lost more of her miniscule number. The Kinases are our strongest rival, but they would have fallen without Midas now that Lethe has defected."

"The city would experience a power vacuum if the gwyllgi were taken out, leaving it ripe for the plucking. That makes it a city matter." I tested my grip, readying myself. "That makes it mine."

"I am willing to let you live," she bargained. "My coven and I have no quarrel with the Society."

The fae part of her ancestry must carry more weight than her witch blood if her plan was to avoid the Society altogether. Its agreement with the Earthen Conclave, the ruling body for fae this side of Faerie, meant there would be harsh repercussions for her actions if civilian necromancers got killed or harmed.

The Society wouldn't be thrilled with losing a potentate, or his protégé, either. Still, she had wiggle room there. The job was dangerous, and accidents happened. Especially to potentates-in-training while their boss was out of town.

"Siemen must not have gotten the memo." I grimaced as my left arm reminded me I was fighting at half-strength. "Did you not catch the part where he tried to kill me? You were standing a few feet away from him. Did you blink and miss it?"

"A truce then," she said, extending her arm toward me, and I noticed her nails had sharpened into metallic, silvery claws. "Will you accept?"

"I can't stand aside while you systematically murder innocents, no."

"How many innocents have you killed?"

"Enough to know even one is too many."

"Your soft heart will be your downfall."

Blue sparks crackled in her hair when she lunged for me. I whirled aside, raising my blade to deflect her claws. With my left arm going numb, I was stuck using one sword when I had trained with two. The POA had warned me not to depend on them, that swords got knocked out of hands during a real fight, but I hadn't stepped up my practice with singles, and that meant I left my already useless side open for her to rake me from breast to hip with her claws.

The stinging burn left me breathless, but I ignored the pain.

Twisting aside, I blocked her, but she met me blow for blow. She had lost more blood, but I only had the use of one arm. I knew who would tire first, and what it would cost me.

A throaty baying noise lifted the fine hairs down my nape, the sweet sound of backup en route, and Bonnie—Iliana?—hesitated.

I ducked under her guard while she was distracted and plunged my blade into her heart.

Beside me, Ambrose licked his lips, and I rewarded him for his good behavior.

Given permission, he pounced on her chest, knocking her back, and began feeding on the dying magic in her veins.

Certain he couldn't overdo it now that her heart had stopped beating, helpful information I didn't want to know how I knew, I sat down to wait on my backup to arrive.

That was the plan anyway, but darkness scooped me into its arms and carried me away.

EIGHTEEN

Midas tore across the distance between him and Hadley on all fours, but he shifted as her knees buckled and caught her against him. Pain shot through him, radiating across his tender abdomen. The healer had sealed the wound, so he wouldn't die from the strain of supporting her. It just felt that way.

Blood soaked her left arm, and bone glinted through exposed flesh. Her right arm twitched, her fingers flexing around the blade she clutched in her hand, the one that had ended a fae life.

"Hadley?"

A moan parted her lips.

"I'll take her," Ford said, coming up behind him. "You're weaving on your feet."

"No." Midas hissed out a ragged breath from between gritted teeth, unable to let her go. "I've got her."

"Suit yourself." He shook his head. "At least let me get the sword in case she wakes up swinging."

"No," she protested, a barely there whisper.

"She must not be dead if she can complain about us taking her weapon."

Her eyelids fluttered. "Ambrose."

"Who is Ambrose?" Midas fought the instinct to clutch her tighter against him, like this Ambrose might walk up and yank her out of his arms. "I don't remember anyone at the OPA with that name."

Black edged his vision, but he put one foot in front of the other on his way back to the healer.

"I'll find out." Ford rubbed a hand over his face. "Goddamn it, Midas."

Grim determination hardened on his face. "What now?"

"That you care? Changes things."

"The case is closed." Midas blinked away the tunnel vision. "Our involvement with the OPA is done."

"You're going to let her go? Just like that?" Ford kept a wary eye on the foliage. "You marked her, Midas. Multiple times. Once is an accident, twice is intent."

"Marks wear off in time."

"You know as well as I do that the more layered and nuanced they become, the more difficult they are to erase."

"What do you want me to say?"

"I want you to admit you did it on purpose. That it was a conscious decision."

"I can't do that."

"The hell you can't. You *won't*. Big difference."

"There is no difference, not when it comes to this." Midas tensed when Hadley made a soft noise then buried her face in his shirt. "I can't be what she needs, so what I want or don't want doesn't matter."

"I'm going to pursue her."

Claws punching through his fingertips, Midas kept walking, afraid of what he might say if he opened his mouth.

The healer waited where they left him. One look at Midas sparked red annoyance in his eyes. The guards were quick to pluck

Hadley from his arms, thankfully before he embarrassed himself by hitting his knees.

"Growl all you want," the healer said to Midas curtly. "Just do it over there."

Healers occupied a peculiar niche in the pack hierarchy that set them on equal footing with alphas in a way. Their high non-rank was the only reason they could treat wounded dominants without serious injury to their patients or to themselves. Even though Midas was a beta, the healer had no trouble staring him down or bossing him around when he felt it was needed.

Ford horned in on them, his brow pinched with worry. "Will she be okay?"

"Shoo" was his answer, which did nothing to unknot the tension coiling in Midas's gut.

"I've seen her take worse." Smiling all the while, Ford launched an elaborate story about Hadley culling a rabid chupacabra from the herd. "She shook that off, she'll walk away from this too."

Midas vaguely remembered the incident from months earlier, and he scowled at his friend for glorifying her near-death experience, but Ford just belly-laughed until he lost his breath.

"You have no idea how bad you've got it." Ford whistled through his teeth. "This is going to be fun."

That was the point when Midas realized the growl he had dismissed as Ford's had been coming from him, was still coming from him, and only got worse when he comprehended the scope of his meaning.

Whether Midas participated or not, Ford had decided they were competing for Hadley.

NINETEEN

Popcorn pinged against the glass lid on my pot while I melted butter in a saucepan on my tiny stove. I had sweet tea, beer, lemonade, and chocolate milk in the fridge. I had a pizza on the way with a side of tongue-torching buffalo wings, and I had an old favorite cued up for when my guest arrived.

I was as ready as I would ever be.

When the knock came, five minutes after my last outfit change, I didn't have to look hard to find a smile. Ford was running early, but that was okay by me. I opened the door and...got a shock.

"Linus." I didn't know what to do with my hands, my feet, my face. "Hi."

"I won't keep you long." His gaze slid past my shoulder. "Can I come in?"

"Oh, sure. Yeah. Come on in. Definitely." I tripped getting out of his way. "What's up?"

"I came to oversee the movers." He chuckled at my shock. "You knew this day was coming."

"I just closed my first case." I smelled the burnt stench of popcorn and rushed to rescue what I could, giving me a second to compose myself. "I have eleven months and change left."

Hands preternaturally cool, he took the pot from me. A snap of his fingers brought Ambrose running, and the POA dumped the blackened kernels into his dark maw before handwashing the pot, turning on the vent over the stove, and starting a fresh batch.

Cooking was one of his many hobbies, and he was better at it than anyone else I knew, so I wasn't going to turn my nose up at his offer of help. My nerves had been jangled before his arrival. They were audibly jingling at this point.

"You don't need me looking over your shoulder." After the first kernel popped, he adjusted the heat and began shaking the pot to agitate the rest. "As you said, you closed this case on your own."

"I didn't picture you as the momma-bird type who shoves her baby out of the nest the second it grows a feather."

"You have the team to rely on, and I'll be three hours away." He dumped the perfect popcorn into a ridiculously gigantic bowl I bought for less worthy snacks, and he managed to evenly coat it with butter and salt without leaving it a soggy mess. "This is the test." He set the bowl aside then loaded the pot into the dishwasher. "You have to prove you can stand alone, and that will be made clear if I'm not in the city."

"What about the coup Iliana was planning? She mentioned a coven. That means there are more of them." Unable to resist, I savored a single buttery kernel. "Did you miss the part in my report where I mentioned they can look and smell like anyone?" Not even buttery perfection could calm me. "Did I mention her kind can hurt Ambrose?" In corgi form, she had done serious damage to Ambrose. "How can I combat their magic without exposing myself?"

"Hadley." He rested a hip against the counter and tucked his hands into his pockets. "There will always be a faction who wants more than what they have and are willing to kill innocents to get it. I've never come up against witchborn fae. I'm not sure what they are, aside from what the name implies—a child born of a witch mother and fae father. You'll have to hit the books, do your research."

"Always with the homework." The gripe reminded of his other potentate-in-training student, and I asked after his fiancée. "How is Grier?" The history we three shared made it awkward, but that had never stopped me. "Doing well, I hope?"

The slightest hitch in his graceful movements told me he was just as uneasy answering as I was asking.

I had tried to kill her once, after all. Ambrose would again, given the opportunity.

"She's growing into her role," he said at last, "a bit quicker than you, but that's to be expected."

Her magic was such that she had bonded with the city, which had no potentate, on her own. That connection, in fact, was what kept Savannah from burning to the ground during the siege. Even without being officially recognized by the Society, she was the Potentate of Savannah, though she had the same year of training left that I did.

The bond she shared with the city made her aware of its moods and whims. Savannah wasn't alive, in so many words, but she was sentient, and she was nudging Grier ahead of the curve. Though I couldn't complain when I was inheriting a crack team with resources I could never imagine, let alone fund, on my own. There was something to be said for inheriting a mantle versus stitching it yourself, piece by piece.

"Once you've bonded with Atlanta," he continued, "you will grow in leaps and bounds as well."

"You sound like it's a done deal." I scowled at Ambrose, who rubbed Linus's ankles like a frakking cat. "We both know it's not."

"You've proven to me that you're fit for this position." High praise coming from him. "I will throw the full weight of my support behind you when the time comes."

An ounce or two of the guilt weighing me down slid off my shoulders. "Thanks."

"The loft will be available for occupancy within the next few weeks," he said casually. "You're welcome to stay here, or move in."

The moisture left my mouth, and I couldn't get my tongue to work. "Move? In? Move in?"

Soft laughter turned his navy eyes lighter. "Yes."

Before I got too excited, I had to make sure of one thing. "Are you offering because of the break-in?"

"No." He glanced around, soaking in the décor. "Consider it a vote of confidence that it will become your permanent residence within the year."

The calculated interest he showed in our surroundings got me thinking about Midas, who I hadn't seen since we closed the case a week ago. All the loose ends were tied, all debts paid. Including the gift card I sent Lyssa with my thanks.

"I'll stick with my apartment." I couldn't look him in the eye, afraid of what he might see. "The loft will make a nice reward when I become official."

"All right."

From there, he walked me through the standard checklist to ensure Ambrose remained contained and cooperative. With that done, we set a date to have the ink on my ankle refreshed so the spillover from Ambrose was contained, eerie laughter and all.

The next time someone knocked on my door, it was Ford, and I found my smile again.

"Oh, hey." He shook hands with Linus, who was on his way out. "I didn't know you were in town."

"I'm not," he said. "I didn't come to congratulate Hadley on a job well done. I'm still in Savannah."

"Riiight." Ford winked. "Still, it was nice not seeing you."

Not until after Linus left did it occur to me he must have known I was expecting company. As plugged in as he was to the city, he likely knew who as well but hadn't warned me off Ford or Midas or gwyllgi in general. He hadn't said a word either way.

Huh.

Almost like he trusted me to make the decision for myself.

"What was that all about?" He shut the door behind him. "I saw movers in the lobby. Are they his? I spotted a portrait of a little girl who was a dead ringer for Grier, but I didn't want to make assumptions."

"He is stalker levels of obsessed with her," I joked, but not really. "Good thing she's obsessed right back."

There was an instant of expectation where he might have wanted me to elaborate on how I knew, but I wasn't about to tell him the truth, that I had witnessed their dark and winding courtship firsthand. Then it passed, and Ford shucked his enforcer obligations.

"I smell popcorn, but I don't smell pizza." He folded his arms over his chest. "The pizza was a cruel joke, wasn't it? You were bribing me to help you with the case, and now that it's over, so is my dream of free pizza."

"Yes." I took a single popped kernel and threw it at his forehead. "That's exactly it. I lured you here with empty promises and plan to —" A third knock on the door set my stomach growling. "Hold that thought."

I dug around in my wallet then opened the door and stalled out with a bill in my hand.

"I paid the tip," Midas said, handing over the boxes. "Dough to Go made the mistake of sending Misha to deliver. He's down in the lobby trying to get into Dan's pants. I thought I would bring these up before they got cold."

"Thanks." I inhaled with a happy sigh. "Sure you don't want to join us?"

"I'm on my way out." A muscle twitched in his left cheek. "You're not the only one with a date."

"Here." I forced him to take the money. "Buy yourself a drink stronger than water this time."

Midas took the cash, careful not to touch me, and I got the message loud and clear.

I had eye-contact privileges, not skin privileges, proving Iliana had been right.

The miasma of charms she wore must have amplified Midas's miniscule interest in me, and mine in him.

'Cause no way was he getting a free pass unless I got one too.

No wonder Ford was in such a good mood. Midas's mark must have finally worn off me.

"I should go." He folded the bill and tucked it into his pocket. "Enjoy your night."

"You too," I said, even though we both knew he wouldn't.

After crossing to the futon, I dropped the stack of boxes heavy with pizza and wings on the floor beside Ford.

Slapping his hand when he reached for the wings, I warned, "Do *not* eat all this before I get back."

"Back?" He stretched out his legs. "Where are you going?"

"Just give me a second, okay?" I barreled into the hall. "*Midas.*"

The elevator doors were closing, and I was too late, and it shouldn't matter, and Ford was waiting...

Midas's scarred arm shot through the gap, and my heart did this stupid little flip.

"Hadley?" Midas held the door. "What's wrong?"

I jogged the rest of the way, stumbling at his expression, what I thought I saw there. "I just wanted to say you have my number if you need a rescue."

"You're on a date," he reminded me, "with Ford."

"A friend date, not a date-date."

"Mine is a date-date."

"I know, I just..." I dug the toe of my sneaker into the carpet. "I wanted to tell you that."

Mortification was slow in coming, but it got there, and I flushed, embarrassed to have run after him.

I walked back down the hall, toward my apartment, as fast as I could and shut the door behind me.

"I started without you," Ford said, his mouth full of pizza. "Hope that's okay."

Grateful when he didn't bring up the topic of my mad dash, though I was certain he overheard it all thanks to the door I hadn't bothered closing, I sank beside him and got comfy.

"A gwyllgi with no self-control around food? Whodathunkit?" I palmed the remote with reverence for the ridiculously expensive TV it controlled for my viewing pleasure. "Now, on to matters more important than how many slices you left me. Do you want to watch *Robot Groundhog Saves the Earth from His Alien Shadow* or *The Thing That Came from the Basement*?"

"Gee." He took a wing, gnawing on the bone before sucking out the marrow. "That's a tough one."

"I'm feeding you, don't disrespect me."

"*Robot Groundhog*."

"Excellent choice."

I flipped off the lights, and we settled in to watch a man wearing a silver groundhog suit do battle with a woman whose left leg kept coming out of her shadow costume.

We ate tons of food, talked and laughed, and generally had a good time. If he asked a few questions that toed the line of professional curiosity, I decided I preferred that to more personal ones.

When the night came to an end, I fit a hug into the space where he hoped for more, if the look in his eyes was any indication. He took rejection well, kissing me on the cheek before he left. All in all, it was a very nice night with a very nice guy, and I ought to feel very good about it.

I *did* feel good about it.

Sure I did.

Of course I did.

A metallic rattle drew my attention to the window, my preferred exit, and my heart stopped when a dark shadow—not Ambrose—flickered on the other side of the glass. Summoning my darker half, I palmed my swords and advanced slowly.

There I found a gwyllgi curled up on my fire escape, right outside my window, like he was guarding me.

Or like he was lonely.

That last thought had me throwing open the window and meeting his crimson stare.

"Rough night?"

The fact Midas came to me on four legs instead of two, in a form that couldn't speak, wasn't lost on me.

The gwyllgi huffed, not bothering to lift his head off his front paws.

"I have leftover pizza and wings."

Glancing past me, he gazed into my apartment.

"You can come in, or I can come out."

He patted the metal with his paw, and I took the hint.

"Do you want your food warmed up?"

A man after my own heart, he shook his head.

"You can't go wrong with cold pizza." I ducked back in the apartment. "Be right back."

I got down my largest mixing bowl and filled it to the brim with water then stacked half of the leftover pizza and wings on a baking sheet to carry out with me. Loaded down with treats, I climbed out onto the fire escape and placed the offerings within easy reach of him before settling in with my back against the building.

Midas ate while I watched the sunrise, both of us content with the silence.

I must have dozed off after I shut my eyes to hide from the light spreading across the horizon.

I woke alone, Midas's visit a dreamlike memory, except for the two words written in the reddish pepperoni grease on the baking sheet.

Thank you.

Him coming to me after what I was certain had been a disaster of a date meant nothing.

Me going to him after I set Ford firmly back in the friend zone meant nothing.

Just like the marking thing meant absolutely nothing at all.

But for a whole lot of nothing, it sure felt like...something.

ABOUT THE AUTHOR

USA Today best-selling author Hailey Edwards writes about questionable applications of otherwise perfectly good magic, the transformative power of love, the family you choose for yourself, and blowing stuff up. Not necessarily all at once. That could get messy.

www.HaileyEdwards.net

ALSO BY HAILEY EDWARDS

Manufactured by Amazon.ca
Bolton, ON